A Love Betrayed

Sylvia Robins

A Love Betrayed by Sylvia Robins

Copyright © 2023

Published in 2023 by Hicken and Co

Copyright © Sylvia Robins 2023

The author asserts their moral right under the Copyright Designs and Patents Act, 1988, to be identified as the author of this work.

All rights reserved. No part of this publication may be reproduced, copied, stored in a retrieval system, or transmitted, in any form or by any means, without the prior written consent of the copyright holder, nor be otherwise circulated in any form of binding or cover other than that in which it is published and without a similar condition being imposed on the subsequent purchaser.

ISBN: 979-8-3980-9096-3

This book is a work of fiction. Names, characters, businesses, organizations, places and events other than those clearly in the public domain. are either products of the author's imagination or are used fictitiously. Any resemblance to actual persons, living or dead, events or locales is entirely coincidental.

DEDICATION

Once again, to all my family who have helped me in so many different ways.

Thanks also to my former Creative Writing Lecturer, Susie Lynes, now an established Author, who taught me so much about writing.

Many thanks to my fellow writers in both of the writing groups to which I belong; Meena Arnold, Alison Barker, Jett Nyx and Ruth Skilbeck have been tremendously supportive and provided invaluable criticism.

Special thanks go to Jett Nyx for typography and other assistance with the cover and Amy Withnall for photography.

Millinery expertise for the cover artwork was kindly provided by Fiona J Timmins.

Sue Dymel read the final copy – thanks so much, Sue.

CONTENTS

Dedication	iii
Chapter 1	11
Chapter 2	17
Chapter 3	22
Chapter 4	28
Chapter 5	33
Chapter 6	38
Chapter 7	43
Chapter 8	48
Chapter 9	54
Chapter 10	59
Chapter 11	63
Chapter 12	67
Chapter 13	72
Chapter 14	81
Chapter 15	90
Chapter 16	94

Sylvia Robins

Chapter 17	103
Chapter 18	111
Chapter 19	121
Chapter 20	126
Chapter 21	135
Chapter 22	142
Chapter 23	148
Chapter 24	153
Chapter 25	161
Chapter 26	171
Chapter 27	178
Chapter 28	184
Chapter 29	192
Chapter 30	197
Chapter 31	203
Chapter 32	209
Chapter 33	222
Chapter 34	230
Chapter 35	238
Chapter 36	246

Sylvia Robins

A Love Betrayed

About the Author   259

CHAPTER 1

May, 1812 The Rose Garden, Beauminster Priory, Kent.

'I love you. Marry me!'

Caroline Langrish looked down at her suitor on bended knee before her,
 and smiled. 'You do not mean it, Gervase. First you disappear to London, we have not seen you for a week, and now you propose to me!'

While Caroline had been cutting roses for the morning-room at Beauminster Priory, Gervase had surprised her by vaulting over the low fence that bounded one side of the otherwise walled garden. and appearing in front of her eyes.

Unobserved by anyone.

Almost out of sight, beyond the massed blooms of white, palest pink and creamy yellow, she could make out the figure of her maid, Sarah, and her footman, Finch, deep in conversation.

'Caroline, I am asking you! Do not torment me!'

Caroline laughed. 'You know Papa would not approve. If he finds out you have met me here…' Though the truth was, her father probably would not care … She looked around, she was alone, all she could hear was the murmur of bees and all she could feel was the heat of the sun. Overwhelmed, she subsided onto a nearby bench. 'Come, sit here with me.'

Gervase rose and threw himself down beside her. 'Ignore me if you must but I wish you and I to consider ourselves engaged, because…'

'Why, Gervase? Surely we go along very well as we are?'

It was true, as a near neighbour, Gervase Thorpe, though only a steward's son, was an occasional permitted visitor in the main house, sometimes even an attendee for dinner. Probably beneath her father's notice. Not taken seriously. A nobody. It might have been different if her mother had lived, Caroline thought. Gervase had undoubtedly benefited from the laxity. Although officially out, she lived quietly at home with her sister. Both had been largely ignored, she felt: their father always preoccupied with his own pursuits since her mother's death from the wasting disease. 'Has something changed?'

Gervase faced her directly, now still.

'With my friend Roland, the Earl of Marlow, I should say, we are off to fight Bonaparte in the Peninsula. Roland has come down from Oxford especially, by the by! I want you to promise me that when I return we shall marry. Yes, a secret engagement. That is what I ask of you, Caroline.' Taking her hand, he kissed it. 'In answer to your question, everything has changed.'

'I do not understand. I thought we would wait until we both came of age?'

'I have prospects now, Caroline. My Uncle Walter has died and turned up trumps, the old - never mind that now. He has left me a small property in Hampshire, and the money to purchase a commission! Providing that I enlist in his old regiment, the Fifty-Second. It is worth a great deal to me. For you know, since my father died I have had no real future - until now, that is.'

'I see,' said Caroline. 'Yes, I will wait for you.'

'Then I will expect your letters. Promise me, Caroline.'

'I promise.' She watched as Sarah left Finch and made her way unhurriedly along the path towards her mistress. The illicit visitor had been observed.

Gervase kissed her hand again. 'Remember.'

And he was gone.

July, 1814 London. Two years later.

Why was the ballroom so infernally hot? Even the curtains at the long verandah windows hung limply to the floor.

And so many candles, in spite of the season, nearly ten o'clock and still light, helplessly guttering all of them, threatening to drip onto the elegant plumed and coiffed heads beneath. Or onto the locks à la Brutus, or even the smattering of gentlemen still sporting hair pulled back into the style of the old-fashioned queue. A sober sort of gathering. As one would one expect with a regal duke at the centre of it, even if not an actual blood relative of the Royal Family.

July had no business aping August. Damn it, the sweltering heat from the Peninsula had followed Gervase here to plague him all over again.

So thought Gervase Vyvyan Thorpe, late of the Fifty-Second Regiment under Lieutenant-Colonel Sir John Colborne, as he eased his shoulders under his close-fitting jacket, trying to get more comfortable and failing miserably. Sweat ran down between his shoulder-blades.

He shot a quick glance at his companion, Roland Francis Sebastian Wendover, Fifth Earl of Marlow, another Fifty-Seconder, though still enlisted, if on half-pay, more fool he.

His friend, Roland, almost his brother, with whom he had grown up.

Roland. Still pale from loss of blood incurred at the storming of Badajoz. He will have recovered in a year, the estimable Doctor Jamieson, physician to the mighty, had pronounced confidently. Gervase was not so sure.

He winced as he shifted his weight from his own injured leg which was still painful. We are both damaged, thought Gervase.

Gervase had most certainly been indulged by Roland's father, the Fourth Earl, who had smiled upon his steward's heir, regardless of rank, as if he, Gervase, were almost a second son.

It had all been a long while ago but the bond remained.

Strengthened if anything, after Salamanca.

Roland was now slightly ahead of him, staring down the ballroom, cool as ever, but with a crease between his brows.

Then the throng in front of them parted to reveal the woman Gervase had come to see.

An impression of a slight figure, seated, wearing a plain white robe but all the more to set off the jewels adorning her... Familiar dark hair, swept up. Diamonds, oh yes, no doubt of that! Diamonds in her hair as well as around her throat. A diamond ring upon her finger making a mockery of the promises amongst the roses so long ago. Gifts from one of the richest men in all England. Damn his eyes.

Even at a distance she was unmistakable and yet, and yet... there was something different about her...

An added poise, a gloss, a sophistication? Never mind the diamonds, the silks, the satins... an additional quality... Gervase's stomach roiled and he closed his eyes for a second, surely the duke had not had the temerity to seduce Caroline before the engagement? Please God she had not... that they had not... What would be left for Gervase to do – but call this scion of some famous house or other out and put the bastard to a slow, painful death.

Had he bedded her?

Gervase shook himself mentally, no, no, he was imagining the worst that could happen... He forced himself to concentrate upon the scene ahead.

Next to her another, younger girl, also seated.

On the other side, a gentleman, standing tall, not close but too damn close nevertheless.

Sounds from the conversations of the guests milling around them and some wretched music hurting Gervase's ears, receded for a moment, then resumed. The scene ahead of him fractured, dissolved and re-assembled itself. Bile rose in his throat - threatened to unman him. Not here, not here!

He must have started because Roland had laid a hand on his arm.

'Yes, she's the one. She's the one who has betrayed me. Caroline Langrish.' Gervase choked out.

But Roland answered not. Obviously knew better. Probably frightened at his friend's imperfectly-concealed emotion. Well, for once, Gervase did not blame him. Sometimes Gervase frightened himself; he had to admit it, they were neither of them the men they were before they set sail for the Peninsula.

The woman who had promised to wait for him, Gervase, while he was away fighting a worthless war. No, not worthless. But damaging, as it had proven. In body and soul.

No letters answered, no, nothing.

And then on his return, to discover the announcement to the world, in print, in the Times, below the Court Announcements, of her forthcoming marriage, to the Duke of, what was it? The Duke of Albion, no less. An unfamiliar name at the time but embedded in his consciousness now and forever. Betrothed. Well, he, Gervase, would see about that!

Remembering how he had felt at the news, on that dark day, as the sun beat down, here in his homeland, far away from Iberia, brought back another wave of sickness and pain indescribable.

Roland's hand on his arm increased its pressure

Had Gervase spoken out loud without realising it or

worse still retched? It was not impossible. 'Let me go, I mean to have it out with her. Betrothed or not!' Gervase looked down.

His friend released him and moved away, his attention now elsewhere. 'Is that her sister next to her? A younger Miss Langrish?'

Gervase hesitated, knowing he almost welcomed the diversion. He knew he had to gather his wits together otherwise he would be all over the place. 'Yes, no, I don't know. It must be. She was not out, well, probably still in the school-room when I last...' Choking, he heard his voice dying away.

'I see. She is the loveliest creature. Shall we proceed?

'Oh, yes, let us proceed, by all means.' Gervase replied. If he could have bitten on a bullet he would have done. It was a pity he had not done so before when his shattered leg was being attended to, but no amount of physical pain could rival how he felt now. As if someone were twisting a knife in his gut. And then giving it another turn, with a maniacal laugh.

Now for a moment of reckoning, long overdue.

CHAPTER 2

Caroline was conscious of feeling both hot and icy cold at the same time. No air was circulating in the ballroom. There were beads of moisture on the back of her neck yet she could not repress a shiver. Madness!

The sick feeling in her stomach had not improved since dinner, though goodness knows she had tried to eat something in order to survive the evening ahead.

Hugo Frederick James Alversleigh, His Grace the Duke of Albion, had offered for her, when she was at her wit's end, and she had accepted. Now here she was, at the celebration of their affiancing.

After all, she and Susannah had been ruined. Destitution had loomed. He had appeared as if a god to rescue her. A betrothal had seemed the answer at the time.

Now she was not so sure.

Perhaps the governess option would have been preferable but there was also her sister to consider.

Mentally she chided herself. With the unlimited means now at her disposal, why should not Susannah, have come out? She deserved a season, a chance to establish herself in the world. Especially with her startling good looks. Just because Caroline herself had not *taken*, still unwed at twenty-two she heard the gossips murmur ... Apart from Gervase, or the Inconstant One, as she sometimes called him now.

There was a name for her choice.

Her too quick acceptance of funds for Susannah. The come-out ball, her sister's court gown, the obligatory curtsey to Her Majesty, The Queen, and finally, a voucher for Almack's, deemed indispensable for entering society's Marriage Mart. The list was endless because it had not stopped there. There were the current expenses of day-to-day living. Living in a style to which, she noticed, Susannah had adapted only too well. An ever-increasing mountain of debt. Everything was possible thanks to the Duke of Albion.

He, Gervase, would not have scrupled to use the word either. *Jade*, at the very least. Or worse. *A kept woman.*

After Susannah's glorious debut, Caroline did wonder whether she herself had entered into some kind of devil's pact out of guilt or even a distraction of such enormity solely to forget the loss of Gervase. Could it have been so?

But what was she supposed to have done after Papa had been found, with a pistol in his hand, lying on the floor, cold. He had gambled everything away at cards, everything, including their home, Beauminster Priory, the whole estate...

And Gervase himself, no word from him. She had heard nothing. No letters. Left bereft. Best forgotten. She battened down the memory.

She forced herself to return to the present.

Why did they have to appear as if in a tableau anyway?

The formalities had to be complied with, her fiancé had informed her with just a slight lightening of his expression. Important for the Duke of Albion. A wry smile. He had intimated that their future life together would be, well, formal. She had bowed her head.

At least Susannah was beside her, although unusually for her, saying very little. The duke appeared to be content to observe the onlookers come to stare at the newly-engaged couple. Perhaps in a moment, she thought, he would deign to speak to a select few.

If she fixed her gaze ahead and took deep breaths maybe calmness would descend.

The crowd gathered on the other side of the room were by now edging forward. A disturbance at the front and a man emerged.

No, it could not be. She had conjured him up.

Gervase was advancing across the ballroom towards her. If he had been wearing spurs, as he so often had, back then, that gleaming polished parquet floor would have rung with the sound, she thought hysterically.

Only now, - her heart missed a beat - his tread was uneven.

'Caro, who is he?' Her sister whispered. 'He looks quite beside himself. Caro?'

Gervase felt overwhelmed with fury, impeding his ability to act. He realised he was shaking. The insufferable heat in the ballroom did not help. Droplets of sweat ran down his brow forcing him to blink his eyes and clear his blurred vision of the three people on the small dais in front of him.

Gervase took the measure of the duke, a tall, well-proportioned man plainly and simply dressed but the suiting of his evening wear was expensive and his physique did justice to his tailor. Not one of your effete aristocrats then. He would shape up well in a fight. The fight that he was going to get before long. The sooner the better. Fisticuffs would be preferable. Flesh on flesh.

He glanced at the sister briefly. Was she Susannah? A diamond of the first water. She would storm the *ton* without question.

And now for Caroline. Modishly dressed as might be expected, ignoring the garish jewels. As befitted a future duchess. What more was there to say? She had the same dark eyes, the same full mouth, the same slender figure. Now that he saw her again he could not get enough of looking at her.

But she had proved so fickle.

The scene swam before his eyes. 'Caroline, why did you not reply to my letters, I wrote enough of them!'

Caroline stared at him, pallid-hued. 'Gervase! I did not hear from you... What is the matter with your leg? Were you injured in Spain?'

'And what have you done?' Gervase spat out, directing a cursory glance at the duke, who was in the process of raising his quizzing-glass to regard Gervase. 'Why are you marrying this man?'

Another moment and he was elbowed out of the way. Roland had caught him up. 'Your Grace, Alversleigh, how do you do? May I congratulate you upon your engagement.' Said with a graceful bow.

'Wendover, good to see you. I'm pleased the invitation did not go astray. Your valiant exploits in the War have been noted. The papers were full of it.' The duke paused. 'I would introduce you to my betrothed. And her sister. But it is more pressing that your companion should be removed forthwith. He, I think, was not invited. The Blue Room.' The duke allowed the quizzing-glass to slide through his fingers and nodded his head briefly.

Gervase swung around, unsure whether to strike the stony-faced duke or Roland first. He did not have to make a choice. Events were taken out of his hands as he was manhandled from both sides by two previously unseen footmen.

Gervase's feet slipped on the floor as the men dragged him away. To avoid complete ignominy, he regained his balance but could not stop himself struggling. 'Unhand me, will you!'

There was no reply and soon he found himself passing before the assembled guests now staring and silent. He was forced through a side-door at the back of the ballroom and out into a corridor. There a servant stationed beside a further curtained entrance allowed their passage. They entered another room, the ungainly little group, where he was flung unceremoniously on a sofa. The two men took their leave but he heard a key turn in the lock. Silence. The entire episode had taken less than a minute he would wager.

Gervase sat up, rested his elbows on his knees and held his head in his hands.

He stared down at the carpet, trying to get his breath back.

To his horror he heard a sob escape him. Good grief, he had just enacted a Cheltenham tragedy!

He willed himself to concentrate on the pattern in the carpet until the offensive blue of the heraldic dragons turned his stomach.

Cautiously he moved his right leg and was rewarded with a familiar pain that shot all the way up to his hip.

At least he had not lost the damn thing as was once feared. Cursing, he lifted it onto the sofa and was relieved as the hurt eased.

He leant back, looking around him. The room he was in was small for a room in a ducal household. No windows and almost devoid of furniture apart from the sofa but there was a screen which divided the space in half. A small table with a basin and ewer stood to one side. He puzzled fleetingly then he knew where he was. He was in a retiring-room, and with no chance of escape.

How long would it be before the expected confrontation?

In the event it was to be merely a matter of minutes.

CHAPTER 3

Caroline could hardly believe the scene that had just unfolded in front of her, her sister and Gervase's friend, not to mention the duke himself!

First she had had to overcome her shock at seeing Gervase appear out of the blue, with all the appearance of having suffered a war injury, only for him to be *dragged,* there was no other word for it, across the ballroom before she could explain... yet, what could she explain?

Then there were his *painful* accusations...

She would think about it later...

All the duke had had to do was to issue a command and the ballroom had been cleared of what His Grace no doubt thought was an *interruption.*

She looked around wildly.

Even now, so soon afterwards, the assembled throng of elegant ladies and sober gentlemen were progressing towards the supper rooms, at the behest of numerous young footmen dressed in the red and gold livery of the ducal household. The chatter was subdued but here and there a tinkling laugh or a sonorous tone broke through to promise the evening would end in a different manner.

Let the audience do as they wished. No matter, she had

to follow Gervase.

Her heart pounding, Caroline rose, allowing her wrap to slip from her shoulders and shimmer to the floor.

She took a step forward intending to alight from the dais but felt herself held back.

'Where are you going, Caro?' Susannah hissed in a whisper as she clutched at the thin material of Caroline's dress.

But on Caroline's other side a firm grip on her gloved forearm restrained her more fully. 'You will not leave me. I shall be back directly to escort you to supper,' Those were the duke's words.

She was aware that Susannah shivered beside her.

Gervase's friend, addressed as Wendover, dropped to one knee to retrieve the discarded wrap but his gaze was fixed on Susannah as he restored the garment to Caroline.

'Your Grace, I beg leave for a word,' he said to the duke. 'In private, if I may. I would like to acquaint you with a little of Major Thorpe's recent history in the Peninsula. But I can assure you I will be responsible for him for the rest of the evening.'

The duke gave a slight bow, stepped down from the dais and the two men moved off together across the ballroom. The duke increased his pace as Gervase's friend harangued him, but then he halted as if to listen more closely.

They too disappeared through the side-door.

Gervase heard a key turn in the lock of the door opposite him. As expected, it heralded the entrance of His Grace, the Duke of Albion, with the two footmen otherwise known as henchmen. With a wave of the duke's hand the men were summarily dismissed. They left the room.

Gervase got to his feet and squared up to his gaoler. 'Why am I here? By what right?'

The duke faced him full-on. 'Well, do you see, I could

not allow you to disrupt the proceedings any longer. I gather you have a grievance, Thorpe. Wendover claims you are a boyhood friend of his, son of his Father's steward. I knew the Fourth Earl from the House, of course. Wendover has acquainted me with a little of your history - that you also have been mentioned in despatches of recent date. It has given me pause; otherwise you would have been quite summarily dismissed. In effect, I suggest we meet again, but on my terms. Would tomorrow at noon suit? In my office here at Grosvenor Square?'

Taken aback, Gervase stammered. 'I will meet you anywhere. The sooner the better.'

'That's settled then. We can discuss the situation man-to-man. Wendover has undertaken to convey you back to his residence. I am afraid you cannot stay here any longer at my betrothal celebration.' There was a slight curling of the duke's lip as he spoke. An infinitesimal bow followed.

Ha, how much had that cost him?

Gervase marched out with as much dignity as he could muster.

There was nothing further to be said. Everything could wait. Even Caroline. He would deal with *her* later.

Not while the bloodlust was upon him.

There were important matters to be resolved.

Man to man.

Yes, that would do.

Caroline started as Susannah's nails threatened the delicate fabric of Caroline's evening glove.

'What just happened, Caro? Why have you kept so much from me?' the inquisition had begun; Caroline turned to face her sister; Susannah deserved to know the truth.

If only Caroline knew what the truth was.

'Susannah, I have not deliberately concealed anything from you. But you were so young and in the care of Miss James at the time…'

Susannah was fanning herself vigorously, her eyes fixed on Caroline.

Time passed.

Caroline began again. 'I was expecting that when Gervase returned from the Peninsula... Well, I thought that we would, that he would...'

Susannah snapped her fan shut. 'You thought he would propose?'

Caroline closed her eyes momentarily. 'No, indeed. I mean, we had already ...'

Susannah's eyes widened. 'You had a secret engagement.'

'Yes. But I heard nothing from him. And then with poor Papa... Well, I thought Gervase was lost to me.'

'So you accepted another offer.' Susannah spoke matter-of-factly.

'Yes.'

'For both our sakes?'

'Yes.'

Susannah went quiet then continued. '*He* did not look well, Caro.'

Caroline felt a constriction in her throat. 'Soldiering can do that to a man,' she replied desperately. Her sister was driving her into a corner. A not uncommon feeling with Susannah.

It was true Gervase had changed in some indefinable way, but then so had she. Was he battle-weary or battle-hardened? Always a lean figure he now looked, if possible, even more so, maybe gaunt would be a better word. Heaven forbid. 'He will recover.'

'He was limping.'

And then there was the injury.

What could she say? 'He may have encountered an obstacle on the journey back to England. He may have had an accident.'

'I think you are not yet free of him, Caro.' Susannah spoke with emphasis.

'It is too hot to argue. I am betrothed to the Duke of Albion. Gervase is the past now, Susannah.'

'I shall talk to you later. I shall come to your bedchamber.'

Caroline straightened her back. 'Very well. Hush. The duke is returning.'

The door at the far end of the ballroom had just opened to re-admit the duke. As he started across the ballroom towards them he was joined by another younger gentleman who had been hovering near the door and casting glances towards them for some time. He bore all the hallmarks of the upper *ton*. Tall and fair, he carried himself well as he accompanied his mentor and talked quietly to him. The ballroom had by now almost emptied of guests. Most had proceeded to the supper-rooms.

Caroline sighed. It was insufferable that they should be marooned here on a dais. Granted the level was only slightly above the ballroom floor but she supposed she must endure the marking out from the rest of the guests, from the less worthy members of the *ton*.

A situation that would be with her for the rest of her life.

The duke approached across the ballroom with his usual measured tread, looking neither to left nor right.

An expression Caroline could not define was on his face as he bowed slightly to her and then to Susannah. 'The Earl of Saint Cross will escort you to supper, Miss Susannah. I wager you will find his company congenial.'

There was a swirling of skirts as Susannah stepped down from the dais and took the arm of the gentleman who had stepped out from behind the duke.

'Miss Susannah Langrish.' The Earl's eyes were wide as he regarded Susannah.

It was a not unfamiliar reaction when confronted with her sister's beauty, thought Caroline.

'I think we may have danced together earlier in the evening, my lord,' was Susannah's graceful reply.

Caroline could not fault her sister's behaviour. Susannah would never be short of offers but her polite acceptance of all overtures meant one never could be sure of her true feelings.

The duke held out his arm to Caroline. 'Let us go down to supper. I have no further desire to mingle with guests at present.'

Caroline responded as was required. Well, if that was what he regarded as mingling!

However, it was with a feeling of relief that Caroline allowed him to direct her towards the supper-room. Too many thoughts were whirling around in her head and she must endure as best she could. When she had retired for the night – that would be the time to go through the events of the evening - when Susannah would continue her inquisition! But Caroline was being unfair; Susannah had Caroline's best interests at heart.

Nevertheless, she still found herself trying to look back into the ballroom but the pressure of the duke's arm prevented her. Gently he pulled her towards him and adjusted her wrap with careful fingers that lingered. 'The Earl of Marlow has taken our unwanted guest home. You will not be bothered again tonight. I shall take further measures tomorrow, rest assured.'

And he acknowledged the servant come to escort them. 'I have ordered one of my private rooms to be set aside for us. We shall not be disturbed.'

Caroline was about to reply, to ask questions and then thought better of it as she walked with him. She must stay composed for whatever lay ahead.

CHAPTER 4

Once released into the corridor after a meeting which could only be described as dispiriting, Gervase found Roland keeping guard close to the door. He was alone.

Looking over his shoulder as he spoke, Roland said, hurriedly, 'As you are unharmed, I think we will wait until we are safely away from Grosvenor Square before we talk, do you agree? I have some information to impart with regard to the Misses Langrish but it will wait.'

Gervase nodded. Speech had deserted him in any case.

Besides, he was not sure he was ready to hear gossip. Even gossip on the subject of the Langrish sisters.

His mind was fully occupied as it was. He was still trying to take in the Duke of Albion's command of the situation which had just occurred in the retiring-room. Had he, Gervase, been worsted? It would seem that he had. But not for long he swore. Justice would prevail. As it always did in the end he reminded himself.

'I have ordered my carriage to be brought around. It should be here directly.' The crease between Roland's brows deepened further as he looked at Gervase. 'Most guests have already arrived, I assume. No-one wants to be late when the Duke of Albion is the host.' The doors to the street were wide open but no personages were visible. 'We can leave inconspicuously.'

'I have no intention of skulking away like a miserable cur. In any case I wish to walk back not be confined in your fusty conveyance. It's far too hot a night.' Gervase was out of the house and down the steps without waiting for a reply.

He strode off down the road hoping for some fresher air. Anything to clear his head.

Roland caught Gervase up several minutes later, unfortunately, and began another conversation, which Gervase could well have done without. Small shards of glass located somewhere within his head and trying to get out were relentless. Not to put too fine a point on it, his head was splitting.

But still his companion went on. And on. 'Very well. We'll walk together – if you insist on going on foot. I've arranged for Jessop to take my carriage back to the mews. That's if you can bear my company? You were adamant you wanted to accompany me to the Betrothal Ball earlier, were you not? Regrettably, in view of the consequences. I mean, a scene in full view of worthy assembled members of the *ton*. If not, perhaps the most *interesting* members, I give you that.'

Gervase grunted.

'But for goodness sake, slow down, will you?' Roland said, breathing heavily. 'It grieves me sincerely that you are the one with the war injury, not I, and we both know why.'

'Have you forgotten Badajoz, then?'

'I meant, of course, what happened at Salamanca, as well you know.'

Gervase strode on, increasing his pace.

He did not wish to be reminded of the incident in which he had nearly lost his leg. Especially not *now*. In any case Roland *had* suffered; even if he had chosen not to remember. Captain Gordon Howard too, yet another Fifty-Seconder, making him a difficult rooming companion for Gervase. In Gordon's case - actual scarring - with some justification. But, had they not all suffered?

The next thing he knew, Roland had him in an arm lock. 'You are wasting your temper on the wrong person, my friend.'

It was true. 'Let go of me.' Gervase was released for a second time and stood rubbing his arms.

'If you are really after revenge, you need to keep a cooler head. I endeavoured to smooth things over back there, my friend.'

'I wish you had not. And what was all that about the Peninsula? I'll thank you to keep quiet. You were mentioned in dispatches at least as much as I was. Or so I was told.' He pulled down his cuffs and straightened his neckcloth. 'The heat is driving me to distraction.'

'You were risking your life in the field – it was a near daily occurrence. Any foolhardy expedition behind enemy lines mentioned and you put yourself forward to lead it. In the end I had to accompany you more often than not. Colbourne went so far as to recommend you were sent back to Headquarters. He swore unnecessary and persistent recklessness was not in his book.'

Gervase said nothing. What was there to say? He had lost hope when he had heard nothing from Caroline. Weeks had turned into months, then years. Life had seemed meaningless.

They both paused in view of yet another square. Just as deserted as the others, dusty and desolate.

But Roland still had not finished. 'Now I know why. You were entangled with Miss Caroline Langrish! Miss Langrish of Beauminster Priory, but you did not think to tell me. and you had received no letters from her as it turns out. I mean the elder Miss Langrish, not Miss Susannah,' said with a sidelong glance.

'I know who you mean. But I don't know what you are talking about. Anyway, to show weakness to the enemy is never beneficial.'

'And the enemy is now the Duke of Albion? It was best to quieten His Grace. Enough disturbance had been caused, I thought. I tried to rescue the situation.'

Gervase gave a hollow laugh. 'Impossible.'

At least there the conversation appeared to have come to an end.

They walked on together across the square and turned a corner into the next street. There was no-one there. In the distance a rumble of thunder promised the night would be disturbed. For once the elements were in tune with him.

Then Gervase bethought himself of the encounter to come on the morrow. If all went very ill it was best that Roland be aware of the circumstances – especially after the recent bruising session in the retiring room. After all he, Gervase, had been locked in. Who knew what might happen? Though who on earth cared, one might ask. Still.

'I have an appointment with the Duke of Albion. Tomorrow.' Gervase volunteered.

Roland halted in his tracks. 'What the devil! Have you indeed?'

Gervase stopped as well. 'I shall challenge him.'

'On what grounds?'

'What do you think?' Gervase retorted. Deliberate, intentional obfuscation. He despaired of Roland sometimes. Who needed friends when all they did was question one?

'I have no idea.' Roland scuffed his heel on the ground releasing a cloud of dust. 'I hate to say it, but I presume Miss Langrish has not been coerced?'

The remark hung heavily in the air between them. A long pause followed, replete with meaning.

At last, as if not expecting a serious reply to such a *reprehensible* question, Roland gripped Gervase's shoulder briefly. 'Shall we continue our discussion over a brandy back at my town house? There is much to discuss for I have news for you.'

Still speechless, Gervase swallowed, then nodded his

head and for once they continued the rest of the way in silence.

He was beginning to feel tired. And sick at heart.

The heat. It was the heat.

CHAPTER 5

Thankfully Gervase accepted the tumbler of brandy held out to him by Roland.

The walk back to the Earl's town house in Mecklenburg Square and up the three flights of stairs necessary to reach the Roland's study had taken more out of Gervase than he would have liked to admit to anyone, least of all his closest friend.

Perhaps liquor would help but he doubted it. He had certainly tried the drinking cure often enough since he had returned to England, what was it, but a couple of weeks ago? Unsatisfactory in all respects. Well, maybe not entirely. For a few hours at least it had produced welcome oblivion.

He suspected Gordon, back at his rooms, might be thinking the same and going down the same route, but with more justification perhaps.

'Sit down over there, I suggest.' His friend gestured to a chair by the windows which had been thrown open to the night air. 'You will be more comfortable.'

But no perceptible breeze entered into the room. The stifling heat had not dissipated at all even though it must be in the early hours by now.

The promise of a storm had receded.

It had been a miasma, an unwelcome reminder of the torrid atmosphere of Spain. Like Caroline's protestations but a few years ago; a false promise.

Gervase knocked back a decent portion of spirits before limping over to the far side of the study and casting himself down as suggested. He placed his offending leg on the footstool that Roland had obligingly put within reach.

Gervase stretched back in the chair.

'If you want some food, Symonds has prepared a cold collation', his friend said, shooting him a quick glance, 'but I fear food is not uppermost in your mind.' Roland himself strode over to a sideboard, picked up some bread and cut himself two generous slices of ham, which he proceeded to eat with gusto. 'Well, Symonds has done us proud tonight. Devil take it, but I am hungry. However, I fear I should not have taken you as my guest tonight. It has not ended well.'

Gervase sat up suddenly. 'Well, I for one am grateful for the invitation. I saw for myself.' He looked down at his hand around the tumbler and realised it was shaking. 'I saw her in her true colours.'

Roland sauntered over to the window and looked down into the Square. 'A pity. Because if the situation were different I should have tried to advance my suit with the fair Miss Susannah Langrish. If you had had no objection?' He paused. 'You will stay here tonight.'

'That sounds like an order. And pray dangle after Miss Susannah if you must, I'll not stand in your way. Perhaps she is more faithful than her sister, but I doubt it,' said Gervase bitterly, staring down into his now empty glass. 'Deuce take it; you are not my commanding officer now. But I will take you up on a room for the night. I am tired.'

He slammed his empty glass down on a side-table. 'Now tell me your news.'

Roland continued, still with his back to Gervase. 'The Duke of Albion is a very powerful man in the land, as well as being a peer of the realm. The rumour is he runs with the Carleton House set. It surprises me as he seems a stickler for form. Well, no one is immune from temptation. Maybe when the Prince Regent misbehaves himself again Albion will reconsider. Whitby said only yesterday there were rumours of debauchery at Carleton House and last week a *contretemps* was narrowly avoided after His Royal Highness misread the signals and propositioned a married lady who turned out to be devoted to her husband. Rare, I know but it happens…' Here he halted, as if aware that Gervase was not paying attention.

Frankly, Gervase could not care less about the Prince Regent.

'And?'

Roland swung around, leant against the window-sill and gave his attention to Gervase. 'Well, more to the point, we have not been back long but long enough for me to discover that we are out of touch. I have not been idle, you know. Were you aware that the Langrish sisters were left destitute?'

'Destitute?'

'It transpires the Langrish sisters were our near neighbours but not known to me. Oxford has much to answer for, I regret to say. I knew them not but it seems you did.'

'What of it?'

'Oh, yes, I had heard of their father and his gambling habit but that was all. Naturally I knew *of* him; his land adjoined my father's.'

'Get on with it, man.'

'Well, I had words with Whitby, whom I ran into while you were ensconced with the duke. Yes, I know Whitby is a windbag but he always has his ear to the ground. On this occasion he was useful, I thought.' He moved swiftly back to the side board. 'Let me re-fill your drink. You may be in need of fortification when I have told you all.' Without waiting for Gervase to acquiesce, Roland un-stoppered the decanter and poured liquor into a fresh glass. 'Here, drink.'

Gervase took the proffered tumbler but put it down next to the other one. This was news indeed; his heart began thumping in his chest. If this was true, what the devil had happened to Caroline's father, George Langrish, the arrogant reprobate? But well-cushioned in the extreme surely, with his huge estate in Kent. A landed gentleman, one of the foremost families in Kent it was said, even though one without a title. 'Tell me more. Destitute? How?'

'I don't know. Well, the *on-dit* is that the Duke of Albion has supported the come-out of Miss Susannah Langrish as well as offering for your intended.'

Gervase shaded his eyes with his hand. 'Go on.'

'There is more.'

Gervase grimaced. 'Well?'

'The sisters are living in a rented house with a hired companion at the behest of the Duke of Albion. Unless, of course, the lady in question is something other.'

Gervase rose from his seat, sending the footstool spinning away. He forced out some words, any words, aware that he needed fresh air again, immediately. 'How many women does he need? The meeting tomorrow cannot come a moment too soon. I have had enough for tonight. I'll not stay here. I'm for home.'

At least back at his rooms in the Albany he would receive no further news that felt like a punch in the gut. Gordon would be a blessed relief after Roland and his topics of conversation.

His friend's face assumed a no doubt purposely blank expression. 'As you wish. Mrs Hammond was delighted with my request to prepare a bedchamber. You are quite the favourite amongst my household staff, you know. Mrs Hammond will be disappointed and I am too.'

Gervase dragged himself away, stumbling over the damned footstool which had inserted itself between himself and the way out. He gave it a good kick. 'Kind of her but I'm not fit company. I'll see myself out.'

At the doors he turned around. 'Is there anything else I should know? Before I go? Did Whitby say anything else?'

'Our talk was cut short. There may be more to tell; he had as good as hinted that there was. I am sorry, Gervase.'

To do him justice he did sound so.

Gervase summoned up what remained of his breeding. To overcome his dangerously feeble state. 'Yes, it is better for me to know. I am more prepared for the assignation with His Grace, the Duke of Albion. Perfidious Albion. Is that not the quote?' He snarled.

Roland could always be distracted by a literary allusion.

'Yes, French, I believe; the Marquis de Ximénèz. Be off with you then. I hope you rest easier than you would have done here. I have done my best.'

Gervase slammed out of the doors.

Too much. Too much to think about.

How had Caroline and her sister become destitute? What had possessed Caroline to accept *carte blanche?* For that was what it was, make no mistake. Indubitably Gervase needed to see Caroline but tomorrow's arrangement with the Duke of Albion took precedence.

Man to man.

At noon.

CHAPTER 6

Caroline stood on the threshold of the supper-room escorted by the Duke of Albion. Her hand was resting lightly on his arm: a pose likely to be repeated on innumerable formal occasions for the rest of her life. Unless...

To her dismay it was as warm in here as it had been in the ballroom. There would be no relief for her in *that* direction. Nor in any other until she and Gervase were together again. And talking. The resulting conversation did not bear thinking about, so it was best to concentrate on her current predicament. Distraction was the key and heaven only knew she had plenty to distract her with the Duke of Albion. She determined to focus on the present.

By the ducal standards set in Grosvenor Square she was faced with a small intimate room, a mere three sashed windows either side of a balcony - its doors thrown open to the night air. A modicum of furniture tastefully upholstered in dove-grey silk would allow a select supper-party to retire here and engage in light conversation or disport themselves otherwise.

A table covered in a white cloth and laden with an array of small dishes, a decanter, crystal glasses and a tureen or two had been set ready for them. A side-board showed a further assortment of dainty sweetmeats and another bottle resting at an angle on a bed of ice in a silver bowl.

Only one white-gloved footman remained, stepping forward from the shadows to adjust a serving dish, moving it an infinitesimal inch or so further to the right. Then he too bowed himself out of the room.

Now they were completely alone. How rarely they were, she thought, looking at her fiancé. As she watched him she saw he was preoccupied with the arrangements in the room. His quizzing glance was already aloft as he observed first in one direction then another, before letting the glass slip though his fingers and nodding his head to himself as if satisfied.

Above all the heat was unbearable. Caroline allowed her stole to slip down a little from her shoulders and fanned herself with slow repetitive movements.

The duke gave her a lingering glance. 'Please sit down, Caroline.' He moved to draw out one of a pair of elegant gilt-edged chairs set either side of the table.

Caroline obeyed him.

Once she was seated the duke did likewise. A gentleman of his stature was not ideally suited to the chair in question but he faced her, formal as ever. He stretched out his long legs at the side of the table and placed one hand firmly down on the table cloth. Not for the first time she sensed the power inherent in him: the broad chest, the well-proportioned legs, a body honed for Corinthian pursuits.

There was a stillness too which she must admit she liked.

Caroline returned his regard.

Just faintly, the rumble of a carriage over cobblestones outside broke the silence. In the distance a clock chimed the hour: one o'clock.

The duke poured them each a glass of white wine from the decanter at his elbow and handed one to her. Their fingers touched briefly.

'Well, Caroline, I feel you owe me an explanation.' His voice was flat, his face betrayed no expression, as he sipped elegantly.

'Your Grace, I...'

'*Hugo*, please, Caroline, when we are alone. I have asked you to do so before. There is a reluctance, I feel. Very proper, but now we are affianced. It would give me great pleasure.'

Caroline felt the colour rising in her cheeks. 'Very well, Hugo. Gervase Thorpe and I were close, a few years ago. After he took colours and left for Spain, I, I did not hear from him again.'

'Just so. You were not betrothed. Yet this Gervase swears he has a prior claim on you. Is that so, Caroline?'

'We were not formally engaged, it is true.'

'But there was an understanding?'

'He did not answer my letters.' Caroline's voice rose higher. 'I have not had an opportunity to talk to him. And now I see that he has sustained an injury...' she choked and raised her hand to cover her mouth.

The duke stilled. 'My feeling is that the situation warrants little of my time but he has attempted to interfere with my betrothal celebration.'

The duke leant forward and took her left hand, caressing the large diamond glittering on her third finger. Then he raised her hand to his lips, and kissed it, his eyes not leaving hers. 'The disruption was unhappy.' He released her and sat back. 'I shall deal with him. In due course.'

'What do you intend, Hugo?' Her voice rose higher still.

He reached over, took the cover from one of several dishes and speared a piece of beef. 'Please eat, Caroline.'

Caroline looked at the assortment of delicacies in front of her, selected a few morsels at random onto her plate and took a mouthful. The food, of whatever kind it was,

was completely tasteless.

They ate in silence for a few moments.

Then at last the duke spoke. 'I understand that Wendover, he is the Fifth Earl of Marlow you know, and Gervase Thorpe have taken credit for daring exploits in the Peninsula.' He threw down his fork and pushed his plate away. Sitting back, he rested his elbow on the arm of the gilt supper chair and supported his head on his hand. 'It is only to be expected that the Prince Regent will have taken note.'

Startled at his words, Caroline looked up at the duke.

Unlikely as it might seem, she was to be beholden for Gervase's safety to the Prince Regent!

The duke met her gaze unflinchingly but a muscle twitched at the side of his jaw. 'And as for you, Caroline, you have been *seen,* the *ton* has recognised you as my future Duchess, the Duchess of Albion. The importance of the evening cannot be emphasized enough, so there is therefore nothing more to be said.' Here he paused and lifted his napkin to pat his lips. 'If you have eaten enough, I think it best if you return home now with your sister. I shall say you are indisposed and I shall visit you tomorrow, when you will be more yourself. We have a long future ahead of us and there will be many occasions when we can be together. And now I have other plans for my evening.'

He rose and bowed to her.

The audience was over.

'As you wish, Hugo.' Caroline murmured and rose, gathering her stole and reticule together.

He escorted her to the doors, which swung open as ever seemingly miraculously aware of the great Duke of Albion's bidding. More likely at the behest of the attendant footmen outside in the corridor. The duke exchanged a few words with a major-domo who had hastened to his master and Caroline was on her way home, she knew, as she was hastened along the corridor. In the distance she saw Susannah with her newly-acquired swain close beside her.

The evening was at an end.

The duke had at the very least answered her question. She would allow him some iota of concern. Although whether the concern was for herself or not she wondered, but at least Gervase was safe for now. Her fiancé would not proceed for fear of damaging his position with the Prince Regent. And he had had the decency to tell her so. A large concession for the Duke of Albion and perhaps even auguring well for their future together.

But was she clutching at straws?

Nevertheless, maybe he understood, in his own cold way, how she had felt about Gervase. Or rather how she still felt, if she were honest with herself.

Her one coherent thought amongst her confusion was that she must see Gervase as soon as possible. But how?

CHAPTER 7

'What the devil are you about?' Gervase ground out when he saw Captain Gordon Howard, flat out, face-down, sprawled on the sofa of the modest sitting-room they both shared at the Albany. The Captain's current position obscured the sabre slash acquired at Salamanca and which lent his features a rather alarming distinction.

Captain Gordon Howard, whose brute strength Gervase had had reason to be grateful for... Gervase hated to admit that his hazy memories of rescue from the battlefield of Salamanca obtruded more often than he would have liked.

Air, that was what was needed, Gervase thought, and which was in such short supply; he flung up the sash in the only window in the room, which unfortunately overlooked a similarly airless space, a small enclosed courtyard at the back of the Albany.

His head was still splitting. The walk home had done nothing to ease the after-effects of a superfluity of brandy which, coupled with heartache was more than any man could decently bear. Certainly he was unprepared to find his companion in a similar state to his own; befuddled with drink.

Though, in all honesty, Gervase did not know of any emotional entanglements on the part of the Captain. Fortunately for him. Though that was not to say that there definitely were not, Gervase admitted to himself. He had been too preoccupied with his own: Caroline and that damned betrothal announcement in The Times.

Gervase had always regarded Gordon as someone who did not take life too seriously. Well, it may have been true before the Peninsular War but his behaviour since had caused Gervase not a little worry. Maybe they had all been scarred in one way or another. Poor Gordon certainly had.

Aware of the inconsistencies in his train of thought, only too ready to condemn others when his own behaviour hardly warranted close examination, he stared down at the comatose Captain. His boots had been discarded but he had made no further progress in divesting himself of his dishevelled clothing.

Gervase had been ready to fall into his bed back at the Albany. Uncomfortable, yes, but a bed was a bed after all.

Now it looked as though rest was to be delayed.

A disturbance coming from the area brought forth, as expected, Nathaniel, manservant and now few would question it, Gordon's friend. Gervase still marvelled at the way in which the former foot-soldier, having attached himself to Gordon, had returned with him from the Peninsula and proved invaluable. It helped of course that Gordon was flush with funds. Nathaniel brought order to the bachelor rooms of the Albany apartment and Gervase for one was heartily glad of it.

Obviously awakened by the noise of Gervase's return. Nathaniel appeared yawning from his own quarters. 'Might you take the Captain's legs, sir, if you're willing to help?'

Gervase nodded.

Together they hefted Gordon from the couch but there was some resistance at first. 'Leave me alone, must sleep.' he mumbled. 'That last bottle of port was a mistake. Best not to mix vintages, Avery said. Too late now. Anyhow

Lydia not here.'

Lydia? Maybe there was a lady in the case.

The two men staggered through to Gordon's room and slung him down on the bed.

Gordon thereupon surprised Gervase by opening his eyes and fixing his stare on his erstwhile companion in arms. 'Oh, you are here too, are you? Told you before, you should not have been left. Told Roland so. Then I lost him too.' And he swore. 'A lot to answer for.'

Oh no, many and various were the battlefield histories of the three of them: Gervase, Roland and Gordon but when it came to it in the end there was only one that counted for Gervase.

The incident at Salamanca.

For all three of them had been affected. Although until now Gervase had not realised that Gordon too suffered with guilt, or so it appeared.

Poor Gordon. The sabre slash had come later and had at least removed Gordon from the battle-field.

It only surprised Gervase that Gordon should imagine himself back in the fray at such an hour of the night, and after so much time had passed. Still there was no controlling memories.

Gervase searched for a proper response but the lateness of the hour and his inebriated state interfered with his ability to concoct suitable words of reassurance.

Fortunately, Gordon promptly turned over and went to sleep.

'A frequent occurrence, I take it.' Gervase realised he was sounding Nathaniel out. How much did he know?

'Yes, sir. But he'll be bang up to the mark in the morning, you'll see,' said Nathaniel, picking up a cover from a nearby chair and throwing it over the snoring man.

Gervase bowing to his superior judgement, shrugged his shoulders and wished the same could be said for himself.

Nathaniel arranged the cover more suitably and

continued talking but without looking at Gervase. 'You'll have been at the Duke of Albion's soirée I expect.'

Gervase opened his mouth to respond, in awe as ever at the information gleaned by all from within a household but Nathaniel had not finished. 'Heard tell, there was a bit of a mill there? Expect you displayed to advantage, mind.'

If only. Not even his best friend could have said so.

Nathaniel gave the covering a final adjustment and stood back, admiring his handiwork. 'You'll be in trouble now, I'm thinking.'

'What?'

'The Duke of Albion. He's a rum cove.' Nathaniel threw Gervase a glance. 'If you was wanting an escort at any time?' He spoke matter-of-factly.

'Whatever do you mean?'

Nathaniel went on hastily. 'Well, I do not have enough to occupy me here, with the Captain - he does not go out much, not nearly enough, you might say, being as the lads returned from the War are so much in demand. The ladies love a wounded war-hero, don't they? Told him so. Not much to take care of, speaking as a valet, you understand?'

'Oh, I see.' A picture was beginning to emerge. Gervase himself had endured a similar spell of inactivity but he had not noticed the same with Gordon. His disfigurement might have had something to do with his reluctance to participate.

'Yes, well, if you need a protector. A groom, say? A groom, now, is never remarked on.'

Gervase might as well come clean. His head was making a wonderful effort to clear itself. 'It is true that there was an altercation. Although I cannot for the life of me understand how you know this. But never mind,' he said hurriedly. 'It is a shame Gordon, the Captain, I mean, does not attend more social events. The Season is not over by any means. Where was he this evening, by the way?'

Again, Nathaniel did not meet his eye. 'Well, in a manner of speaking, he was here, with the Earl of

Dulwich, who he calls Avery, sir.'

'Yes, yes, I know.' Another Fifty-Seconder. Were they all in London, half-pay or not? Gervase was beginning to think they were.

'The Captain was drinking deep, he was. Says he doesn't want to go out no more. So His Lordship visits him and they drink.'

Gervase decided to bring the conversation to a close; his head had started throbbing again. He had enough going on without being burdened with another man's troubles, sympathetic though he should be.

'If I need a guard as you call it, I will certainly ask you. I will have a word with the Captain tomorrow about the other matter.' He glanced at the mantel clock; it was past three. 'Now I need my bed. I have an early start.'

'Sir.' Nathaniel bowed and made to leave the bedchamber.

'Oh, by the by, who is Lydia?'

'No idea, sir. Now I'll be off.' And he duly left.

No further enlightenment there but Gervase realised he had another problem, albeit minor, on his hands. A Fifty-Seconder with no desire to participate in the Season, when invitations lay thick on the shelf in their sitting-room.

It was scarcely credible but understandable in view of the disfigurement. Maybe there was something deeper at work.

Well, he for one would have a brandy or two before turning in; there was much to ponder over. He went over to the sideboard and poured himself a decent glass.

As well as the enigma of Gordon, he pondered over the question of whether or not, he, Gervase, a man regarded as being beneath the notice of the illustrious Duke of Albion, really needed some kind of bodyguard. Perhaps after the meeting tomorrow in the duke's offices he would!

With what Gervase had in mind he sincerely hoped so.

CHAPTER 8

Caroline entered the Lilac Drawing Room with Susannah, closely followed by their companion, Mrs Farley, who had met them on their return from the Duke of Albion's town house.

Even now, after nearly three months Caroline was not used to her surroundings. Number Thirteen, the house in Brunswick Square had been taken for the season, the duke had informed her. Perhaps so but Caroline could not help believing that the contents bore all the hallmarks of the taste of a former courtesan; richly opulent if somewhat faded; furniture that had seen better days. No good comparisons could be made with Beauminster Priory's inherited elegance. He had entreated her and her sister to make themselves comfortable. It had certainly been a very grand setting for Susannah's come-out dance.

However, Caroline could not like the Lilac Drawing-Room, the all-pervasive pale purple drapery more resembled a boudoir. Was it necessary to place four chaise-longues upholstered in the same shade of lilac watered silk around the room?

If only the curtains would billow in the wind instead of hanging there sullenly and adding to the oppressive atmosphere.

Caroline placed her reticule and wrap on a draped table, also a becoming shade of well, puce. She began stripping off her evening gloves. It had been a long evening.

Throwing off her stole too, Susannah immediately took herself off to the far side of the room. Wielding her fan vigorously she positioned herself by the open windows. 'It is too hot. The heat in London is insufferable. I wish we were still at the Priory.'

'You know that can never be,' replied Caroline quietly. How many more times would she have to say those words.

'Will there be anything else tonight, Miss Langrish?' A voice close to Caroline's ear. A waft of lavender with undertones of an unfamiliar scent drifted past. Yesterday the perfume had been different, more exotic. A woman of many moods, but all well-concealed.

Caroline started, recalled to her senses. 'No indeed, Mrs Farley. We are well taken care of, as always.'

The elegant lady beside her was dressed modishly in blush pink silk. An ensemble that was discreet, yet expensive. Rather like the widow herself.

Not for the first time Caroline wondered what the exact relationship had been between the duke and the obliging acquaintance conjured up at such short notice. Or if the past tense should even be used.

But she gave a modicum of decorum to the unusual arrangement of two sisters living alone at the duke's expense. In great splendour. Caroline was unsure whether for once the duke had not succeeded in his aim.

Maybe it did not concern him.

'I am sure His Grace's Betrothal Ball was conducted with his usual attention to detail,' the smooth voice continued.

Until now Susannah had remained motionless by the open windows. Now she swung around; her finely-arched eyebrows drew together and her gaze was sharp and attentive.

'Oh indeed, yes.' Caroline replied in what she hoped was a colourless tone. 'If you will excuse us we are both worn out by the festivities.' And suiting herself to her words she threw herself down on the chaise-longue nearest to her. She motioned to Susannah, who for once obeyed her cue and subsided on the one nearest the open windows. A faint breeze lifted one of the drapes as if somewhere a god had taken pity on mere mortals.

Mrs Farley smiled. 'I shall bid you good-night then.' She gave the slightest of curtseys and glided from the room. The doors closed noiselessly behind her.

'I feel as though Mrs Farley is watching us all the time, Caroline! I declare she is a spy. The situation is impossible!'

'You should not allow the heat to disturb you so, Susannah. And Mrs Farley is our companion and chaperone while we are living here alone.'

'At the courtesy of your fiancé.'

'Yes, but,' said Caroline wearily. 'We have discussed the matter so many times. Did you not enjoy your come-out ball?'

'If Mrs Farley is our chaperone, why did she not attend upon us tonight?'

'Well, I suppose as I am engaged, I was considered chaperone enough for you.'

'I wonder you can bear, well, everything,' replied her sister, spreading out the struts on her fan and examining them closely. Of a sudden, she snapped the fan shut. 'Never mind. Let's to Gervase, your hitherto unknown suitor. Unknown to me at any rate.' Her eyes brightened, she laid down her fan and crossed the room. She threw herself down on a small foot stall the better to observe Caroline no doubt. 'Tell me all!'

'Very well.'

Caroline did not need to close her eyes. She was back there, back in the rose garden at Beauminster Priory. A few snatched moments of time with Gervase before he left for the Regiment, for the Fifty-Second, for death or glory in the Peninsula. And it had turned out to be the glory. But at what cost? And what of the injury to his leg? More to the point, what was his state of mind now... aggravated by her conduct...

Beauminster. How many aeons of time ago was that? Before everything fell apart, before the misery of Papa, before the knowledge of the extent of his gambling debts.

Before the Duke of Albion.

And still the unanswered question, why had she heard nothing from Gervase?

'Caroline? What are you thinking about, Caroline? You promised me, did you not? To tell all?'

'Well, I told you before, Gervase and I were...'

Yet what were they?

'Betrothed?'

'Yes, but it was not widely known. It was to be a secret engagement.'

'Then why are you so upset? Is it because...'

'Susannah.' A note of warning crept into Caroline's voice. 'You go too far.'

'You promised to wait for him. You have broken your promise.' Susannah leant back on the footstool, a slight smile on her face. With care she re-arranged the silk of her overskirt so that the folds were more becomingly disposed about her. 'I think Gervase is your first love and now you are embroiled with the duke and you do not know how to extricate yourself without being name-called as a jilt!' She shot a glance of satisfaction at Caroline.

Sickness washed over Caroline.

'But I am right, am I not? 'Her sister said, mercilessly. 'what are you going to do?'

'Don't forget, the Duke of Albion arranged for your come-out. And paid for it. Mrs Farley spoke of a small fortune having being expended. Not that I necessarily believe her,' She added hastily. 'Are you not grateful?'

Susannah had the grace to look ashamed but did not reply.

The terrible thing was, Susannah had spoken truly.

Caroline rose from the chaise-longue, swept past her tormentor and crossed the drawing-room to the open window. Now it was her turn to seek fresh air. She leant on the window-sill and looked down into the gardens at the back of the town house. Heavy scents rose from the darkening shadows in the gathering dusk. Moths fluttered here and there but not a sound dared to disturb the private world of one of the town houses belonging to the *haut-ton*. The domain of the Duke of Albion.

'I am indeed in trouble,' she murmured quietly to herself.

But Susannah had followed her and now spoke again 'I think you must arrange an assignation with Gervase. No good will come of it if you do not. Cannot you send word to the Earl of Marlow, his friend? He must know where your lover is lodging?'

'He is not my lover,' replied Caroline. 'But I agree. I must do so.'

'Send a note to the Earl of Marlow, I insist. They were comrades in arms and surely he will have Gervase's wellbeing at heart. You know I am right. I am always right. Dear Finch will convey the letter. He is very loyal. *He* is not best pleased to be here in such a strange household. His tales of the goings-on below stairs... well, never mind. I don't want to shock you.'

Susannah stepped away from Caroline, picked up her fan and gathered up her wrap. 'You should listen to me. I should have been the older sister, not you.' She laughed.

As she made her way towards the doors, she halted before several antique portraits hanging on the wall. 'So ill-favoured. Yet the Duke of Albion is not so, do you think? Quite the reverse. But so cold in his demeanour. Are you the one to pierce his armour? I wonder. Or have you already done so? It bears consideration. I think you will not easily escape. Or do you not want to at heart?'

She favoured Caroline with another of her well-known

stares. 'However, he did not escort you home, did he? Is his ardour cooling?'

'You forget we had outriders.'

Susannah laughed again. 'Oh, yes, I had forgotten. To puff up His Grace's consequence,' and she flounced out of the room.

Caroline followed her, aware that she now had a headache. Susannah had a habit of tiring Caroline by shifting the conversation so quickly from one topic to another.

And her words were just, Caroline would rather not admit it, truly rather not. How had her sister learned to twist her, Caroline's, not to be faulted, point of view into something completely other? She put the thought away, for now. There were more important considerations.

A plan was beginning to form in her mind. She would not write to the Earl of Marlow. No, it was well known that to speak to someone in person was always to be preferred. A visit to the earl. As soon as possible. His address could be easily found and Finch, the loyal servant, would accompany her. Best not to tell Susannah in case she performed a *volte-face* and relayed the news to Mrs Farley. One could never be entirely sure with Susannah. If Caroline left her sister a pleading note maybe that would be sufficient.

The Earl of Marlow. He would help. He was Gervase's best friend. He would be certain to give her support and details of Gervase's lodgings. *He would, surely.*

Tomorrow. Tomorrow would be a step on the way to regaining Gervase's trust, she hoped.

But what then? She was an affianced woman.

CHAPTER 9

An almighty banging woke Gervase the next morning.

He turned over in his bed and groaned, his mouth felt dry and his throat was sore, he ached in all the wrong places and especially where he least expected to receive the release he so much wanted. His injured leg was nothing to it.

Noting unsurprised that he had slept in his shirt and breeches, he dragged himself in his stockinged feet to the chamber window, pulled back a curtain and looked down into the cobbled inner courtyard, already dazzling the eye with reflected light. He groaned again.

A scene was there unfolding; a tall, willowy lady robed entirely in bright cerulean blue, so bright it hurt Gervase's eyes, was deep in conversation with Nathaniel. She wore an extremely modish hat with a fine set of plumes which nodded vigorously as she spoke. Even the brim was lined with the same brilliant colour and looked to be made of silk. Who was the fashionable apparition?

The interlude was soon over. Shaking her head, the lady turned smartly on her heels, and clattered across the cobbles and through the archway leading to Piccadilly. Nathaniel had proved his skills as a gatekeeper.

The clock on the mantel chimed the hour with a sound that did little to help Gervase's headache. Ten o'clock and later than he had intended.

It was time to get ready for the meeting at Albion's.

Gervase stumbled through to the sitting room to find Nathaniel laying out an ample breakfast on the sideboard. Gervase's gorge rose.

'Hot water, please, Nathaniel, and quick about it. I have an appointment at twelve.'

'Certainly sir. Would that be with His Grace of Albion?'

'Yes,' replied Gervase. He was not sure he wanted the former soldier as a companion, either openly or secretly. Not yet, for sure, even though doubts had been raised on the score of Gervase's personal safety.

But Nathaniel did not comment further and made his way towards the green baize door.

'Tell me, who was the lady?' Gervase asked.

Nathaniel sniffed. 'Lady Lydia Vellacott. Come calling. Her ladyship knew the Captain before the War. I saw her off.'

'Whatever for? She might have nursed your master back to health.' Lady Lydia in all her glory looked more than capable of affecting a man in the best possible way. Gervase wished that Caroline would do the same for *him*.

'Not a word since we left. Only now we are back does her ladyship show herself. My master deserves better than that.'

Gervase gave up. There sounded to be too many similarities with his own circumstances. He had no time to dwell on another's distress, his own predicament must occupy his attention fully.

At this point as Nathaniel disappeared in the direction of the kitchen area, Gordon, pale but looking more presentable than earlier in the morning, emerged from his bedchamber and made for the sideboard. 'Hells bells, but I have a devil of a head this morning,' he said, turning his back on Gervase and piling a plate with cuts of what looked to be undercooked beef.

Gervase did not think the remark was worthy of comment. Besides, he was in the same way himself.

He was pleased to see that the pangs of conscience that had affected Gordon the previous night showed no signs of reappearing. Gervase could do without his compatriot's no doubt worthy remorse at not conveying Gervase from the battlefield sooner. The strong and muscular soldier did not suit such mawkish sentiments. Besides Gordon *had* returned the following day, with Roland. In time to prevent the worst from happening by all accounts. Gervase thankfully remembered little. Well, little that could be rendered coherently, that is.

High time to direct one's thoughts elsewhere. 'You had a visitor this morning – a shame you were not here to receive her.'

Gordon stilled, fork poised in mid-air. 'You don't say?'

'I most certainly do. A most comely widow or maybe a lady looking for a cisbeo?' Remarks ventured at random. Almost. The lady was indeed comely and with a decided air. No shrinking violet there. Who knew whether she had not a spanking new coach and four waiting in Piccadilly. Gervase rather thought it was likely.

'No idea who she was.' Gordon's attention returned to his breakfast as he added a chunk or two of bread from a wicker basket. He made his way to the small table by the window, sat down and began to eat. 'Nathaniel knows better than to disturb me for no good reason at all,' he mumbled through his food.

'Lady Lydia Vellacott, Nathaniel informs me. The lady looked worthy of your attention, I think. Although early for a morning-call, don't you agree?'

'Oh?' Gordon carried on eating.

Really Gervase wondered why he was bothering with his Albany brother; just the small matter of the Regiment, he supposed. *And the debt incalculable from Salamanca.* 'Come on, Gordon, you are gammoning me.'

When Gordon continued to ignore his friend's words, Gervase tried a different tack. 'How is old Avery, by the way? I hear he is here most nights.'

Gordon sat back, every last morsel having been consumed. 'Seems right as a trivet to me. Sometimes a man just needs company, don't you know?'

Gervase did know.

'And he's got a damn fine cellar, what he doesn't know about wine ain't worth knowing.' He shook his head. 'Brings a selection in a post-chaise, would you believe? Fact is; I might have been a bit disguised last night.'

'I never would have guessed it,' was Gervase's reply.

A crease appeared in Gordon's forehead as if he were concentrating. 'Nathaniel said you and Wendover went to, was it Carlton House?'

'Hardly. I do not move in such circles.' Although Albion certainly did and Roland could, if he chose to. All in all, not a topic Gervase wished to discuss with his luckless rooming companion. 'Now I must leave you, I have an appointment.' For Nathaniel had re-appeared carrying a tray with ewer, basin and other washing utensils, and went through in the direction of Gervase's room.

'Well then, I'll no doubt see you later,' came Gordon's reply, as he waved and bustled off back to his room.

Later, before leaving the Albany, as Gervase added a few final flourishes to his cravat, he wondered whether he could contrive a meeting between Gordon and the undeniable beauty who had made such fruitless efforts to gain entrance to the Albany and Captain Gordon Howard's person. Gervase doubted whether Gordon's scar would incommode the visitor so recently sent away.

But to the matter in hand – the meeting with the Duke of Albion, curse him.

Gervase slammed out of the doors of the Albany and walked towards Piccadilly noting that there was no sign of Nathaniel following him. Maybe he had thought better of it for now or perhaps Nathaniel regarded the meeting as likely to be innocuous.

If he had only known what Gervase had in mind Nathaniel would have been ten paces behind at the very least.

Now, for the duke.

CHAPTER 10

'Pray take a seat, Mr. Thorpe.' The Duke of Albion graciously condescended to Gervase.

'Thank you, I prefer to stand.'

'As you wish. Would you take some refreshment… coffee, or perhaps something stronger?'

Punctually at noon Gervase, unaccompanied by Nathaniel, had been ushered into the private office of the Duke of Albion by his secretary, who had introduced himself as Charles Swinton; a lean, spare young man, he had effaced himself with almost indecent haste. The circumstances led Gervase to surmise that the ensuing meeting promised more than a dressing-down. Gervase hoped that it did. He supposed a bout of fisticuffs was too much to hope for.

They were in a large room, dark, with a thin haze of dust hanging in the atmosphere.

A small army of scribes had vacated their desks at a wave of the hand of a head clerk, who had remained a little longer but had also made a dignified retreat.

Gervase was alone in the august presence of the Duke of Albion.

Presumably the duke did not often frequent these

particular rooms. The large desk showed no signs of recent use, although a small side-table was set with a suitable array of decanters and an assortment of brandy glasses. A heavily-curtained opened window allowed the rumble of carriages to enter from the square below, but no breath of air.

The duke strolled over to the table. 'Well?'

'Nothing for me, Your Grace.' Gervase shook his head. That would be the last time he would use the honorific, he swore to himself.

The duke filled a glass with care, and sipped from it; it looked to be water, as Gervase might have expected. The duke must have registered Gervase's mood, because he swung around, cold as ever. His face was expressionless apart from a slightly raised eyebrow. 'Very well.' He took a long look at Gervase. 'You caused a disturbance last night. But it was dealt with. Now I have a proposition to make to you.'

The duke had cut to the chase and no mistake. Gervase faced him. He felt calm. He knew what he was going to do. But he would hear the old devil out. It would at least be interesting to hear and ignore. 'A proposition,' he repeated.

'Yes. My man of affairs will arrange all the details. Charles, he has just shown you in.' The duke cleared his throat. 'Shall we say, ten thousand?'

'What!'

'Is that not enough, do you think? A payment, a sole payment we shall understand, in recognition, of your, shall we say, of your prior *interest,* in my betrothed. Five now and the rest after you have left town. The latter by banker's draft. At Drummond's Bank, naturally.'

Gervase blinked and swallowed hard to prevent himself from retching. The duke's words had shocked him beyond anything. An insult of quite such magnitude! But secretly he felt triumphant, it made everything that he had planned easier. Much easier. His action to come would not now be so extreme.

Very slowly, Gervase undid the top button of his jacket and reached between his waistcoat and his shirt. Carefully he withdrew a dark brown leather riding glove and shook it out to remove any creases.

He stared at the duke and was rewarded with a reciprocal stare. Not a muscle moved in the duke's face. Not that it ever did.

Gervase lunged forward and slashed the Duke of Albion across the face with the object of retribution. 'I shall treat that remark with the contempt it deserves. I demand satisfaction. Name your seconds. The Earl of Marlow will do duty for me.' He added recklessly. Well, Roland had damn well better, with Gordon as backup if need be. Gervase was pleased to see that the force of the blow had left a red mark. It would quickly fade; more was the pity.

The duke staggered back a pace or two. He raised a hand to his face, passing his fingers down over his cheek with care as if to remove any taint that might have been left by an article from one of the lower personages given space amongst the *ton*.

Gervase thought he caught a glimpse of his rival's state of mind. *He does not know what to do.*

He himself felt better than he had in an age. Caroline would come back to him. She must. 'Well?' Now it was his turn.

Time ticked by.

'Naturally I accept your challenge.' The duke spoke strongly. Appeared to have recovered himself. Afterwards Gervase wondered whether he had imagined the momentary lapse from absolute dominion over all creatures on earth. 'I suggest tomorrow morning. And pistols.'

'Agreed.' Well, Gervase was not going to argue the point, but frankly he regarded *himself* as the injured party. Notwithstanding the glove episode: the choice of weapon should have been his.

Then with a lurch of his stomach he noted for the first time that the duke was wearing a ring on the third finger of his left hand. Admittedly a heavy gold signet ring with a ducal crest but why? *She* could not have given him that, surely. Nonsense, of course not.

'I shall ring for Swinton. He will see you out and make the necessary arrangements.'

'Your servant, sir.' Gervase clicked his heels as the duke walked away towards the back of the office and pulled the bell-rope.

The secretary duly appeared. 'Please to follow me, sir,' was said with a bow.

As Gervase left, he had the satisfaction, looking back over his shoulder, of observing the Duke of Albion, that lofty scion of nobility, close to a looking glass on the far wall, examining his face.

Everything would be alright now.

The die was cast.

Gervase had done what he was minded to do from the beginning, all along. To call out his rival. No, not his rival, the very word gave undue importance to the man. Gervase would not dignify the Duke of Albion as a love rival. No. Not even if he wore a ring on a significant finger, like a woman. In fact, Gervase could not think of an appropriate name. He would forget it. Never mind. Deuce take it, it did not bear thinking about. But he would, at a suitable moment ask Caroline for an explanation of the ring …

Caroline.

At last.

Gervase would put all thoughts of the duel to come out of his mind – it was time for Caroline.

CHAPTER 11

'Gervase, Gervase, ...' Caroline was drowning: drowning in a cool green river, green and full of leaves fallen from overhanging branches, the water shifting in the sunlight, pulling her down, whispering to her ... but then she was encircled by strong brown arms, Gervase's. Heaven was here and now; she must never leave his embrace. Never. She heard his voice, 'Caroline, Caroline, why have you forgotten me? Why?' The echoes faded away.

Caroline cried out in her sleep and awoke. A dream so real, so vivid she realised her breathing was shallow, disturbed, almost hysterical. Now fully awake, she sobbed, 'No, no, I have never forgotten you, stay with me! Gervase!'

If only she were still in his arms, if only.

Caroline leapt out of bed, and crossed to the window. Hints of dawn were traced in the sky; it promised to be another day without relief from the heat, or from her captivity.

The day had begun; it was the morning after the fateful ball. She could hear sounds from below, the servants about their duties: raised voices from the servants of Mrs Farley.

Normality returned; it had been a dream, a figment of her imagination: an impossible dream.

Today she would search for Gervase, to explain her apparent faithlessness. *That* would not be easy. But it was not true, she screamed in her mind, not true.

To the business of the day, to find Gervase's lodgings. The Earl of Marlow, he would know.

'Caroline, what are you about? Why are you dressed to go out?' Susannah had entered Caroline's dressing-room and was now poised with her hands behind her still clutching the doorknobs as she leant forward for all the world like a ship's figurehead. A slim, elegant figurehead. Poised, yes, that was the word. In an *eau-de-nil* watered silk morning ensemble worn with black fingerless gloves of some mesh construction chosen only the other day. Highly unsuitable.

It was useless to try to keep anything from Susannah. It was a blessing they did not share a bed chamber.

Caroline, after her unquiet night, was seated at her dressing-table, attempting the impossible task of winding a flimsy muslin scarf neatly around her close straw hat.

Her reflection in the looking glass before her was not encouraging. 'If you must know, I am going to visit Gervase's friend, the Earl of Marlow and endeavour to find out the whereabouts of Gervase's lodgings. *If* the Earl will tell me.'

That he would help her was not a foregone conclusion, knowing how close the two friends were. What would his attitude be towards Gervase's erstwhile love? 'The Earl must have Gervase's best interests at heart. If he will not, I shall endeavour to persuade him.'

But how? Caroline did not know but any sign of weakness on her part would be instantly pounced upon by Susannah.

Caroline sat back and considered the figure she presented in the mirror, swathed as she was in draperies.

'I told you to write a letter but for once you have had a much better idea. Here, you are making a mull of that,'

Susannah said and came over, tutting crossly.

With a few deft touches Susannah contrived the veil in such a way, that really… Caroline saw herself reflected in the hand-mirror Susannah had picked up from the dressing table and was now holding aloft.

'Yes, that is much better,' Caroline conceded, as she turned her head this way and that to admire her sister's handiwork.

Susannah smiled and turned her attention to her own hair. 'Lizzie favours the latest Egyptian mode, what do you think? I am not so sure it suits me.'

And then, relinquishing the hand-mirror reluctantly, she placed it back down on the dressing-table. 'Shall I come with you?'

'No,' replied Caroline, picking up her gloves and reticule. 'It is better that I go alone. Besides, are you not interested yourself in the Earl? It would be folly for you to risk your reputation. For myself, I care not, not at all. I shall leave by the area stairs and take a hackney carriage from the stand across the way. Finch has promised he will escort me there. He knows where the Earl of Marlow lives while in London.'

Finch was the sole servant who had come with them from the Priory, even Sarah, Caroline's maid, had been dismissed. Fortunately, the Dowager Countess of Westborough had happened to need an abigail and the new post suited Sarah; it was a blessing. Finch, for reasons unknown had been kept on. Perhaps it had been an oversight, or was he supposed to spy on them and report back? Caroline smiled; for his loyalty was beyond question.

Susannah lifted her shoulders in one of her familiar expressive gestures and flounced away. 'I am not sure the Earl of Marlow and I would suit. He is undoubtedly excessively handsome and has such address. But I am besieged by suitors, I do declare. But it is you who are undertaking a clandestine adventure. You, Caroline! But what about *la* Farley? Have you thought of her, when she finds out?'

'Well, maybe you could distract Mrs Farley?'

'Oh yes,' said Susannah, hand to mouth. 'I shall request her opinion on the Earl of St. Cross. We merely had supper together last night but I swear he is on the verge of offering for me. So tedious. I suspect he is frightened of the Duke of Albion though. An excellent idea. I shall go to her room now. You know she rarely stirs before noon. But I shall watch you leave from my bedroom window first.'

Hurriedly buttoning her drab-coloured pelisse, for the more concealment the better, Caroline followed her sister to the doors.

Caroline had not divulged to Susannah how apprehensive she was. The Earl of Marlow, though a friend of Gervase's, had been invited to the Betrothal Ball.

Why? Because he was a friend of the Duke of Albion.

It would be only natural for the Earl to have divided loyalties. Most gentlemen of the *haut ton* would not hesitate to choose the path of duty and reward… The rarefied air in which her betrothed lived precluded any acquaintances other than those of the upper ten thousand…

Gervase did not stand a chance.

And then she wondered why the premonition of doom was with her. She squared her shoulders. The Earl of Marlow would help her.

He should.

No, he must.

CHAPTER 12

By the time Gervase arrived at Mrs Farley's house, an aptly-numbered Thirteen Brunswick Square, the afternoon was far advanced but still there was no lessening of the persistent heat. It was to his advantage he thought that he was inured to the relentlessness of the sun's rays, absence of shade and airless shuttered rooms in countries far from England. Gordon had once remarked upon Gervase's stoicism in the face of the burning skies of Spain, or had his friend shown sarcasm for once? No, mere discomfort was no reason to abandon Gervase's quest for Caroline - nevertheless, he was aware of feeling not quite himself.

Gervase was admitted with ease, rather to his surprise. And so he entered the residence of Mrs Farley, the mysterious companion and her two charges, or *acolytes,* who were to be instructed in the feminine arts, or *worse,* he thought sickeningly. Perhaps they were best described as prisoners, if that was not a step too far. Although prisoner was better than some of the more vulgar terms of reference that could be used.

Eventually he had been shown into a large drawing-room, all the furniture of which had been upholstered in delicate shades of lilac, rose and grey. He was not sure how to describe the pastel shades that confronted him - except that they made him feel distinctly unwell.

'The Lilac Drawing Room, I believe,' the butler had whispered in Gervase's ear, 'it is the most suitable.'. How the man managed to make such a trivial remark sound suggestive Gervase failed to understand and why on earth was it necessary for the butler to lick his lips as he spoke? 'I shall see if the Misses Langrish are at home.' And the manservant had bowed his way out.

Gervase was amazed he had achieved so much. His calling card, hastily made-up on his return to England, had not been rejected. Earlier, while Gervase had waited in the massive entrance hall, tiled in lustrous gold and black squares, the butler had held the item some distance away as if it were distasteful. He had given Gervase a second glance, making him wonder if he was becoming known, if not notorious. Maybe even now intense discussions were afoot in the servants' hall, awash with rumours, all agog and awaiting the next developments…

He suspected the household here, if respectable *now*, had not always been so. The butler, a man of considerable height and stolid build, had also shown significant damage to his left ear.

A hollow feeling returned as Gervase surveyed the so-called Lilac Drawing Room. Why was he so affected by the atmosphere? He could almost believe there were incense sticks, unseen, wafting poisonous vapours. Why was he feeling so disconnected, alone and faint? He struggled to remember when he had last eaten and reproached himself. It was well-known that self-neglect gave rise to many flights of fancy.

A drawing room; that was all it was, not a haunt of vice. Everything here pointed to the abode of a mistress, and no ordinary one at that, but one upon whom much had been lavished.

Carte-blanche indeed!

He wandered aimlessly amongst the assorted sofas,

ottomans and reclining couches, some strangely separated from one another by screens heavily swagged with silk. But still he dreaded to think what might have gone on in secret corners of a room designed for dalliance.

On the mantel-piece a pile of invitations that had mounted up on a silver tray, caught his eye.

He crossed to the fireplace, now mercifully empty, and idly picked up one or two, glancing through them. An impressive roll-call - including a dinner invitation to Carlton House no less! He dropped the card back as if scalded.

The doors to the drawing-room swung open and a discreetly elegant lady he did not recognise entered together with the sister but no Caroline.

The ladies arranged themselves either side of the entrance and posed as it were. The sister's ravishing looks had not diminished, if anything daylight became her better. Bur she was not Caroline.

Gervase quickly switched his attention to the other. A completely different kind of beauty. Faded, yes, but she had a quality, even a power …

Of course. The house and all its accoutrements, the air of exotic tastes indulged in an expensive manner and now grown ever so slightly shabby… Everything must be hers. It was her setting.

Unwittingly he must have stared more than he should have done at the lady for he saw a faint bloom arise in her cheeks. There was a coldness in the atmosphere. The elegant one curtseyed but before she could speak, Gervase forestalled her. 'Gervase Thorpe, at your service.' He executed a courtly bow in what he hoped was his best aide-de-camp manner. Wellington insisted upon impeccable behaviour from his officers – in society at least. It was slightly marred by an involuntary stumble.

'I am Mrs Farley,' replied the hostess.

Neither lady moved as they regarded him silently.

At length the sister hurried forward. 'And I am Miss

Susannah Langrish. I saw you at the Betrothal Ball. Please sit down, Mr Thorpe,' she said, in a soft, musical voice, full of interest.

Gervase found himself sitting down rather more quickly than he had intended on the nearest silken seat. The room had unaccountably blurred.

'It is Miss Caroline Langrish with whom I wish to speak,' he said, as if from far away, holding onto the wooden arm next to him. And damn uncomfortable the chaise-longue proved to be. He looked up to see both ladies were now much closer.

'Miss Langrish is not receiving callers at present.' He thought it was Mrs Farley who had spoken.

'I shall tell my sister you were here,' her companion pursed her lips and favoured the other with a quelling glance. 'I am sorry you have had a wasted journey.'

Gervase dragged himself to his feet. The weakness whatever it was, had passed. 'Thank you. Please do so. It is most important.'

He bowed again and realised a footman had appeared and was waiting to escort him out of the building. The two ladies curtseyed again and said nothing as he left the drawing-room.

What had just happened there?

One possibility was that the duenna, or whatever one chose to call Mrs Farley, had assumed that he, Gervase, was another suitor for the apparently much in demand Miss Susannah Langrish, and had come to act as chaperone. He knew that Roland was already smitten; there would be soon be a long line of devastated young men. But was Caroline being deliberately kept from him? Should he storm the upstairs rooms in search of her?

Once Gervase found himself back in the black and gold entrance-hall, he tried to decide upon a plan of action even though another heavily-built manservant had opened the doors in preparation for the visitor's exit.

As Gervase hesitated, he heard a swift rustle of skirts

behind him and almost before he had registered her presence, Miss Susannah Langrish had slipped an envelope into his hand. He saw her disappear away up the staircase. The doorkeeper took no notice. Maybe it was a common occurrence in a house of secrets; Gervase was sure there were many such assignations afoot.

He hid the paper in a waistcoat pocket and removed himself from the Brunswick Square house. He had found the atmosphere overpowering. The stifling air outside felt cleansing.

Gervase crossed the road to shelter under the shade of one of the many trees imprisoned in the Square gardens and with its foliage overhanging the railings.

Opening the envelope, he drew out the thick sheet of vellum and smoothed it flat. It was difficult to read and had obviously been scribbled in a hurry. He squinted down at the crossed and re-crossed writing.

Dear Mr Thorpe,
My sister has escaped to visit your friend, the Earl of Marlow, to find out where you are like to be. She is desperate to see you, please make haste
Ever yours,
Susannah Charlotte Langrish.

Gervase's heartbeats speeded up and the blood thundered in his ears.

If only he could believe the sentiments in front of him. He did not. He did not believe Caroline was 'desperate to see him' nor was he convinced that she needed to 'escape'. Miss Susannah Langrish was a completely different personality he was sure.

It *was* heartening that Caroline was searching for him via his friend of course. Gervase hoped to God she had not hired a hackney carriage!

He stuffed the note back into his waistcoat. He would indeed *make haste* to Roland's town house.

Regrettably Gervase also needed to see Roland about the damned duel.

Sylvia Robins

CHAPTER 13

'I am Caroline Langrish and I would like to speak to the Earl of Marlow.' Caroline stood on the steps of the town house belonging to Gervase's friend, and spoke to the austere doorkeeper.

He looked down upon her from some height; his mouth had dropped open a little but his expression lightened when he appeared to see that Finch was behind her and had drawn closer. She was glad she had arrived accompanied at the domain of an aristocrat. Not, of course, that that weighed with her at all.

The door was opened wider, reluctantly, but it was enough for Caroline. She made her way in before the servant could change his mind. 'My groom, Finch,' she said, for Finch had exerted pressure on the front door, and had followed her.

The entrance hall in which she found herself was wide and spacious though sparsely furnished. Sunlight streamed in through fanlights set above in the lofty ceiling.

Several staff were now visible all along one of the two corridors either side of the main staircase and were led by a distinguished-looking elderly man who must be the butler. 'Yes, Ingleby?' He intoned.

The doorman hurried to him and exchanged a few hushed words.

The butler rose magnificently to the occasion. 'Please to follow me, my lady,' he said to Caroline. 'Finch may accompany Phillips, our second footman, below stairs.'

Finch duly followed the servant as directed.

'Thank you,' replied Caroline and followed the butler along one of the corridors to be ushered into the first room off the hall. It turned out to be a small dark room; a study, she supposed.

'Please take a seat and I will inform the Earl of your presence. I am sure he will receive you.' He gave her a slight smile, bowed and left her alone with her thoughts.

Caroline looked around her and saw a desk, several hard-back chairs and a small library in a bookcase. Crossing the study, she looked at the spines of several of the books. The classics predominated: Homer, Ovid and even Cicero. A scholar as well as a soldier.

Moving on to the window, she looked down onto the street. Hastily she drew back when she saw a couple of young men looking up. She had no wish to be seen before her errand had even begun! Hurriedly she retreated.

The sound of the door opening made her turn to see the Earl of Marlow in the doorway. 'Miss Langrish.' He came forward into the room with an easy manner and held out his hand to her. As she surrendered hers and sank into a curtsey, he bowed and kissed her fingers.

As he let go of her gloved hand and straightened up she marked his athletic build which his elegant mode of dress could not disguise. But she also noted his spare frame, the fine lines around his eyes, and his colouring reflecting time spent under a Spanish sun… There were lines etched in his forehead, which as she watched, came together to show signs of worry. 'My dear Miss Langrish, how may I help you? I hope there is nothing serious to bring you here to call upon me so unexpectedly. Is everything at Brunswick Square as it should be?'

Had he been thinking of Susannah? No, surely not, so soon. After all the pair had hardly met, she dismissed the thought.

'Oh, yes,' said Caroline, aware that her colour was rising. 'It is about another matter entirely.'

At that the Earl looked away for a moment before replying. 'I expect you are seeking the whereabouts of Mr. Thorpe. Am I right, Miss Langrish?'

She nodded. 'I am, my lord.' Before she could say any more, he took several steps closer to her.

'I own I was expecting to hear from you in one way or another.' He hesitated. 'My housekeeper is in the next room. I can summon her – she will unfortunately not be regarded as a duenna but … You see, I am in want of a lady of respectable birth. I mean no disrespect to Mrs Hammond. I have no married sisters here, much to my regret.'

She admired his address, his command of the situation but it was too urgent a matter to worry about such social niceties; she shook her head.

Surely he could not seriously believe her reputation was at risk from a visit which would be as brief as possible as far as she was concerned? Gervase's whereabouts were all that mattered. She would not, could not give her attention to such a minor matter.

Was he worried he would be compromised? Ridiculous. Although it showed his awareness of the rigid rules of the ton.

But still he persisted, with a slight smile. 'Would you like me to fetch the good Mrs Hammond?'

'It will not be necessary. I am only here to request the name of Gervase's, I mean, Mr Thorpe's' lodgings. And you need not be concerned about me.'

'Very well. I am still most concerned for your welfare though. If I give you Gervase's details, you must allow me to send you home in one of my carriages. I insist. Even then, if you are seen… I am afraid the Duke of Albion will not take the matter kindly. Beside there is the heat of the day to consider as well.'

Caroline felt her gaze slide away from the direct look the Earl had given her. 'Yes, indeed,' she agreed. How could she admit she cared not? 'I must hope that I am not observed.'

'Gervase is lodging at Number Fifteen, the Albany, as a courtesy from a mutual friend of ours, Captain Gordon Howard, also of the Fifty-Second. You will understand my place in town was always available but Gervase could or would not reside here. He had his reasons, I expect. But we are a close-knit bunch, you must understand, Miss Langrish.' He laughed as if to lighten the atmosphere. Or was he too on edge? She could not tell.

'The Regiment,' she said and paused but then quickly added, 'Thank you, my lord.'

She was grateful but now that she had achieved her purpose, and so quickly, the temptation to elicit more information from Gervase's close friend was too tempting. 'Pray tell me, Mr Thorpe, I mean Gervase's injury, how came he by it? How bad is his leg? And was it so difficult to send word from the battlefield?' Her words tumbled out over one another and she realized she was short of breath.

'My dear Miss Langrish,' the Earl took hold of both her hands. 'Let me request some refreshments for you. Please take a seat. Here by the window.'

'Thank you, I am quite well. I am not in need of anything.'

Except an explanation of the events of the past day or so.

'As you wish.' The Earl released her to stride over to the sash window, which he threw open wider, allowing cooler air to sweep into the room. Caroline followed him and sank down onto a window-seat. Drawing over a chair, he took a seat beside her. 'I think it best if Gervase tells you his story. But I can assure you that he will recover from the leg wound. In time. Trust me.'

Worse and worse.

'In time?' Caroline said, hearing her voice unnaturally high. 'My lord, I beg you to tell me the details. Gervase and I have been unable to exchange more than a few words since he,' she hesitated, at a loss then recovered, and in a stronger vein continued, 'disrupted the Duke of Albion so…'

The Earl smiled again. 'Yes, Gervase did. The duke behaved in an irresponsible manner I am afraid. He brooks no interference in his affairs. But I am not entirely convinced all his actions are self-interested. Where his relations with those subjected to his sway are concerned - but I say too much. I am aware of your engagement.' Here he rose and took a turn about the room. Returning, he stood over her. 'The subject is impossible to discuss with you, my dear Miss Langrish, please forgive me. It is of no consequence.'

Caroline was shocked beyond measure. What could he mean? Could he be in the right? Subject to the Duke of Albion's sway must mean servants, or perhaps even herself and Susannah? They were in his power, supported by his immense wealth… Or was the Earl considering Mrs Farley?

For now, it suited her to ignore the Earl's remark, but she put it aside to think about later.

There were more important matters to discuss. 'Please tell me about Gervase's wound.'

Her companion resumed his seat beside her. He appeared to be making an effort. 'Well, I have asked Gervase, several times to see the good Doctor Jamieson, you know. He is highly regarded amongst the *ton*.'

'He will not?'

'Not as yet but I have hopes. It is my opinion his leg is not perfectly healed.'

Caroline gasped. 'How came he by the injury, my lord? Is there anything else I should know? Please tell me.'

A wash of colour swept over his face. 'Please forgive me, Miss Langrish if I do not recount the precise details. It is still painful for me, and I regret to say that he may be unwilling to tell you, but I beg you to ask him.'

Aghast at the effect upon the Earl, Caroline looked away. What had happened?

He swallowed and started again. 'That is the extent of his physical injuries. But…'

She waited.

'There are other injuries, other damage that a war may cause. Not observable perhaps as such… Forgive me, Miss Langrish.'

Gervase's impetuosity, his barely-reined in temper, it all fell into place.

The Earl had not done. 'Some of the sorties, some, especially those behind enemy lines were foolhardy in the extreme… he volunteered at every opportunity. I feel I should tell you, Miss Langrish. His bravery was not in question, quite the opposite, but it was noted, and brought to the attention of Sir John. That is, Lieutenant-General Sir John Colborne, ma'am.'

He took a deep breath. 'More often than not I went with Gervase. In the end, well, we were both required to present at Headquarters. I was expecting a dressing-down at the very least, on the lines of, putting our men at unnecessary risk. But it turned out to be quite the reverse. A promotion in fact. Admittedly there was a requirement for another two *aides-de-camp* and the Duke of Wellington prefers those with certain social skills.' Again he laughed. 'Believe it or the ability to dance a decent *quadrille* stands one in good stead with the Duke. And, how shall I say,' he hesitated, 'he prefers young officers of a certain rank.'

'But Gervase is not a peer. I do not know about his dancing ability,' she said cautiously.

'No. That is true certainly.'

Caroline's mind leapt ahead. 'You used your influence, you took him with you, did you not?'

'The Duke needed two more staff and we were removed from the front-line. It was a mutually beneficial arrangement, as it were.'

Caroline faced him; it suddenly seemed important to

understand exactly the meaning of Gervase's closest friend. 'You accompanied him?'

'Yes, certainly. Both in the field and at Headquarters.' Again the Earl looked away. 'I was worried about him. What he was likely to do… in the event of being left on his own.' He sighed. 'Now I have definitely betrayed a confidence. It would please me greatly if you would forget my last few words. Please, Miss Langrish.'

'I promise.' Feeling sick by now, Caroline found herself saying and dreading the answer. 'Was this because Gervase had not received my letters?'

The Earl nodded. 'It would seem so. I was not aware at the time, of course. You must understand he did not take me into his confidence.'

'I see.'

But there was still more to learn, while she had the Earl captive. Maybe an opportunity such as she had here would not arise again, who knew.

'Other letters were received, I mean, from other… families?'

'Yes.'

It was a bald answer. She had expected as much. Caroline stumbled to her feet. She did not think she could bear much more. 'So correspondence reached the lines.'

'Yes, it did.'

'You must believe me when I swear I wrote.'

'I do.'

The explanation must have lain elsewhere. Her father – had he intercepted her letters? She would never know the answer to that question.

The earl was now looking away from her, as if gazing into the past. 'Later we were both returned to the front line.' He paused. 'It was necessary, for military reasons.'

'My lord, I should like to go now. Thank you for giving me details of Gervase's lodgings.'

She had no wish to hear more.

The Earl also rose to his feet. 'Before you go Miss

Langrish, I hope your sister is well. I would like to be further acquainted with Miss Susannah Langrish and have it in mind to call upon her very soon.' There was a questioning slant to his words but he faced Caroline directly. 'I know you are deeply concerned about Gervase so this is not the best of times to plead my case.'

Caroline could not be thinking of Susannah. 'We are both under much constraint at present. I am sure my sister wishes you well.'

She was not surprised at the Earl's smile at her remark, only the quality of it. He must be deeply enamoured.

He bowed slightly and made for the door. 'Of course. I will arrange for one of my carriages to come around now. Brunswick Square, is it not? Your groom can travel up with Jessop.'

Caroline murmured her thanks and followed him back into the high-ceilinged entrance hall, now empty of company apart from a solitary footman.

As Caroline half-listened to the complicated instructions being given by the Earl of Marlow to the young man, her mind was pre-occupied with the wealth of information the Earl had just disclosed about Gervase.

There had been too much to think about in the Earl of Marlow's words. He had unburdened himself. Truly. She was amazed to be the recipient of his confidences, which evinced a high degree of *trust*, there was no other word for his behaviour. He must be worried about Gervase, his friend.

However, she was no closer to knowing how Gervase came by the damage to his leg. The Earl had prevaricated on *that* score.

The more she thought about Gervase, the more fear gripped her inside, a roiling fear that had no limit...

'The carriage will be brought around from the mews in no time at all,' said the Earl, now devoting his attention to her once more, as the footman hurried away to do his lordship's bidding.

Taking deep breaths, she managed to control herself, but she saw the Earl 's brows come together, concern etched on his handsome face. 'Miss Langrish, are you not well?'

She nodded and he took her arm, saying 'Let us walk up and down here in the entrance hall, while we await Jessop.

The Earl did not speak to her again and they turned slow, measured circles together on the cold tiled floor. A welcome relief from the heat outside. A hushed silence surrounded them as if nothing could ever trouble those who dwelt in the aristocratic confines of the Earl of Marlow's town house. Calm descended upon her. Perhaps all would be well.

Very soon she would be with Gervase again and the threat of the Duke of Albion and the future mapped out for her for ever and ever would recede.

The Earl halted and looked down at her. 'My carriage is here; I can hear Jessop's voice.' He bowed low, and released her. 'I will escort you to the door but no further, I am sure you will forgive me.' He was gone before she could thank him.

The door keeper reappeared, the doors swung open, and Caroline was out into the heat of the day to the awaited carriage, drawn up close to the small flight of steps. Finch was already seated beside the coachman and a groom was holding the carriage door open for her.

Everything was prepared to take her home.

But it would be the work of a moment to re-direct Jessop to number Fifteen, the Albany. She brushed aside a lingering doubt that he might not be amenable. She would deal with the situation if and when it arose.

The Earl of Marlow had told her much - but not enough. He had been singularly unforthcoming on the subject of Gervase's injury and how it had come about.

She needed to see Gervase as soon as possible. Too much had happened and they were still apart

Sylvia Robins

CHAPTER 14

Gervase left Caroline's residence at Thirteen Brunswick Square, one could not call it a home exactly, *gaol* was his preferred name for the abhorred building, and set out for Roland's town house, wondering whether Caroline would be there.

Then there was the small matter of the duel. In that case, time was of the essence. It was a great pity his friend had no inkling of his responsibilities - yet. As second, Roland must make contact with the ducal adversary's supporter, and soon. Arrangements needed to be made; it was Roland's task; Gervase could not be involved. And the duel was fixed for tomorrow morning. Frankly he did not care where the venue was to be; the gates of hell would suit, for example.

The distance between Brunswick Square and Mecklenburg Square was no distance at all. Neither as the crow flies, nor by the laborious circuitous route, he, Gervase, had had to take to avoid the intense heat as far as he could. Not far, but far enough. The pressure of the constant repetitive motion on his right leg had already played havoc with his injury.

He felt, not to put too finer a point on it, at the end of

his tether.

Gervase leant on a convenient balustrade fronting Mecklenburg Square gardens and was grateful to rest under the shade of a tree. Damn it, his wound was still paining him. He would have to see a saw-bones about it before too long. Especially if the sore had not properly healed... He cursed long and slow and felt better.

It was quiet here; all lulled into a kind of afternoon *siesta*. Once again the comparison with Spain almost made him laugh. To be back in London and still to be suffering from the heat!

Now he was ready to go on.

At all costs he must not show weakness in front of Roland. Otherwise the devil knows what his friend might get up to – he would probably try to stop the duel, but it was not *his* honour that was at stake. Gervase loosened his neckcloth in readiness as he prepared to face the glaring rays from above.

He was about to cross the road when the somnolence of the Square was disturbed by a carriage rounding the corner at some speed. From the direction of the adjacent mews, if his memory served him right.

Gervase stepped back. As the vehicle swept past sending up a cloud of dust, he recognized the coat-of-arms on the side; the coat-of-arms belonging to Roland, the Earl of Marlow; *argent, chevron sable*. At the window the curtain swung back and forth revealing a tantalizing glimpse of Caroline Langrish.

Hell's teeth, what the devil was she up to now? She had indeed been looking for him!

Acting on impulse, with a sudden rush of energy, Gervase found himself running after the carriage and shouting to Roland's Head Coachman, Jessop. His companion beside him high up on the driver's seat was Finch, if Gervase was damn well not mistaken. Finch, whom Gervase had last seen at Beauminster Priory, back in days of yore, longer ago than Gervase cared to remember in fact: Finch, who had been ever the loyal servant but was now Jessop's companion. He was inclining his head, a mere inch or two with studied neutrality. Oh well.

Afterwards Gervase could not remember exactly what he had said. But it had had the desired effect. With the snorting horses loudly complaining, the carriage came to a lurching, juddering halt.

Jessop leant down and tipped his hat to Gervase. 'Mr Thorpe, your servant, sir! Good to see you again. Just like old times, back with the brigade!'

Unable to help himself, Gervase gave Roland's coachman a mock salute.

Caroline meanwhile was leaning out of the window. 'Gervase!'

'Let me aboard and then drive to Hyde Park, if you will, Jessop.'

'Right you are, sir,' came the reply and Finch showed enterprise by dismounting from his seat next to Jessop to assist. Wasting no time, Gervase pulled down the steps, wrenched open the carriage door and was inside a moment later.

Time for a reckoning. Caroline could hardly escape him now. At last.

Involuntarily Caroline shrank back against the squabs; Gervase was here again in front of her.

The Earl of Marlow's magnificent, luxuriously-appointed carriage, all done out in the deepest blue velvet with hints of carmine in the facings adorning each window and trimmed with golden tassels now busily swinging backwards and forwards as the vehicle gathered pace, up until then appearing spacious, had now became suddenly too small. Too small.

She had heard the slamming of the carriage steps upwards, then a slight pause, a call to the horses and the vehicle had proceeded on its way. No need for a knock on the ceiling. For all the world as though nothing amiss had occurred, just an additional passenger taken on. Listening to the conversation Caroline marvelled at the camaraderie of the Regiment, from the lofty elite of the staff officers down to the humble but necessary foot soldier. At least she assumed the coachman must have been from the other ranks, otherwise how did Gervase know Jessop? Some might call the situation collusion.

Gervase angled himself into the opposite corner of the carriage, one arm along the back of the seat and the other taut against the door, his hand grasping the window strap.

A quick movement and he leant forward and pulled down first one window blind and then the other, closing the curtains for good measure, intensifying the heat in the carriage.

In the flickering sunlight, as the blinds swung back and forth rattling against door-frames, Gervase regarded Caroline for what seemed like an age.

'You betrayed me!' His voice was raw and thickened with an emotion which she could not name. Disgust perhaps.

'That I did not!'

'What did you call your behaviour then, if not betrayal?'

Again silence descended.

'Let me see you again, Miss Langrish. I dare not call you Caroline anymore. I have forfeited the right. No, you have decided that.' And he disturbed the veil hastily resumed after leaving the Earl of Marlow's house, grazing her cheek with cool fingers. 'Did you hope to escape my notice, that I would not recognize you? When all I ever dreamt of in that hell of Salamanca ...' He stopped abruptly, winced and rubbed his thigh as if in pain. He recovered and leaned forward to her, 'And why are you in the Earl of Marlow's carriage may I ask?'

'Gervase... I merely wanted to find out where you were lodging.' *That* at least was easily answered, if not the rest. Her throat dried. His stare transfixed her. She clutched the edges of her seat. The question was where to begin.

The carriage gathered speed, then turned a corner with a sudden jolt so that Caroline was thrown across the well of the coach and into Gervase's arms. He whispered to her. 'Hyde Park will give us plenty of time. Time to discuss your past and your future with me. Damn your fiancé. It has been too long. Caroline, you must, you will… Caroline?'

She remembered the scent of him, sandalwood, she remembered, oh, she remembered too much, yet not enough. The linen of his shirt slipped and slid against his chest under her hands. But she was not restraining him, she knew it. His mouth was close to her lips and then was withdrawn. 'Caroline?'

'Yes!'

He untied the strings of her straw hat, which fell to the floor, unbuttoned her pelisse to her waist …

He was kissing her. Hundreds of kisses on her face, cheek, neck and below.

There was no more holding back: no more words.

It was as if she had been transported into another world. Aware that she was responding as voraciously.

The carriage slowed. Had they reached Hyde Park so soon …

Then Caroline did halt his attentions, capturing his hands, afraid that she was out of control.

But the jolting resumed, they were on their way again. Caroline felt Gervase brace himself, one booted foot jammed against the carriage door, the other against the opposite bench seat, both arms gripping her tightly as he shifted her body so that she was positioned more securely on his lap, or to increase his arousal beneath her. Her heart leapt as he buried his face between her breasts, murmuring incoherently.

Any lingering doubt that she would feel the same way, the way she had felt back then, back in the rose-garden at Beauminster Priory, was gone forever.

And then, 'No, it is not the time nor the place, Caroline!'

The words sounded wrung from him.

Just as quickly as the tumult had begun it was over. Gervase released her. She fell back onto her side of the carriage and he slumped back in return.

Time passed. The carriage rolled on.

Where Caroline was she neither knew nor cared.

Gervase stared at the blanked out window. With a shaky voice, he said, 'Caroline, forgive me. Your first time should not be in a carriage. We will wait. You should be in a marital bed, mine. You deserve better.'

Caroline had no answer.

A different expression came over his face. One that she could not name. He spoke urgently. 'Why did you not answer my letters? I wrote most every day. Except, after Salamanca, after the bullet was removed. When I had recovered... I had given up by then. Why are you not saying anything, Caroline?'

Caroline looked down, smoothing her dress, trying, unsuccessfully, to obliterate some of the creases. 'And I wrote to you, too, Gervase. I swear I did. I sent them to be franked by my cousin, Jonathan. He was a staff officer with the Duke of Wellington, you know. I thought... Well, I thought they would be safe.'

'I did not receive them. And mine?'

'I did not receive yours either. You must believe me.'

'Enough of the letters. Perhaps in the end your father *did* interfere.'

'I had thought Papa did not care.'

It must have been a casual cruelty, Caroline thought. *Her father was capable of acting in just such a way.*

'Yet it will not do, will it?' He jeered. 'You are an affianced bride. I asked you before, Caroline, at the *so-called* Betrothal Ball,' Gervase sounded as though he were choking, 'And I will ask you again, why are you marrying the Duke of Albion?'

When she did not immediately reply, he continued. 'And he wears a ring on the third finger of his left hand. Why? Unusual is it not? Did you give him a token of your love for him, perish the thought?'

'No, I did not.'

'Then why?'

Caroline swallowed. 'I think, I think, I may be wrong but I think he has chosen to wear his, his ducal ring. As a token of his regard.' Then she added, softly. 'We have not talked about it but it may be so.' She was afraid to look Gervase in the eye.

He fell back against the carriage.

It was her opportunity. 'Gervase, so much has happened.'

'Indubitably.' His voice was grim. 'We are no further forward. I am still at a loss.' He shook his head and looked down at the floor. 'Give me my dues. At least try to explain.'

'My father, he gambled.'

'As do many men.'

'At White's, one night, he wagered, well, everything. Our home. The Priory.'

'And then?'

'Papa was found, the next morning.' She swallowed. 'Everything was lost.'

'Everything?'

'Yes. And – I accepted the Duke's offer. He was – very prompt.'

Gervase flinched. 'That does not surprise me. He saw an opportunity. When you were at your lowest ebb.'

'Why do you say so?' She flared up. 'I had considered, becoming a governess, but I felt responsible for Susannah. I felt I had no choice.'

Gervase hunched a shoulder. 'Responsible enough to marry a fabulously rich aristocrat.'

'You were not there. You were away in the Peninsula, fighting, goodness knows where. He promised me he would arrange Susannah's come-out. I wanted her to have an opportunity, to meet... Well, not to have to fend for herself. Gervase, you have seen my sister.'

'Yes.' He looked away. 'She cannot hold a candle to you. But we waste time,' he went on. 'You decided to take advantage of the duke's offer and now you are to marry him. What about me? Let us leave the precious Duke of Albion for now. He has made you an offer you chose not to refuse. Ostensibly for the sake of your beloved sister. Now to the delightful duenna.'

Caroline felt sick. When would the interrogation end? 'You mean, Mrs Farley?' she replied.

'Yes, obviously a former mistress of the duke's.'

When she did not answer, Gervase laughed. 'Oh, come. And how do you know she is still not? Although the *on-dit* is, he sees no-one but you.' He looked away. 'However, that is by-the-by. Is she schooling you?'

'I do not know what you mean.'

'I think you do, Caroline. Is she tutoring you in the special ways in which the duke likes to be serviced?'

'You are beside yourself!'

'Now to the most important question. I know your intended has supported your beloved sister. You are both indebted to the Duke of Albion. Do not pretend, for the *ton* knows, I have it on good authority, from the Earl of Marlow no less, you are a kept woman!'

'Kept I may be, but soon to be married,' she hissed.

'Are you his mistress? Has he bedded you, for God's sake!'

'How dare you!' Caroline raised her hand to strike him, but Gervase caught her wrist, wrenching her forward across the distance that had opened up between them.

'Gervase!'

At that, he let go, fell back across the divide and rested his head in his hands, jolted back and forth with the unsteady passage of their prison, which lately had been a witness to their near coming together.

Blood pounded in Caroline's head. 'Was it your intention all along, to seduce me? Well, you have not succeeded, have you? To ruin me, for the duke?'

He looked up. 'For God's sake, Caroline! I am like a man parched in the desert. You have never seen Spain, the heat, the dust, the blood. I am too far gone, to scheme!'

The carriage halted, rocking from side to side.

'I must leave you or I shall do something I will regret! And seduction is not what I have in mind, now. I have other plans.'

He snapped up the blind covering the window next to him. 'Hyde Park. I shall instruct the coachman to return you to Brunswick Square. I need to see the Earl of Marlow.' Gervase hesitated and glanced at Caroline, 'about quite another matter.'

Gervase opened the carriage door precipitately and leapt out, slamming it behind him.

'What other matter?' Caroline called after him but her words were worse than useless.

Gervase had gone.

She had said much that she regretted. Had he too?

CHAPTER 15

When Gervase finally arrived at the Earl of Marlow's town house in Mecklenburg Square it was not before time, Gervase admitted to himself. A moment longer and he would have been good for nothing.
He was ushered into one of Roland's many receiving rooms, a room used as a study, judging by the usual gentlemanly accoutrements of papers, books and an assortment of newsprint scattered liberally across an ancient desk.

A faint, lingering scent of roses perfumed the air. If he had not known, he would have guessed that Caroline had visited.

For a while he walked up and down, trying to compose himself. It was not easy after what had just happened. Had he intended to seduce Caroline? He could not say for certain. There was no doubt he had been out of control. But she had been equally willing...

No, he should have taken responsibility earlier. Another unpardonable offence.

To despoil her for the Duke... No.

The list of his sins to be dwelt upon later was accumulating rapidly, he thought grimly. A very long list.

All to be thought about later.

But now he must focus on the event that would take place on the morrow.

The duel.

In an attempt to distract himself, he read the names on the spines of the three volumes which appeared to have been most recently selected from the bookshelves; he was not surprised to see that they were all Greek classics. Soon he felt calmer.

He swung around when the doors were opened and his friend strolled in.

'Gervase, good to see you. I'm for White's later. Will you join me? The Earl of Marlow came forward into the room, resplendent in dark blue suiting and preoccupied with fixing a white sash across his body. 'My man Melville has not tied the damn thing correctly, I'll swear. I'm expected at St. James first,' he said by way of an explanation.

The final adjustment to the silk made, Roland straightened his jacket, and spoke, without looking directly at Gervase. 'What do you say, will you take supper with me at White's? Or have you other plans for tonight?'

'For tonight I have not but tomorrow morning is another matter,' replied Gervase. His throat felt unusually dry. 'My plans may affect yours, I fear.'

'Now you have intrigued me.' Roland looked at Gervase closely. 'Sit down, won't you? I hope the worst has not come to pass, as I feared. You look done-up.'

Gervase threw himself into one of the two leather armchairs arranged either side of the hearth. 'By the by, when were you going to inform me that Miss Langrish had visited?'

'Miss Langrish merely wished to know where you were living; I gave her your address. I sent her home in one of my carriages. I take it you do not accuse me of anything improper?'

'As if I would.' Gervase carelessly replied. *But Gervase*

knew the state he was in, he may well have done. 'No, she has told me all. I have – encountered – her already.' He felt hot, as he realised his friend was fixing him with a look of concern. 'I have enough to deal with, without calling you out as well.'

'As well?'

'There need to be some arrangements made, I gave your name. As my second. I considered Gordon as a remote possibility but thought better of it.'

Now that the knowledge was out in the open as it were Gervase felt drained.

Roland strode over to the side board, un-stoppered one of a pair of handsome decanters and filled two glasses with brandy. 'The meeting went as expected I see. I told you not to get involved with the Duke of Albion. He is a power in the land.' He returned, handed a glass to Gervase and knocked back his own drink in one go, before seating himself opposite Gervase. 'But you know you can always count on me. Brothers in arms. Pistols, I presume?'

'His choice. Naturally.' Gervase swirled the liquid around in his glass and drank some. It had a bitter taste, so much so that he nearly spat it out.

'Naturally.' Roland sat back. 'He is a crack shot, you know. There was a meeting with Lord Brancaster, I remember now, before we left for the Peninsula.'

Gervase could have lived without the information but forced himself to reply with a semblance of interest. 'Brancaster?'

'Brancaster tried to lure Albion's latest *chère-amie* away, before the *affaire* had run its course. A mistake, by all accounts. Everyone knows Albion brooks no interference. Besides, he always retains an interest. Witness Mrs Farley. Supported for life, no less. You see, I have had more words with my Lord Whitby. I thought it would be beneficial, windbag though he is. But I digress. More brandy?'

Gervase held out his glass though he was not sure it

would help. 'What was the outcome, may one ask?'

Roland took the glass and rose, then hesitated. 'Brancaster survived but he no longer frequents society. I shall do all that is required – after I have descended upon my lords at St. James. Meet me at White's or have you yourself preparations to make? Perhaps with Miss Langrish?'

'By no means. I have preparations to make as you call it but no, I shall not see her again, not before the morning. White's it is then.'

He could ill afford further distractions at such a time.

Still Roland held back. 'You have not seen Miss Susannah Langrish since the ball by any chance?'

Gervase roused himself out of his stupor. 'Oh, the wind lies in that quarter, does it? Yes, I called unsuccessfully at the dark tower. Rest assured, the object of your desire is as lovely as ever, I imagine there is a long line of suitors; you will have to join the queue. Albion will no doubt vet them all personally.'

Here he noted a darkening of the expression on his friend's face and made up his mind to desist. 'On second thoughts I will pass on another brandy, I do have one or two letters to write before morning and arrangements to make.'

Perhaps a will, though there he had little enough to leave. The letters might be more problematic. He was not going to find it easy. He might be fully occupied before White's.

A feeling of overwhelming tiredness swept over him. Gervase stumbled to his feet and made for the doors. 'I'll see myself out. I shall walk home and clear my head.'

Roland waved a hand in dismissal.

Once out in Mecklenburg Square again he braced himself. What had he to do really? He could rest back at the Albany. Then, a few letters to be written, of no consequence, a few words with Roland at White's then oblivion until the morning, when revenge, he hoped, would be sweet.

    Unless the Duke of Albion lived up to his reputation with his weapon of choice.

CHAPTER 16

The return from Hyde Park had seemed interminable to Caroline. Once she arrived back at Brunswick Square all she wanted was some time to herself – to adjust, to think things over, to… to decide on a course of action. Yes, that was what she needed to do, she thought, as she stumbled up the stairs to hers and Susannah's rooms…. Unfortunately, she would not be alone that was for certain.

Caroline crept into the small, private dressing-room given to herself and Susannah.

As expected, her sister was already seated at the dressing-table leaning forward regarding herself in the looking-glass. With a quality of complete absorption in her own reflection that only Susannah could achieve. Undoubtedly waiting. For Caroline.

Sunlight filtered through the draped muslin nets over the window. With a sighing sound, the material fluttered in a slight passage of air and then returned to stillness.

Although it was getting late the heat was not diminishing, especially in a small room, so unlike the accommodation the Langrish sisters had taken for granted. Times had changed.

Just for a moment Caroline closed her eyes and

remembered how it used to be. With her own apartments, growing up at Beauminster Priory. Mama, the legion of servants and above all the luxury.

But it had not been a rosy dream after all. The past must ever be, well, the past. Her father's gambling, the raised voices, Mama's muffled sobbing. Caroline could go on, she knew it. Then, the final catastrophe, long after poor Mama's death.

At least the ignominy came later.

Ruin, the threat, only too real, of penury and her sister... could Susannah have borne it? Or had Caroline been unfair to her sister? Maybe there were underlying qualities not yet called upon but which would have stood her in good stead... Who knows? Then, lately, a change so slight that it would have been easy to miss, had Caroline not known Susannah so well... And here, thrown as they were closer together and in an altered milieu ... More time was being occupied with Mrs Farley. Why?

Or, worse still, was it *she*, herself, Caroline, who could not bear the thought of... destitution? Perhaps she was deluding herself.

And no word from Gervase.

Years had passed. Sometimes she doubted herself, her own recollections. Had she and Gervase really been engaged? Had she imagined the promises made in the rose garden? The secret betrothal?

It was hard to say. The more she concentrated, the more elusive the recollections became.

And then along had come the Duke of Albion. Descending from the august ranks of the haute-ton. Introduced by Lady Jersey herself. The occasion had been Caroline's last attendance at Almack's, with an old family friend of Mama's, Lady Melrose, persuading Caroline, against her will. But the word was out. The Langrish sisters were without means. It was meant to be a last society outing. A farewell.

The hushed silence at Almack's as His Grace had advanced across the ballroom with the illustrious patroness. Almost leading her.

Certainly in charge.

A gentleman never before seen by Caroline. No, not even at the most fashionable of her previous soirées or any social event of any kind. Was she known to him? She had doubted it. To be taken up in such a way. Inexplicable – unless… a fancy? A whim? Or something else?

Memories flooded back: a tall, broad-shouldered gentleman with a decided air of authority. Expensive suiting. Tailoring exquisite. A considered mode of dress

(Later she was to be assured by Albion himself of the confidence of centuries of breeding through the English Shires, Eton, Oxford, White's. Not to mention the royal connection…)

Meanwhile Lady Jersey's words floated away into nothingness. Everything receded. Rising from a deep curtsey, Caroline had caught a look of such intensity in his almost handsome, impassive face she had gasped.

Flushing, she had had to look away, unable to meet his gaze.

She who never blushed.

The introduction. Lady Melrose immensely gratified. The quadrille. The supper dance, followed by refreshments in a private room. Almack's was notorious for its sparse provisions, but still. The attention.

Everything had changed then.

Caroline's future assured.

And Susannah's. Her come-out followed. Suitors appeared, cognisant of the sisters' place in society once more.

Sometimes, looking back to that fateful evening, would she, Caroline, have been the duke's first choice had Susannah, with her looks, stood beside her.

And what would happen now?

What would His Grace do… when he found out Caroline had had a tryst in a carriage with her former lover.

A lover until recently completely unknown to the noble duke. Well, he knew enough now. Enough but apparently not enough to break off the engagement.

So far.

But if he were to find out what had taken place? What would happen then?

Caroline knew she had nearly given herself to Gervase. But he had refused her...

Her sister's voice broke into her reverie bringing Caroline back into the present. Her eyes snapped open.

'Caroline, is that you?' Susannah swept around on her chair with one of her usual graceful movements. 'La, Caroline. What an age you have been. I thought to have to invent another tale for our gaoler!' She was wearing Caroline's leghorn chip straw hat with the wide brim. Caroline's favourite.

Something must have shown in her face, for Susannah resumed looking at herself in the mirror. Catching sight of her sister in the mirror and making a *moue* with her mouth Susannah unravelled the wide blue ribbons, laced into a wide bow under her chin. Now free of the modish hat, she dangled it between her fingers.

'Mrs Farley is not our gaoler,' replied Caroline mechanically, as she rescued her favourite hat from further damage. 'I have told you often enough. Susannah. I am feeling unwell. I think I shall lie down.'

Susannah turned to face Caroline and rested her face on her hand with her elbow on the dressing-table top. 'Well, maybe not, but she keeps a close watch upon us both. You have been an uncommonly long time away. Tell me, did you see the Earl of Marlow?'

Caroline sank down on a sofa by her sister. 'Yes, and also Gervase.' There was no use pretending otherwise.

Susannah fixed her with stare. 'No.'

'Yes.'

Silence fell between them.

Caroline looked down. At her own dishevellment.

'What are those marks on your neck? Are they bruises?' Her sister was beside her, with her arms around her. 'What has he done to you, Caroline?'

Heat rose in Caroline's face. She began to struggle. 'Let me go, Susannah. He has done nothing.'

'Nothing!'

'Yes, nothing.'

Susannah released her. 'I do not believe you. I shall fetch Mrs. Farley.'

Caroline started to laugh hysterically. 'Mrs Farley. After all you have said. No, no.'

She took Susannah's hands in hers. 'Look at me. I swear Gervase has not harmed me.' She took a breath. 'Whatever I did, I did willingly.'

Her sister was no longer looking at her. With a toss of her head she rose from the sofa and crossed the room to pick up her wrap and reticule. 'I do not understand. I wish you would tell me what has happened between you both. Perhaps it is best I should not know. But I will leave you to rest. Besides it is better that I go downstairs and engage the duke's mistress in conversation. As a distraction. I shall tell her you are overcome by the heat.'

'I do not believe Mrs Farley is the duke's mistress.'

'Is that because you desire the duke yourself?'

'You know nothing of such matters.'

At the door, Susannah halted. She turned to look at Caroline. 'I may be ignorant, but what are you going to tell His Grace?'

'I do not know.' And Caroline truly did not.

'I think you cannot marry him now. He will not be best pleased.'

'I am betrothed to him.'

'That may be the right of it but you love Gervase!' With those terrible words, Susannah left the room.

Now that there was no longer any distraction from Susannah, Caroline wondered how often she had used the excuse of concentrating on her sister's moods, foibles, imperfections, whatever one cared to call them, to avoid the situation they were in. Or rather the situation *she*, Caroline, was in, if she were honest.

Now there were decisions to be made, decisions about the duke and Gervase.

The mighty Duke of Albion protects us: Susannah and I. He protects from the censure of society as much as from want. From the whispered discussions of society matrons behind closed doors as much as from the gaping onlookers when we are conveyed hither and thither in the various carriages belonging to His Grace. Below stairs, who knows the ribald comments being banded around on the subject of the luckless Langrish sisters, brought low by their father's gambling debts and death by his own hand.

Unable to halt the cascading thoughts and aware of an impending headache, Caroline retreated to her bedchamber. Any action to be taken would have to be on the morrow.

An idea was beginning to form in her mind.

There was also the nagging worry as to why Gervase needed to consult the Earl of Marlow so hurriedly…

And she still did not know how Gervase had come by his leg injury.

Distractedly, she crossed the room to her dressing-table.

The jewellery box.

Her maid, Constance, had moved it to the centre of the dressing-table.

After her father's death there had been nothing of value left. Her mother's jewels, her father's signet rings, her grandmother's pearls nearly the size of duck eggs or so it seemed, first pawned then sold. In the end, she had ceased to care.

She lifted up the mirrored lid and stared down at the replacements. And there were many of them. Could they be called replacements? Certainly she would not so call them.

The sapphires, always, always, the deepest, darkest blue – the duke of Albion would have none other.

She could hear his voice now, flat, devoid of emphasis.

She recalled the obsequious jeweller clad in dusty black abasing himself, almost to the Aubusson carpet, in front of them both. Any lower and he would have been kneeling.

In the duke's drawing-room, as the duke himself sat in a high-backed chair receiving. At ease, which in itself was a state not usual with His Grace. A glass of wine at his elbow. His clothing, she noticed, was loose about his person, especially about his nether regions. Most unlike the duke. Never had she seen him with such a mode of dress; she could have been in his dressing-room, almost. While Caroline herself watched from a low chaise-longue a small distance away; her throat dry, her pulse throbbing. Why she knew not. She suspected an advance would likely follow. She was unsure how she would behave if called upon…

After the departure of the jeweller the duke had risen and approached her.

Leaning over, he caressed her cheek lightly. Caroline shrank away, unsure of his advances. He murmured something which she did not hear and his hand went to his falls, already partially unbuttoned, but then, as if registering her slight dismay, he retreated.

As Caroline had not wanted his attentions he would wait until she was ready for him, until their wedding night, if need be. Those were the duke's words. And he had smiled.

Had he been aroused? She thought that he had.

The dreadful truth was that she, herself, yes, she, Caroline, had also felt an unfamiliar leap of the heart as she allowed her imagination to encompass the awful possibility that His Grace the Duke of Albion might prove a not unworthy, and certainly would be an experienced, lover.

Shortly after he departed.

Another occasion had been devoted to the rubies, flashing their blood-red fire; a particular necklace had passed through the jeweller's fingers slowly, reluctantly, heavily, to remain coiled, snakelike to view.

Joining the other wares in a heap in the top drawer of a display cabinet which had been wheeled in earlier by an underling.

The rubies were soon to be added to her collection.

That time Caroline was wary both of herself and her would-be lover. Temptation suppressed. She had worn a high-necked morning-dress in a sombre shade; the duke left her alone.

Emeralds followed, evil in their intensity. Again, she appeared to be safe now from his notice. For whatever reason.

And from herself.

Did he know?

An added frisson was that she suspected he had guessed.

But above all, there were the diamonds! The duke remarked that she should be clothed in diamonds, and once married and they were together, she would be. Well there were diamonds aplenty in the box – her necklace and tiara worn at the Betrothal Ball. And the engagement ring of course. How much more did he intend to bestow on her?

The future Duchess of Albion must be seen to be adorned.

As befitted the future wife of the Duke of Albion.

It was necessary.

So much had been deemed necessary by the duke.

She pulled out the velvet-lined drawer from the bottom of the box and marvelled at the ring with its solitary hard-edged jewel resting on the soft black material.

Her betrothal ring. Even now she was loath to wear it. But she had – until the visit today to the Earl of Marlow, when she had deliberately forgotten to place it on her ring finger.

Caroline, you are to be envied. Beware, by marrying Gervase, you will be relinquishing untold wealth. Wealth beyond your dreams…

The voice insistent in her ear.

Caroline shuddered as she snapped the box closed,

removing the dazzling display of jewels from sight.

If her heart truly belonged to Gervase, an unknown gentleman from obscurity, she must extricate herself from the entwining arms of the all-powerful Duke of Albion. And her own darker side. For she suspected she was not averse to his advances after all.

If she decided to do so - it would not be easy.

What would he do to her? To be jilted - after the Betrothal Ball, which had taken place with all due ceremony, in front of the massed ranks of the ton.

The Duke of Albion, scion of the nobility, with his close links to the Prince Regent.

Would she ever free herself from his coils?

And in her worst moments, she wondered whether she would ever forget when she nearly fell for the attractions of unlimited wealth, power and influence; a future where her unslaked desire would have been satisfied many times beyond question by an accomplished aristocratic lover, with years of experience in his clever hands. Skilled in the ways of the world and no doubt taught by masters.

An illicit dream; it was Gervase she loved.

And what would be the consequences for Gervase? Physical violence was not out of the question, she suspected.

CHAPTER 17

Gervase turned the corner from Piccadilly into the narrow street leading to his lodgings at the Albany. He was aware that he was being followed. Why he had not noticed before showed the extent of his preoccupation with the events of the day and those still to come. He halted and swung around. As he had guessed; it was Nathaniel: a short distance away, now lounging against a wall belonging to one of the buildings on Piccadilly, and affecting an air of innocence.

'Well?'

Nathaniel was swift to answer. 'Being as you were at my lord's, the Earl of Marlow, I took the liberty to take some time to myself, so as to speak. Will you be going out this evening, sir? '

'White's this evening, Nathaniel. So you can rest easy. Unless of course, the Captain needs you?'

The likelihood of Gordon stirring from the safety of the Albany rooms seemed remote to Gervase. Unless of course the startling Lady Lydia Vellacott had succeeded in gaining entrance. After all, Nathaniel had been keeping watch over Gervase and neglected his gatekeeper duties. Gervase turned on his heel and continued walking, or rather limping, towards the august building of the Albany. He was in dire need of the sanctuary of his own room for a few remaining hours. Rest, rest, that was most needed.

Before writing the necessary letters.

The last time he had done so had been before Salamanca but one letter at least would be more difficult after having encountered Caroline again. *Then* he had hoped against hope that she was waiting for him at Beauminster Priory. *Now* he knew how she had passed the time while he had been fighting in Spain. Everything had changed.

He climbed the stairs to his chambers dragging his injured leg behind him. But as he approached the door he thought he heard the sound of laughter. Gordon was not alone and the voice sounded female, surely, but not one that he recognised.

He opened the door and made his way in.

The small, dull sitting room was transformed. A paisley shawl had been thrown over the couch and, Gordon, supported by a welter of cushions, was lying there, full length, at his ease. Shirt open to the waist, breeches undone he held a glass of wine aloft with one hand, while the other was clasped around the waist of a lady also in a state of déshabillé and sitting astride him. Today the Lady Lydia Vellacott, for it was she, was clothed in a brilliant emerald green dress which shimmered in the half-light. A decanter of red wine was to the fore on a low table next to the chaise-longue. There was no other glass so perhaps the lady in question had no need of further stimulants. An all-pervading scent of some exotic hothouse flower perfumed the air and the curtains of fine net had been drawn.

Unhurriedly, the lady extricated herself from her lover's embrace, rose and assumed a graceful position in front of Gervase. She proceeded to shake down her skirts which rustled as she did so. 'You find us quite à la mode, Mr Thorpe. An afternoon siesta is quite the thing in Spain I am told.' Lady Lydia smiled and looked back at Gordon from beneath lowered lids in a most engaging fashion.

Gordon placed his glass back on the table none too carefully. He sat up to busy himself adjusting his clothing, buttoning his falls and tucking in his shirt. 'Lord, yes, between sorties, that is. I thought you would be away for the rest of the day, Gervase. My room is so cursed confined; don't you know? Lady Lydia here needs lots of space to, er, move as freely as she wishes... Met her before, before we went off to fight Boney. What brings you back so soon, eh?'

'I have some business to attend to, I regret to say. And letters to write.' Gervase stumbled over his words, trying to conceal his shock and embarrassment at coming upon the unexpected scene. Finding his Albany compatriot in post *flagrante delicto* was almost beyond belief. Yet, really, why not? Gordon was a man of normal appetites; it was he, Gervase, who had suffered from rejection. The sharp pain of jealousy returned.

He moved aside to allow Lady Lydia to pass, as she gathered up a wrap of the same brilliant green silk from a chair and moved gracefully away from both of them. She blew a kiss to Gordon by extending a palm upwards and pursuing her lips into an even more elegant shape if that were possible. 'I shall see you tonight at Vauxhall, my dear Captain?'

'Oh dear, yes, Lady Lydia!' Gordon leant forwards towards her. The draping and cushions on the couch fell to the floor boards. He rose to his feet and followed her. In vain he attempted to catch hold of her hands but she eluded him and was out of the doors before he could detain her. Ignoring Gervase, he moved to the window, where he flung up the sash and leant out as far as he could. After a few minutes, his shoulders slumped and he returned to throw himself on the couch and stare moodily at the decanter of wine. Eventually he poured himself another glass and drained it. Turning the glass upside down he replaced it on the table, shaking his head. 'Not the answer.'

A step forward indeed. In spite of himself, Gervase was interested. Perhaps Gordon needed further encouragement to leave the safety of the Albany. He could not stay locked up for ever. 'I take it you will not disappoint the fair Lady Lydia tonight?' Although of course Lady Lydia's hair was as dark as a raven's wing.

Gordon hunched a shoulder and said nothing.

Gervase persisted. 'Well?'

By way of an answer, Gordon retrieved the paisley shawl from the floor and flung it over his head. Lying down on the couch he turned his back on Gervase, muttering a few indecipherable words as he did so. It sounded like a curse.

Finding the sight unedifying, Gervase made his way to his own quarters.

He had much to do; letters to write. Letters that would prove surprisingly difficult without a doubt.

Later, much later as it turned out, letters written, Gervase prepared to drag himself out to White's gentlemen's club.

He needed to satisfy himself that all the arrangements were in order for the next morning's duel. He was sure, as directed, to find Roland at White's, but bearing in mind Roland's presence had been required at the Court of St. James earlier in the evening, matters of such import relating to his friend, Gervase, could have slipped his mind.

Then Gervase smote himself. To doubt the Earl of Marlow, when he had proved a steadfast companion during the years they were in Iberia. Gervase would not care to dwell on some of exploits from which he had been rescued by Marlow. Gervase closed his eyes as the memories flooded back – especially of the blood and gore at Salamanca. Had he, Gervase, deliberately courted danger, flouted the statutes of war, perhaps even endangered his own men? No, no, he had always denied *that* charge, even when tasked with his conduct by no less than Sir John Colborne himself? No, it did not bear thinking about. No, impossible. He shook himself and returned to the present.

He compressed his lips together. To the letters.

Now that he had fulfilled his beloved uncle's wish by enlisting in the Fifty-Second Regiment and serving his time in the Peninsula War he had property to bequeath. His will had already been made but he needed to acquaint a certain George Kilmartin Thorpe, a distant cousin. Truth to tell, he barely remembered the youth. Still at Eton, when was it? Ten years ago? The lad would inherit the property in Hampshire, being Gervase's heir, so it was best to acquaint him of the fact. A mere question of minutes to scrawl a few lines on a piece of paper and thrust the brief note into an envelope. There was no other family, no-one else who required a letter - apart from Caroline.

Miss Caroline Langrish.

The letter to Caroline? A vast quantity of vellum had ended up being shredded and disposed of in the hearth. Pity was it that high summer ruled, else he could have had the pleasure of grinding the offending papers beneath his booted heel and thrusting them into the flames thereby burning his words in a cleansing fire.

Gervase realised he needed to get a grip upon himself.

The letter.

Well, in the end Gervase had had but few words to write, shocking though it was. And shocking they were.

My dearest Caroline,

Have I even the right to call you so, for no longer are you mine, just the affianced bride of the all-mighty Duke of Albion...

That was beginning of one version that would not be sent...

The final letter written in the end in haste was bald and to the point.

Caroline,

A Love Betrayed

It is my sincere wish that any regrets you may harbour concerning myself should be forgotten and I wish you every happiness with the Duke of Albion.

Gervase Vyvyan Thorpe.

There, that should do it. A place should now be reserved for him in the halls of redemption. Though not given to prayer, except he reminded himself, in the extremity of agony when he had received the ball in his leg at Salamanca, he prayed Caroline would remember him, when she was enjoying her married bliss…

Once more Gervase was forced to exercise control over himself. He was becoming maudlin. He was in want of strong drink – or perhaps some banter with Gordon. Although judging by the state in which Gervase had left his erstwhile companion-in-arms it was unlikely to be forthcoming. Gordon at least had been well-known once upon a time for not taking life too seriously. And had emerged apparently unscathed from the horrors of war. Or had he? One never quite knew but staying in drinking with Avery suggested that that was certainly not the case.

However, there were hopeful signs.

Judging by the sounds of whistling, interspersed with snatches of song, emanating from the Captain's rooms, it was obvious he was preparing for the evening engagements, and would most certainly be unwilling to indulge in any diversionary conversation.

Gervase shrugged himself into his jacket, picked up the two slight letters and prepared to face the night ahead.

When he walked out from his quarters into the main sitting-room he was shocked to see how much time he must have spent concocting what amounted to very little in the way of written material. The night was far advanced by the mantel-piece clock, ten o' the clock; though the quality of the light was as one might expect on such a summer's evening. For Gervase himself, the way he was feeling, he would be glad when winter had set in again. If indeed he lived to see it.

Captain Gordon Howard, having emerged from his rooms at much the same time, gave Gervase a brisk nod and, still whistling, walked smartly across the floor towards the doors to their small entrance hall. There he became pre-occupied with assembling gloves, a high-crowned beaver hat and a Malacca cane on a small table. Retracing his steps, he peered into the looking-glass on the mantelpiece and made a minor adjustment to his cravat.

'What do you think? Nathaniel tells me it is a Gordian Knot.'

The scent of sandalwood lay heavy in the air.

Gervase coughed. He would definitely need a drink at White's. 'A Gordian knot indeed, sir! I'm glad the Lady Lydia at Vauxhall Gardens will not be disappointed.'

She must have worked wonders. If only his own entanglement with Caroline could have been resolved as easily as that of Gordon and the bountiful Lady Lydia. And whose fault was that?

Gervase reverted to his own, more pressing affairs. 'By the by, would you take care of these letters for me? I have not had time to have them franked. Tomorrow I may be busy.' And he thrust the slim envelopes in the Captain's direction.

Without an acknowledgement, Captain Howard took the missives, barely glancing down, and stashed them behind the mirror on the mantel-piece. 'Harcourt, Tolland and old Falconbridge, you remember him, from Toulouse, don't you? Falconbridge paid me a visit while you were attending to business. He has hired a carriage and we make up a select party for the Pleasure Gardens. Avery will meet us there. Lady Lydia has procured a box for the evening, which may give some privacy.' And he laughed.

'Yes, I remember Falconbridge,' said Gervase. 'How is he?' It was good that the loss of an arm was not preventing Falconbridge's social engagements. 'By the way, I shall be leaving early in the morning.'

Captain Howard smoothed down his jacket. Picking up

his hat, cane and gloves, he said. 'I'll not see you then.'

He departed without further ado. Gervase heard the sound of his boots echoing down the stairs below to the street.

Dismissing Gordon from his mind, Gervase set out for White's at least a couple of hours later than he had intended and without the benefit of liquor.

CHAPTER 18

To White's.
To discuss the duelling arrangements for the following morning.
Not one of Gervase's usual haunts; actually he had only ever set foot in the place once before, in Roland's company of course. A fact which had probably slipped Roland's mind. How Gervase was to gain entrance was still in question.

More to the point was whether he, Gervase, had a haunt as such at all?

Since his return to the shores of England with Roland, Gervase had found himself almost unconsciously and certainly not by choice in a spell of semi-seclusion in his lodgings. Rather like Gordon himself, Gervase was ashamed to admit. How had that happened? And how long had he spent incarcerated? Even Roland himself had had to use his undoubtedly powerful powers of persuasion to get Gervase to stir abroad. First to Roland's own town house and then later, by degrees, out and about, in town.

Although after the news of Caroline's engagement broke, Gervase had taken to the other extreme, wasting vast amounts of energy endeavouring to find out her whereabouts, leading to the disastrous attendance, (courtesy of Roland's invitation), at the Betrothal Ball.

Oh, to Roland, White's, *The* Gentlemen's Club of choice to all the *ton,* was a second home. Not of course that one could choose it exactly, more likely one was chosen or not as the case maybe. Certainly not for persons of the ilk of Gervase. He suspected the club was an escape for Roland, an escape from his responsibilities for a short time. Somewhere to relax and pass the time of day with his equals as much as his elders and betters.

Gervase knew he was being unfair to his friend. Anyone less likely to shirk his duty would be hard to find. And when had Roland ever pulled rank or used his superior position amongst the *ton* to his own advantage in front of Gervase? Never. Quite the reverse.

It was worth repeating that White's was not for the likes of Gervase, only son of a steward, but tolerated as an acquaintance of one Roland Francis Sebastian Wendover, Fifth Earl of Marlow.

Gervase paused at the top of the steps in front of White's.

Damnit, but he almost wished he had the illustrious Captain Gordon Howard's cane as support!

It was not only that Gervase was not a frequenter of the Club, but the events of the past few days had taken their toll. He halted to get his breath back as much, he told himself, as to gather his wits about him. Although the latter state of affairs was becoming increasingly common since his return from war.

His thoughts were rudely interrupted by a couple of lords, braying loudly, and clearly half-cut, sauntering in front of him. 'After you, sir,' one said to the other as they swayed into the hallowed precincts of White's.

Emboldened, Gervase stepped over the threshold after them. His entrée at last.

He followed in the wake of the pair who waved aside the footman ready to divest them of their outer garments. They continued unsteadily down the corridor leading off the hall.

'To the gaming rooms, Fortescue,' said the taller gentleman who Gervase now noticed was possessed of a white sash. Had he too attended at the Court of St. James with Roland?

His more slightly-built companion nodded and Gervase closed the distance between them. Definitely the favourite choice. If Roland was not known for gambling tendencies, those among his company most definitely were.

Doors along the brightly-lit corridor were open but displayed nothing of any consequence: coffee-rooms mostly empty due to the late hour, libraries for assorted dozing lords, private sitting-rooms for various nefarious activities but who cared? Those chambers were for the more retiring of those of noble birth. But the gambling rooms were the place to be.

The gentlemen of the *ton* meanwhile had started squabbling between themselves, with surreptitious glances over their shoulders in Gervase's direction.

The one named as Fortescue finally turned around and fixed Gervase with an unfocused stare. 'Studley, I do declare!' His speech was slurred.

Gervase shook his head. The other shot a cursory glance at Gervase, then gripped Fortescue by the arm and dragged him away. 'Not with us,' he muttered, 'anyway, here we are.'

And there they undoubtedly were.

Diverted, Gervase stepped in line with the *tonnish* pair, who now feeling at home, turned their backs on him and disappeared off in the direction of raised voices.

Gervase, transfixed, took in the scene ahead; beyond the double doors, now wide open to the world as it were, well, at least to the rest of White's, was an exceedingly crowded gaming room; its plentiful candles dimmed by smoke. Overall there was a strong smell of liquor.

One of the select gaming rooms at the back of the establishment of White's then.

Gervase struggled to find the whereabouts of the Earl of Marlow amongst the sea of gentlemen far gone in their cups.

Narrowing his eyes against the fetid atmosphere, he spied a group of men around the furthest gaming table from the doors, an assortment of gentlemen, amongst them the still prized green or red jackets of the victors.

Well, they are entitled to their moment of triumph, Gervase thought. But at what a price.

Banishing such pointless reminiscences from his head, he wove his way over but his progress was slowed for some time by two waiters with long aprons, each carrying drinks on a silver tray. Gervase cursed beneath his breath, irritated that he could not make headway.

He sidestepped the pair.

At last Gervase found himself at the Earl's table. His friend was seated but leaning back, listening to a younger man in Rifleman green whispering in Roland's ear. Probably regaling him with some choice piece of gossip.

As Gervase approached the officer wandered off.

All the other gentlemen participating presumably in the card-game, whatever it was, were also at their ease: one, much younger than the rest, so much so that he was resting his head on his arms on the green baize itself. And snoring to boot.

'Thorpe,' Roland pushed back his chair and rose elegantly from the table. The movement was too controlled to be anything other than the sign of a man who had drunk enough if not yet too much. He was no longer wearing the white sash. 'We have had a most convivial time at St. James's Palace.'

Snorts of laughter issued from more than one of the gamesters in the circle.

'We are between rubbers, awaiting fresh cards. Sanders here thought the last pack was not quite the thing,' Roland went on.

A cue for more laughter.

Stepping aside from the players, he caught Gervase by the arm and lowered his voice, 'I bespoke a private room earlier where we can talk. It is ours for as long as we like, all night, if necessary. More convenient than returning to my town house. Now, to the arrangements, you know.'

'Yes, yes,' replied Gervase, quickly, his jaw clenching. 'I shall, of course, return to the Albany later.'

'As you wish then.'

Roland turned back and spoke to the rest of the company. 'Gentlemen, you must continue without me.'

The Rifleman who had now returned said loudly, 'What are you up to, eh, Wendover? Will you be moving on in search of female company?'

'Hold up, at least give me a chance to recoup my losses,' came a plaintive voice from the back of the group.

And there was an answering groan from the table-resting youth, who sat up with a jerk and looked around with a blank expression on his face.

'Pray send for Wembley's carriage, will you, someone. He has been out too late. Or should I say too early?' These were Roland's words.

More hilarity ensued but two of the persons addressed took Roland's commands seriously enough to heave the lad out of his chair and endeavour to stand him upright.

The power of a commanding officer, thought Gervase silently.

He went with Roland, glad to be out of the hell-hole. Gervase had too much on his mind to stomach such frivolity.

On the other hand, if his second was already foxed maybe the best option was for Gervase to follow his example.

Gervase followed Roland into the private salon. It had minimal furniture, just two well-worn leather chairs, each with its own small wooden side-table, drawn up either side of an open window, and a sideboard laden with refreshments. In Gervase's opinion therefore little in the way of comfort. For their purposes it was enough, he thought. He envisaged a brief discussion, then a return to the Albany for rest, and then the encounter.

The noise of late-night revellers drifted into the room but little air entered from the street. No chance of any relief from the oppressive heat.

'I have directed that we should not be disturbed,' said Roland as he strolled over to the sideboard. He frowned as he regarded the chafing-dishes. 'I ordered a cold collation,' he said. He removed a cover and dropped it down on the cloth. Swaying, Roland held the dish of meats up to his nose. 'It will serve, I suppose,' he said as he slid the plate back down on the table next to its cover. Having forked a strip of blooded beef into his mouth he chewed and swallowed. 'The quality of the wine at the Palace was remarkable. Truly remarkable. But it leaves one with an unsatisfied desire for, one knows not what,' his voice tailed off.

He gestured towards the food but Gervase shook his head. His senses had been assaulted more than enough by the smell of roast meat.

Instead he joined his friend at the sideboard. The decanter of brandy beckoned. He grasped it by the neck and poured out two glasses. With detachment he saw that his hand shook.

Roland made himself comfortable in one of the armchairs. He accepted his drink from Gervase and saluted him with a flourish. 'Your health.'

Gervase sat down opposite him. 'Well, what news?'

Roland leant forward, 'I have made the arrangements.'

'Yes, and?'

'The venue agreed upon is Hyde Park.'

'Hyde Park?'

'Yes, Hyde Park.'

'Yes, it is unusual. The form is,' Roland hesitated, 'One would normally expect a coach ride for some little distance to a secluded glade somewhere so that both parties may reflect on whether they wish to meet their Maker in such an untimely fashion. An apology might then ensue, but it is not to be.'

Form, yes, Roland was knowledgeable on form but he must have guessed at Gervase's dismay: an appointment so near to the beating heart of London town.

Gervase rose from his seat, brandy in hand and took a turn about the room. 'Would not Putney Heath at the very least have been more, well, remote? Is not Hyde Park a trifle, close to town?'

'You are fortunate it was not Green Park.'

'Green Park!'

'Yes, I managed to dissuade the duke's second, whom I have met before, by the way, the Marquess of Longville. I drew to his attention the early morning activities of the dairymaids in Green Park. In the end he allowed Hyde Park to be the venue.'

'Good of him.'

'He said the duke did not wish to travel far. He had a morning engagement which he had no wish to break.'

'So be it. His choice of course.' Resigned, Gervase resumed his seat. He took a heartening gulp of brandy.

'It may interest you to know that the assignation is with a lady. A much sought-after widow, rumoured to be his next *chère-amie.*'

Immediately Gervase felt a violent churning in his gut. Unable to see, let alone focus, he struggled with his feelings. Uppermost was disgust. Hell's teeth, the duke was a rake after all.

Gervase had thought, yet what had he thought?

That Albion was as in love with Caroline as he, Gervase, was? Madness.

'How come?' He choked out.

'It is the way of the world, Gervase. More brandy?' He rose and went over again to the side-board. 'The Marquess let it slip.'

'Certainly,' replied Gervase. It was his turn to hold out his glass. His hand was steady.

Roland, nursing the decanter, came back and topped up first Gervase's glass and then his own. He resumed his seat and placed the decanter within easy reach on the side table nearest him.

'Longville and I agreed a time of five.' He glanced at the clock on the mantel-piece. 'In two hours' time, or thereabouts.'

Gervase was now past caring. He was still trying to digest the news of the villainy of Caroline's betrothed.

'Doctor Frankenthaler as surgeon will be there.'

A piece of information that was of no interest to Gervase: it did not merit the dignity of a reply.

'As recommended by the *haut ton*, I believe.'

'It is immaterial to me.'

'Oh come now. Surely you want your defeated adversary to receive the best of care?'

'If it is the done thing.'

'It is. Before we discuss my duelling pistols which I have sent for from my town house…' Roland hesitated.

'Yes?'

'There was no question of an apology? Longville and I were in agreement. The situation had gone beyond that?'

'Beyond everything. I struck the bastard.'

'Just so.' Roland rose. 'Laurence, my secretary should be on his way now. They are Mantons, naturally.' He walked over to the bell rope on the wall nearest the doors and rang. 'Then I think we are done.'

The doors swung open and a club servant entered followed by a neatly-dressed younger man, who pushed past him and presented Roland with a carrying case displaying the crest of the Marlow family arms in gold.

'Thank you, your services will not be required now,' said Roland in dismissal to the older man, who bowed his way out. 'Good work, Laurence. Have you the correct set?'

'I came in all haste, my lord.' Laurence gave a quick

nod to Gervase. 'The duelling pistols you required.'

'Excellent.' Roland snapped the lock and opened the case, revealing the fire-arms resting, Gervase dared swear, on a bed of red velvet.

Gervase rose.

'Here, feel the weight in your hand.' Roland removed one of the pistols and passed it over to Gervase. It did indeed fit well into the hand. A smooth, gleaming article. For an instrument of death.

Gervase had to admit he was impressed. 'Well-balanced,' he conceded, turning it over several times. He lifted the pistol and straightened his arm, aiming at the clock on the mantel-piece which as if instructed, proceeded to strike the hour. Three o'clock.

Raucous laughter rose up from the street below.

Roland moved over and slammed down the window. He leant back against the sill, crossed his arms and regarded Gervase with a grin. 'Is it not exquisite? It feels like an extension of your arm, does it not? I paid sixty guineas for these beauties. I doubt whether even the duke has such a pair.'

'You were not short-changed by any means.'

Roland came forward, took the pistol away and returned it to its home. The case was handed back to Laurence.

'Now, let us have another drink. Laurence, send for another bottle of brandy, will you? Look in downstairs and accompany us later. We shall make a night of it.'

Once the secretary had left the salon, Roland returned to his chair and sat down. Leaning over he picked up the decanter and held it aloft, squinting through the glass at the ceiling. 'My secretary. An excellent man. He will be a useful support.'

'How so?'

There was the briefest of pauses.

'Longville says there will be quite an entourage there. Albion does nothing by halves. And the word has spread one hears.'

Gervase snorted. 'An audience. The more the merrier.'

'That was not what you were saying earlier.'

'I have changed my mind.'

Roland shot him a quick glance. 'Well then, let us drink long and deep, my friend.'

When barely two hours remained!

'By all means,' said Gervase recklessly. 'What have I got to lose?'

Oblivion beckoned for a few hours at least.

CHAPTER 19

'A toast, to the fair sister!' Roland's speech was slurred.

Gervase raised his glass, drank, and then on an impulse hurled the crystal goblet into the empty grate. 'May she be more faithful than Caroline!'

He knew that soon, very soon, they would both be very drunk indeed.

Stepping backwards, he fell into one of the armchairs positioned either side of the fireplace. He was having trouble focusing on Roland, who would make a habit of weaving around in front of him.

Next Roland too was seated.

It was essential that Gervase fully understood what was to happen on the morrow. He leant forward but the words would not come.

'When were you intending to tell me about your entanglement with Miss Caroline Langrish, Gervase?' Roland, however, had become unexpectedly loquacious. And also unexpectedly sharp.

Admittedly they were both well into their cups but the turn the conversation had taken did not suit Gervase at all, no, not at all. 'It was neither here nor there. What was the point?'

A Love Betrayed

'Very much to the point, I should say. At the time I merely thought you had a death wish. Here let me find you another glass.'

Gervase did not say anything as Roland somehow managed to reach the side-board at an unsteady pace and returned with another, filled goblet. Gervase did not refuse the drink.

'Had I known what I know now, that there was a lady in the case, well...' Of course Roland could not be deflected.

'Yes?'

'I should have spoken to Colbourne earlier.'

One small blessing at least. That he, Gervase, was not removed earlier from the ranks. 'I did not know it was you who saw the Lieutenant-Colonel.'

Another piece of the puzzle had fallen into place.

'It was not solely my doing. Your reckless, foolhardy behaviour had been observed by others, not myself alone. Trust me.'

Roland had accompanied Gervase from the Regiment to the illustrious tents of the Staff Officers.

But for himself, it was bad enough as it was - being selected from other worthy, much worthier, if truth be told, officers for *aide-de-camp* duties at Headquarters. Gervase still felt sick when he remembered that particular time in his army career. Army career, ye gods!

What had Lieutenant-Colonel Sir John Colbourne thought?

However, by the time of the Battle of Salamanca, the Lieutenant-Colonel himself had been invalided out, for a very long eleven months, so not a witness of Gervase's current leg injury and how it had been acquired. Colborne might have thought his Staff Officer singularly unlucky or much worse, still uncontrollable. Gervase closed his eyes.

Roland must have shaken him because Gervase started and became, as one sometimes does, instantly awake and aware of a profound human truth. 'It was payment, wasn't it!'

Now it was Roland's turn to prevaricate. 'Payment?' But his glance slid away at Gervase's words.

Now they were really getting somewhere.

Unfortunately, it was somewhere in the past, when they had been young. Before the aging effects of service in the Peninsular War... Back at Roland's father's estate, Stretton Manor, before he moved to the family seat at Marlow Grange. Stretton Manor had been managed with the utmost care by Gervase's father, John Thorpe, as Gervase himself was now fully aware with hindsight. Not that either Gervase or Roland took notice of such matters at the time.

One specific day came to mind in particular.

How old had they been? They had been mere striplings that was for sure.

Gervase had come upon Roland fishing, in the river that flowed through the estate and on this particular occasion in spring was running more strongly than it was wont. Roland, casting with more hope than experience, lost his balance in the process so that Gervase had to jump in and before he knew it they were both drenched and spluttering on the bank together. The fishing rod was lost and it was forever in doubt as to who had rescued whom ...

There had been numerous such situations.

'If you are thinking of one of the many scrapes we indulged in? A ridiculous notion. Put it out of your mind.' Roland replied at last.

'As you wish.'

Maybe they had both been at fault. Hotheads, as the very young often are. By now, Gervase had a headache and felt increasingly old.

'I think I would like another brandy,' he said and held out his glass.

Roland obeyed and it looked as though all would be well. Both were satisfactorily replenished with the necessary drinks, silence ensued and Gervase was on the verge of believing a critical moment had been passed. Perhaps they could have some peace before morning.

But it was not to be. Roland, shading his eyes, elbow on arm-rest of his chair, leant forward and started again. 'Still have nightmares about Salamanca.'

Oh no. Now Gervase came to think of it, he realised the incident had never been discussed, which everyone knew, was the best way. 'More brandy?'

'As your second I should keep a clear head.'

There was no arguing with that.

'Gervase, am trying to say, should have come back for you that night. Not left it until morning.'

'I survived.'

Just.

'Should have done so. Should have come back for you.'

'But you did, and so did Gordon.'

Eventually.

Gervase had been told subsequently that it had been nearly too late.

Gervase felt suddenly very tired. The turn the conversation had taken at such a late hour was in danger of sobering him up. A state which he had hoped to avoid until the next day. For once, Roland was the one in need of reassurance. Remarkable but Gervase owed his friend *that*, at least. 'I shall ring for coffee.'

Roland shook his head. 'Not on my account,' and after a pause, 'Owe you so much.'

The conversation must be halted. 'It was no more than you would have done for me.'

That at least was the truth.

Now they were both in the way of becoming lucid.

Gervase rose to his feet, marched over to the sideboard and pushed aside the empty decanter. Fortunately, another bottle of brandy was at hand, brought in by the estimable Laurence no doubt, although Gervase did not remember noticing. He poured himself out a generous measure and turned to Roland.

'Well, we were both mentioned in despatches, the world knows our story. Let us leave it at that. Or do you want to talk about our joint and fruitless efforts at Badajoz or your little excursion and its aftermath at Salamanca?' Two could play at the game of reminiscence.

There was no reply.

Afterwards Gervase's recollections of the evening spent at White's before the duel were not to be relied upon, he thought. There was a vague recollection of various toasts including one to Miss Susannah Langrish, by Roland, but little else.

Had they truly discussed the events at Salamanca? It was scarcely credible but they had.

Roland was usually as loath to revisit the past as Gervase himself but perhaps on this occasion the earl had imbibed more than Gervase. Certainly Gervase thought that his friend had, while Gervase in the end contrived to hold back; not entirely having given up on the necessity of keeping sober for the morning and the duel.

CHAPTER 20

Gervase awoke to find himself being shaken by Roland. 'It is half after four.' His friend stepped back. 'Are you up to the mark?'

Gervase hefted himself out of his chair; only his mouth tasted sour, his head throbbed and as his left leg touched the floorboard the familiar pain was his again. 'Certainly. Let us leave now.'

The sun was already up as Gervase strode out with Roland, closely followed by the secretary, valise in hand, down St. James Street towards Hyde Park. The brief respite from the heat of the previous day was fast vanishing.

'It promises to be another fine morning,' he heard from Roland next to him. Their boots rang out across the cobbles, disturbing the early-morning quiet. Inconsequentially Gervase noticed they were in step. The silence between them felt companionable as the two friends traversed the short distance towards the appointed meeting-place.

As they turned into the Park a slight mist swirled and lifted to reveal a green grass expanse surrounded by trees on all sides, save where the path on which they were entered the arena.

An arena indeed.

Some distance away two lines of carriages were drawn up one on either side of the grassy space, the horses mostly quiet apart from a pair of matched bays that moved restlessly back and forth as a groom endeavoured to quieten them. Assorted gentlemen were gathered into small groups idly chatting, or smoking or drinking from flasks. On the whole the noise was subdued but there was a definite increase when the newcomers were marked out.

Aghast, Gervase stopped. He did not draw back but he had to admit he was shocked. He did not know what he had expected after all. But not this, surely?

'I thought as much,' said Roland tersely. 'White's. Some of the voyeurs may even have walked here, as we did. Making a night of it. Or rather a morning. News travels fast.'

Gervase drew Roland to one side. 'I have a few words to say to you but time is short.'

'Just so,' Roland was squinting at the sun, 'I think the light may be in our eyes, more's the pity.' He looked around. 'I do not see the duke. I do not think he is here yet. Ah, but that must be the doctor, over there.'

'I have left some letters at the Albany. Will you see that they are delivered? Captain Howard is not the most reliable of men.'

Especially at present with Gordon's erratic behaviour; first confined to quarters and then out on the town with the jade, Lady Lydia Vellacott. With a pang Gervase admitted to himself the pair seemed inordinately happy with each other. If the worst were to befall him today he would never have had the satisfaction of *that* with Caroline.

Roland reached into his jacket and produced a hip-flask, which he offered to Gervase. 'Of course. Here, a fine brandy, try it.'

Gervase rook a deep, satisfying draught and handed it back. The fire coursed through his body, providing temporary relief. 'If anything should happen… '

'It will not,' was Roland's voice, loud and strong. He too took a long drink from the silver flask.

'Say nothing to Miss Langrish.'

Roland, in the act of emptying the flask into his mouth, half-choked. He took out a kerchief and wiped his mouth. 'Forgive me. What did you say?'

'I do not mean Miss Susannah Langrish, I wish you joy in that quarter.' Gervase began again. God help him, what was he about to say? The duke would never deserve it. 'Miss Langrish. I do not want her to be unhappy,' he went on, 'If the worst befalls me.'

Redemption. At a price. But that was enough of self-flagellation.

Roland was still coughing. He straightened up. 'You have my word.'

'Now I mean to kill the bastard.'

Roland shot him a quick look. 'Your choice.'

There was no more to be said.

A town coach, larger than one might have expected for an assignation supposedly secret, rounded the corner behind them, followed by another, and another. Gervase would have laughed out loud if he had not been the other main player in the scene that was to unfold.

The crowd fell silent.

The carriages, each bearing an emblazoned coat-of-arms, swayed and lumbered to a halt, the horses skittish and jumpy.

No-one descended.

'Time is getting on.' Roland's voice sounded rough. 'We shall be discovered by the constables or worse if we do not begin soon. Where the devil is Longville?'

'Is that him?'

A gentleman in a long drab greatcoat had detached himself from one of the small groups and was making his way towards them, flourishing a cane with some panache, his coat swinging in the long grass.

'Your servant, sirs.' He executed a bow. 'Doctor Frankenthaler at your service.' He addressed Gervase. 'I must in all duty suggest you apologise to the duke and I can try to persuade His Grace to forget the whole sorry episode and we may all return home.'

Gervase stared at him. He did not trust himself to speak. Moments passed. He shook his head. Had it not been made clear?

The doctor gave a brief acknowledgement. 'I will inform His Grace.'

He made his way back towards Albion's retinue.

Activity was at last visible amongst the latest arrivals. An underling appeared and pulled down the steps from the first carriage and opened the door. The Duke of Albion descended.

There was an answering murmur from the crowd.

Another gentleman likewise made his entrance from the second.

No-one exited from the third.

'Ah, Longville,' said Roland. 'I shall meet with him now. Laurence, the pistols, if you have them. Come.' He beckoned to his secretary. 'I shall return in a few minutes.' So saying he was off across the field with Laurence struggling to keep up. Gervase watched them go

The duke was a still figure in the distance, Longville, for it must be him, lounging beside him, and the doctor a short way back. An impressive array of servants or other vassals of Albion had appeared out of nowhere and gathered behind rather as if posing in a landscape for some court painter thought Gervase irrelevantly.

He sighed. He had rather it would not all end here. He had emerged relatively unscathed from the Peninsula, with the exception of his damned leg. It would indeed be ironic if...

What were they playing at?

Roland and the Marquess of Longville were discussing

something or other, heads together. Now Laurence had been beckoned forward to display the pistols. The lofty Duke of Albion, flanked by the doctor, stood a little distance away. Immobile.

In spite of himself Gervase owned to feeling agitated. He tried unsuccessfully to ease his shoulders under his jacket. It was too tight. He wished Roland had not recommended Weston as a tailor. Stripping off the offending article he cast it aside onto the grass. A good kick and Gervase felt better.

Further discussion between the men and then Roland was on his way back across the grass, once more, with Laurence hurrying behind.

'Well?'

'My duelling set has been rejected. We must use the duke's pistols.' Roland sounded out of breath.

'The Mantons not up to scratch?'

'Yes. In spite of my secretary's care.' Roland frowned and waved Laurence away. 'We are using their set. Regrettably. They pass muster however. Here you are.' He handed a gun to Gervase.

'No matter.'

'Good. Fifteen paces. I agreed. Longville has chosen the spot.'

'Fifteen paces?'

'Yes.'

Gervase shrugged his shoulders. 'So be it.'

'I suppose it's no use asking you not to kill him?'

Gervase did not bother to reply.

In the middle of the grassy field the Duke's second could be seen stamping down the grass with a well-shod boot.

Gervase straightened the cuffs on his shirt. 'I am ready.'

A hush had fallen over the assembled gathering but one gentleman called out as Gervase set off though what the exact words were he neither knew nor cared. All he knew was that at last, at last, God help him, he had a chance to right a wrong. How dare the Duke of Albion aspire to marry Caroline? He was not fit to come anywhere near her. Already selecting a new mistress indeed!

As Gervase stalked to the centre of the clearing he saw the duke unhurriedly making his way over. He too was now in his shirt sleeves. Too long, too heavy the linen. Not the kind of shirt he, Gervase would wear.

Neither spoke when they met only to turn their backs on each other.

The signal was given; the Marquess indicated.

Gervase paced out the required fifteen paces and turned sideways to view his adversary, arm up and ready.

For the second time Longville's services were required. The handkerchief came down.

A blaze of light came through a space between the trees dazzling Gervase as he fired.

His shot rang out almost simultaneously with what must have been Albion's, Gervase felt rather than saw a rush of air. Albion's bullet had passed him by.

But the duke was prone on the ground.

Good God, the bullet had found its mark.

It was the Peninsula all over again.

Even at a distance blood was evident. First a bloom on the freshly-laundered sleeve. Then more than evident. Soaking the ground. Gradually working towards making a shape in the grass approximate to the owner of the body.

Silence.

Gervase could only stare.

Roland shook him. 'Your aim was truer than you knew.'

'I did not mean to kill him. The sun blinded me.'

'Just so.' And Roland was off again running to the other side of the greensward.

The silence was succeeded by uproar. Large numbers of gentlemen rushed pass Gervase as he remained there stunned. Brushing past him.

The duke's men had come into their own. At least four were busy at the mysterious third coach, unpacking rugs, blankets and Gervase could scarcely credit it – a makeshift stretcher. What was this, a ducal infirmary? Doctor Frankenthaler had opened his bag and was now kneeling beside the apparently lifeless Duke.

Gervase's view was obscured by the press of people around the interesting and vanquished opponent.

Gervase turned away and began cleaning his gun, looking down.

What next?

Roland, pushing his way through the melee, appeared once more.

'Well?' Said Gervase.

'Well indeed,' his friend replied. 'All hell is to pay.'

'Dead then?'

'Not as yet. He is bleeding profusely but they are trying to stem the bleeding.'

By now the pair were left behind on the fringes of the event. Onlookers almost, Gervase felt.

The sun was rising higher in the sky. A solitary bird began singing, to be joined by another and then a chorus.

'We should leave.' Roland looked around him.

'Too late.'

Roland shaded his eyes with his hand. 'Hell's teeth. Someone must have laid information against us. I thought too much talk was rife in White's. The duke will not be best pleased.'

'I think he is not likely to notice in his present state.'

'Perhaps.'

A man who could only be a constable was approaching on the path down which they had earlier arrived. Behind him were two young henchmen.

One or two of the carriages on the verge of the entertainment were swinging around prepared for departure. The crowd surrounding the Duke of Albion thinned perceptibly. Gentlemen scattered to their various equipages. Some walked off and disappeared into the wooded areas of the Park. Nearby one was seen relieving himself against a tree while another vomited noisily in the same space.

There was still the duke's retinue. The doctor had fastened his bag and was standing beside the stretcher with the duke lying full-length on it. There was a generous display of bandages on his right arm.

Gervase chose to ignore the law officers bearing down upon them. 'What news of the devil duke then?'

Roland hesitated. 'I will ask. You winged him, badly. He may lose an arm. If he does not bleed to death. Wait here.'

'I am not likely to leave.'

'Good man.' And Roland was off again across the grass.

Gervase stared at the constable. They were the same height so it was eye to eye.

'Duelling is against the law.'

'Just so, officer.'

'I shall have to take you into custody.'

'Very well. It was worth it. I shall come willingly.'

The constable indicated to the two young lads who each took hold of an arm of Gervase's. 'I need to speak to the other gentleman. Come with me.'

The group moved off across the green to the Duke's entourage.

The duke had been well and truly trussed up. His fine linen shirt had been ripped apart and his arm covered in bloody bandages appeared to have been strapped to his body across his chest. So much for Doctor Frankenthaler, sawbones to the *ton*. It must have been exceedingly uncomfortable for the duke; his adversary had been brought low.

'His Grace the Duke of Albion.' The doctor spoke up. Loudly.

The previously blank expression on the constable's face

lifted a little. 'Duelling is illegal. Your Grace.' He turned to Gervase. 'I shall take the gentleman…'

Roland interrupted him. 'Gervase Thorpe. Late of His Majesty's Fifty-Second Regiment. Under Lieutenant-Colonel Sir John Colbourne. Distinguished service in the Peninsula. Salamanca, Toulouse. Need I go on?'

The constable's lips firmed. 'The practice of duelling is illegal.'

A sound from the bier on the ground fixed the attention of the onlookers. 'I am Albion. Release him.'

'Well, I don't know about that, Your Grace.'

'Walters?'

One detached himself from the serried ranks and stepped forward. 'Your Grace?'

'See to it.'

And the duke closed his eyes again. 'Take me home.'

Obediently the four men at each end of the stretcher lifted it up off the ground and moved off in the direction of the third coach.

The minion reached inside his jacket and withdrew a sheaf of banknotes.

The constable shook his head. But Gervase was released. Roland grabbed Gervase by the arm. 'Let us leave now. Before he changes his mind.'

As they prepared to leave Hyde Park Gervase glanced back over his shoulder. The Duke of Albion's carriages were moving off at a stately pace.

It had been a magnanimous gesture but the situation was unresolved. Was he, Gervase, being spared for future torment?

CHAPTER 21

'The ladies are not at home to visitors,' sniffed the man masquerading as a butler at the Farley mansion in Brunswick Square. He appeared even more *louche* than before: neckcloth awry, soiled gloves and a waistcoat stretched over a burly frame. His manner was, as always, vaguely threatening and appeared to foreshadow degradation and torture, amongst other delights.

Still, it was nothing to Gervase. His heart was still beating fast after the contretemps in Hyde Park with its unexpected result. Quite uncalled-for. At the very least Gervase had expected to be worsted. So much for the expert shot that Albion had turned out not to be.

Gervase had decided he must speak to Caroline as soon as possible.

'Thorpe, if you please. Take my card up to Miss Langrish,' said Gervase shortly. He wondered whether the man had recognised him from Gervase's previous visit but maybe that was too much to ask. Never mind, he had plenty of calling cards, he could afford to lose one or two.

The doorkeeper advanced a little and leant forward to peer at the card thrust forward in his direction. It obviously did not jog his memory. 'Mrs Farley has an appointment,' he paused, 'elsewhere.'

'It is Miss Langrish I wish to see.' Gervase was aware that his temper, never at its best in the morning, was threatening to break through the carefully controlled manner he had endeavoured to assume. Maybe it was the accumulated effects of the events of the day but he and Roland had parted abruptly at the gates of Hyde Park with a promise to meet soon. They had both drunk deep the previous night and Roland gave every indication that he was tiring of the physical and emotional turmoil and needed some respite. There had been a hasty discussion about the relative merits of an escape to the country, - Gervase had scorned the idea of a flight abroad, besides the Continent was still in a state of turmoil, – so Gervase had come to the conclusion that an immediate journey into Hampshire and a hurried wedding was the answer.

After that, with Caroline safely his, a visit to the smallholding which so far he had not deigned to cast his eyes upon, would be in order. His uncle would turn over in his grave if he knew how far from Gervase's thoughts the prized patch in Hampshire had been. But the time had come to take up his inheritance. Modest, compared with the Duke's wealth but it would suffice. He hoped Caroline would agree.

The visiting card had been taken again and the butler was carefully turning the card over and over in his gloved hand. Mere time-wasting or could he not read? It had not bothered him before. An impasse. But an unfamiliar pang of conscience struck Gervase. 'Gervase Thorpe,' he repeated.

As there was still no response, Gervase reached inside his jacket, found a coin and held it out to the butler. Maybe times had become harder since Gervase was last here, what, all of two days ago? One never knew.

The token was swiftly taken and the gate-keeper's expression definitely lifted a notch or two. 'Follow me, sir. I shall see if Miss is receiving.'

Once more, Gervase found himself in the monstrous entrance hall; his footsteps echoing on the gold and black tiles. He prayed he would be spared the Chinese drawing-room but he need not have concerned himself for he heard a swish of skirts from on high, and looking up he saw Caroline herself looking down upon him over the balustrades of a landing at the top of a flight of stairs, or rather two which led either side down to the hall below.

'Mr Thorpe,' Caroline called out, and hurried down to him. In a different tone of voice, she spoke to the butler, 'Thank you, Sawyer, that will be all. Mr Thorpe is expected.'

But Sawyer stood still. 'Mrs Farley will not be back until four o' the clock, as I was given to understand, Miss.'

Gervase jumped and snatched out another coin, which, glancing down, he saw to be a sovereign. Recklessly he handed it over. 'Here, take it, Sawyer.'

It served its purpose because the butler inclined his upper body slightly, pocketed the largesse and disappeared down one of the two corridors leading away from the entrance hall. Into Mrs Farley's spider's web, Gervase swore.

'Come. There is an ante-chamber here. It is not in use.' Caroline said. 'We should be safe for a while before your presence is reported to Mrs. Farley.'

She opened the double doors and he was led into what seemed to be a room of no apparent purpose.

Swathes of pale fabric, suspended from the rafters, hung down from on high, festooned pictures and fell to the floorboards, where they pooled untidily. Holland covers concealed chairs, draped small tables and rendered shapeless nameless pieces of furniture.

'We shall be safe here for a while… for a while…' she whispered as she vanished from sight behind a concealing curtain which fluttered in a faint movement of air…

Everything was obscured, faded, ochre, sand…

Feeling momentarily dizzy, Gervase felt himself

swaying, the floor reaching up towards him and then falling away. A memory of the tents of the encampment, *his* encampment, threatened to drag him back to the plains of Salamanca.

Everything receded as he bit down hard on his hand and forced himself to concentrate.

'Gervase, are you unwell?' Caroline's voice was nearby. He felt her warmth against his side and then miraculously they were seated.

At least his surroundings had now satisfactorily settled back down to earth, Gervase thought. He watched with a sense of detachment as Caroline rose from the couch.

'I will let some air into the room,' she said.

He was aware that he was still not entirely himself again. Although thankfully he appeared to be no longer in the camp amongst the cypress trees, choking from the dust of the baggage trains and with the sound of drums beating in his ears. Mercifully *that* at least had ceased. Only a feeling of suffocation remained and if he were honest the temperatures of London town bore little resemblance to that of Iberia.

Caroline threaded her way carefully through the masked furniture with only a quick backwards glance at Gervase. Drawing aside the muslin curtains, she opened the sash window and leant out a little way. He heard her sigh. The heat in the room was palpable.

Or was it the burning fire deep inside him?

No current of air, however powerful, could cool his ardour.

'Caroline,' he called to her, 'Do not leave me!' and then was ashamed of his pathetic words.

She turned and leant back against the windowsill. 'Gervase, I think you should see a physician. Maybe your friend, the Earl of Marlow, can help you?'

'When I have time, I will.' He dismissed her words.

Now to the purpose of his visit.

'Caroline, I have told you often enough of my inheritance. The small property in Hampshire. We can marry – you are of age – and we can live there. You are not beholden to this man, at least not in any way that counts, in my opinion!'

'Gervase, that is not true. I am betrothed to him.'

'What does that matter!' Gervase felt sick at the thought that once again she was evading him.

It was enough. She crossed the room and was in his arms again. He kissed her once, twice, hard and held her back so he could look at her. 'Let us escape tonight. Or even now. What do you say? Let the Duke of Albion rot in hell.' He kissed her violently on the mouth and trailed kisses down her neck and onto her delectable bosom. Her creamy white skin. Feeling dizzy the thought came to him that the lack of sleep the night before together with the events of the early morning had conspired together to make him, well, temporarily unhinged.

Caroline must have become aware for she gently disentangled herself from him but still retained his hand. 'Dearest, you know I cannot. I am betrothed to the Duke of Albion. And then there is Susannah…'

'Ever Susannah! She will fare well in the marriage mart. Offers aplenty no doubt. The Earl of Marlow…' Here he broke off, and glanced away. 'It is not my place to say, however. You cannot marry Albion.'

She did not answer.

'You cannot marry Albion.'

'No, but I must be honest with him.'

'The devil you will! Forgive me, Caroline but this does not bear thinking about!'

'I must have time.'

'What about me?' Gervase heard his own words and swallowed hard. Really, he was behaving like a child.

'I cannot answer you now.'

'Very well. I will give you one night to consider. Not that the Duke deserves it. I shall return tomorrow for your answer.'

Unbidden the painful recollection came to him of their time together in the rose garden at Beauminster Priory, all those years ago. A time of innocence and leisure and, and all the happy foolishness of youth. *Had* Caroline promised to marry him? Or not? He racked his brains but all he could remember was her promise to wait for him. And to write letters. Well, the letters had been written, if he believed her, and he did - but not received, at a terrible cost to himself.

What devil was playing havoc with his mind? Putting aside thoughts that threatened to overwhelm him, Gervase rose reluctantly to his feet. There was the small question of the other matter. He did not want her without full knowledge of the implications of his actions in Hyde Park. 'I have something else to tell you.'

'I thought so!'

'I have fought a duel with the damned duke. Early this morning. There, I have told you. I suppose now he will have all your sympathy.'

Caroline looked up at him suddenly white; there was more colour in her pale dress. She clutched at her throat. 'I knew you would do something rash. A duel! But you are unharmed! What happened? Tell me! Is the duke wounded?'

'He is indeed!' There was a note of satisfaction in his voice which he could not hide he knew it.

Caroline shrank back and Gervase felt sick, his vision blurred for a moment and he sat down again. Could it be that she was more involved with Albion than Gervase had thought?

Heaven forbid. Gervase leant back against the dust covers and passed a hand across his eyes. 'You concern is touching in the extreme but it is not what I want. I wish I *had* killed him,' he added savagely.

Getting a grip on himself with several deep breaths he rose from the sofa and made for the doors.

As he halted there, he turned to look at her. Caroline appeared bereft of words, her gaze still fixed on him.

'This changes nothing.' Even to himself he sounded unconvincing.

'Gervase, how badly is the duke injured?'

'He is still living. Well, I only winged him.' He looked down and then added reluctantly. 'I am not sure of the exact nature of his injuries but he undoubtedly lost a lot of blood. Surely you do not expect *me* to feel remorse?'

But Caroline was not returning his regard. She was pleating the material of her dress and looking down. Had she shed a tear? Unbelievable! 'I must know more,' she said quietly. 'After all, I am betrothed to him.'

'Well, you will not hear it from me,' he shouted, as he slammed out of the doors. 'Until tomorrow. I await your decision.'

His final words echoed past a startled footman for Gervase found himself in the entrance hall again.

CHAPTER 22

'Unhand me! What the devil do you think you are doing?'

For Gervase, much to his surprise, (yet after all who would be surprised at *anything* that took place in this house of sin, he thought to himself) found himself being manhandled and marched across the marbled hall into a room quite other. A room not unlike a broom cupboard! A room full of upturned chairs, drab vestments, and even what looked to be a silver swordstick propped at a threatening angle.

Here he was released and as he shook himself and pulled down the cuffs of his jacket, his two jailors stood to one side.

One of them was Sawyer, the doorkeeper, again. So much for the largesse Gervase had distributed earlier; it had been a waste of effort. Perhaps he should have taken up the offer of Nathaniel's guardianship but it would not have helped within the confines of the Farley household. The other menial frowning at his boots was not dissimilar. Usefully rough.

Sawyer coughed into his hand. 'Mrs Farley wants a word.' And had the gall to sound apologetic.

So saying, with a brusque gesture, he beckoned to the

other man.

Before Gervase could call them to order, the unsavoury pair had left by the same door through which they had just dragged him, and he heard the familiar turn of a key in a lock.

Inwardly swearing at himself for once *again* not paying enough attention to his surroundings Gervase knew he had only himself to blame. One moment he had been back in the preposterous entrance hall still smarting over Caroline's implied rejection, or at the very least her request for *more time,* and the next, two of Mrs Farley's henchmen had him surrounded. Well, obviously, not exactly surrounded but he *had* been taken by surprise.

He sighed, when would he ever learn? He needed to be as wary as if he were back *there,* back in Iberia. Truly.

Also, unpleasant memories of his temporary incarceration at the hands of the Duke of Albion came to mind. At the so-called Betrothal Ball. He was not doing too well back in London.

Before he had time to become even more despondent he heard the key turn in the lock and Mrs Farley was before him. A high colour, eyes glittering like diamonds and her mouth set in a hard line.

And yet once again he felt that there was something disturbingly beguiling about her.

Fury certainly became her.

And furious she was. From the high crown of her chip straw hat tied at a becoming angle to her face to the tips of her elegant half-boots just visible beneath her skirts. Skirts which were still in a state of animation from her dramatic entry into the room. Her bosom heaved attractively above a bodice cut low in the fashion of the times, he supposed.

As if aware of his scrutiny he saw her regain control on front of his eyes. He could not help it; he had to admire her in her distempered state. The moment passed. She was herself again. Her breathing had evened out.

Removing her hat and casting it aside, 'Mr Thorpe,' she

began.

Her voice had 'the ice-brook's temper' as Shakespeare would have had it - Gervase could hear Roland's words, quoting from his favourite poet.

'I have just returned from His Grace's residence,' she continued, wide-eyed and staring. 'It goes without saying how *distraught* I found the household there. And it was all your doing, Mr Thorpe, I learn.'

As if unable to hold herself in check, she moved away from confronting Gervase to pace the room to the small closed window, which let in precious little light either.

Kneading her hands together, she turned to Gervase, without her usual self-command. 'Have you any idea of the turmoil you have caused?'

Gervase threw back his head and laughed. 'No, and I am past caring. In short, I prefer not to discuss this morning's events with you. The state of *His Grace* is immaterial to me.'

Yet how bad was he, Gervase wondered.

'His Grace will not take your behaviour lightly. From now on, you are a marked man.'

Gervase laughed again. 'Well, he refused to report me to the constable.'

'A magnanimous gesture. So like His Grace. *And* you should not have been admitted here. Sawyer will be disciplined. The Misses Langrish are not your concern.'

'There we must agree to differ. Miss Langrish is most definitely my concern. Miss Susannah will do very well for herself one way or another, I feel sure. I shall release Miss Langrish, Caroline, from her prison. Now if I may…' He gave an exaggerated bow and moved swiftly to the door. But there he hesitated, loath to leave; there was more to be said.

'I repeat, Miss Langrish is of no interest to you.' Mrs Farley turned back to look out of the discoloured window.

Silence fell between them.

Then she began again, twisting her hands and sounding

far away. 'After I heard that His Grace was injured I wasted no time. I went straight to Grosvenor Square.'

'How did you hear?' Asked Gervase, suddenly curious.

'I have my sources in His Grace's household. When I arrived, I would have stayed but it was made clear to me that I was not needed. Not that a mere housekeeper would have stopped me. I was shown into an antechamber, hardly a drawing-room. One would not call it that. Not luxuriantly appointed, no, not at all. Nondescript.' She sniffed. 'I had expected nothing better. Naturally.'

'Naturally.'

'There was a message from his secretary, that His Grace thanked me for my concern but that he would be better resting. And then I heard from, well, never mind who, that His Grace had been calling for her. While the fever was at its peak. *Her*!'

Gervase, in spite of his desire to leave the building as soon as possible, watched and waited. It was as if she were talking to herself now. He was a mere observer. Still, good to know the Duke of Albion could cry in vain.

Really when he thought about it, Mrs Farley's features were remarkably fine. Her mass of dark hair was loosened: one long tendril had escaped from the arrangement, and rested on a slim, sharply-angled shoulder. Very soon the whole edifice of waves and curls would escape control completely and tumble down. The whiteness of her upturned collar was only matched by the paleness of her throat where a pulse throbbed beneath the translucent skin. Surely she was overdressed for the heat? In some kind of an open robe of a dull brown stuff, which in her disarray had fallen open from the waist down, to reveal an underskirt shot through with shades of purple and red. The material edging the ruffles thus exposed, caught what little light there was in the room and appeared to glitter.

Once again, he was struck by her allure.

A distant throb of drums ...

Gervase closed his eyes.

When he opened them all was as it should be.

Just another remembrance of Spain when he had been tempted as only a man near the end of his tether, worn out, a shadow of his former self, could be.

Gordon had already chosen from among the beauties and could be heard swearing undying love...

But Marlow had come to Gervase's rescue, with his sensible words. It had all happened at the very last minute, in camp, as they were about to embark on the journey home. The wine had been plentiful, the atmosphere thick with smoke and dust, the company raucous, and a particular beauty from amongst the camp-followers had promised sweet oblivion for a few hours at least ...

But he had not succumbed.

Mrs Farley meanwhile was still keening. 'You see; His Grace usually visits *me*.'

A pause.

'It is in the order of things.'

Another piece of the puzzle fell into place. Mrs Farley herself was enamoured of the Duke of Albion. Hard to believe. Did that make two of them? Devil take it, and he was back to Caroline.

'I shall see myself out.' A farewell of sorts, he supposed. Enough of time wasting.

But Mrs Farley was still lost in thought.

Gervase left Mrs Farley to her dreaming. Or was he intent on leaving his own fantasies behind - Roland would probably say so.

On his way out he had not been accosted by any ill-tempered menservants, or indeed by anyone at all. The entrance hall was deserted, the main door way unhampered. He was unobserved as he walked out into the Square.

Gervase was half-ashamed to say that he did look up at the windows above the porch, hoping to catch a glimpse of Caroline but to no avail. A wasted effort. Admittedly he had no idea exactly where her rooms were. Probably at the back if he knew anything of the ways of Albion and Mrs

Farley.

He took several deep breaths to rid himself of the stale airs and enticements of the Farley household before deciding what to do.

But it was a foregone conclusion. Unburdening himself was of paramount importance After all, what were friends for? Gervase would make for Roland's house. Also the damned leg was painful again. Maybe he would ask the name of the sawbones his friend had recommended. Doctor Jamieson, was that his name?

On the other hand, he would take a night's rest first. Devil take it, but he was tired.

For Gervase's next plan of action with regard to Caroline required all his strength.

CHAPTER 23

On entering his shared quarters at the Albany, Gervase found Gordon seated at a desk staring out of the open sash window at the gathering dusk, already a deepening blue.

The colour of the evening sky heralded the melancholy thought that the year was passing, and still Gervase was unsure of Caroline's feelings towards him. Now he was awaiting her decision. He swore he would not give up; he would seek her answer as soon as possible tomorrow but by necessity after he had made arrangements for their departure from London. The property in Hampshire was becoming like a distant dream of paradise.

The rhythmic sound of horses' hooves, the raucous shouts of young bucks on the town and sounds of high-pitched laughter drifted in from Piccadilly to remind all that the night was young and no time was to be lost in participating if one so wished. For soon the season would be over and the *ton* would return to their country estates if they were fortunate enough to possess them. The Duke of Albion alone was rumoured to own half of Yorkshire.

Participation in society was furthest from Gervase's mind so he most certainly did not so wish. It was in the balance if his Albany compatriot did. By the inattention Gervase thought it was unlikely.

It was not difficult usually to gauge Gordon's mood but tonight Gervase was at a loss. In a different man he would have said Gordon was deep in thought or more poetically, in a reverie.

Gervase stumbled as he attempted to make his way across the room, hopefully unobserved, towards his bedchamber and dressing-room. Sometimes the whole damn setup in the Albany felt more like being back in barracks, more's the pity. He swore quietly under his breath; the events of last night, the drunken reminiscences, and the duel this morning had made him bone-weary and careless. Not to mention Caroline's hesitancy; the memory of which gave him a sharp stab of visceral pain.

Gordon turned around and with a sense of shock Gervase saw the Captain had a pen in his hand, there was an inkwell close by and several pieces of crumpled paper were lying on the floor.

'What are you about?' Gervase said before he could help himself and then instantly regretted his words. Why should his friend not write a letter?

Gordon answered quickly. 'Fact of the matter is, I ain't the greatest at this sort of thing, Thorpe.'

Gervase came closer to his companion and stared down at the ink-blotted vellum.

'You see, thought I would write to Lady Lydia. Instead of … well, enough of that. Too damn crowded in the box last night at Vauxhall. Have you ever been?'

Gervase shook his head, still staring bemused at the piece of paper. Gordon had written a love-letter if Gervase was not mistaken. He looked away, ashamed of himself for prying.

'You know, *she* says she doesn't mind my scar at all, in fact she says it makes my face more interesting. What do you think of that!'

When Gervase did not reply, Gordon carried on, 'Lydia

too popular by half though. Harcourt insisted he brought two friends, to crown it all. And had to throw Tolland out, definitely misbehaving, half-cut. Have suggested to Lydia we meet again tomorrow, at Gunther's Tea Rooms. That should suit. Need to have a word when no one is imbibing so as to speak. Just got to find Nat now for delivery.'

Gervase failed to see the Lady Lydia Vellacott and Captain Gordon Howard in such a staid setting but as Gervase had enough troubles of his own to deal with, he moved away from Gordon, who was now busy sanding the paper. 'I wish you luck; Lady Lydia Vellacott has many admirers.'

At that, Gordon, in the process of addressing an envelope, retorted, 'Ah, but I am going to make a serious offer!'

Interested in spite of himself, Gervase halted. 'What kind of an offer?'

Gordon tapped his nose. 'Wait on it, you'll see. I'm not my father's son for nothing.'

Gordon's father had been notorious amongst the *ton* for a long string of mistresses and for all Gervase knew he still was.

A dawning realisation swept over Gervase; incredible though it was, Gordon must be more flush with funds than Gervase had ever comprehended. Yet the evidence had been there all the time - Gordon *had* taken Gervase in at a moment's notice when they both returned, savaged by battle, to London from the Peninsula. Gervase had not wanted to impose upon Roland's goodwill more than he already had. Besides, Roland's palatial surroundings had been dismayingly imposing – sharing an apartment in the Albany seemed relatively modest by comparison.

'Are you going to offer Lady Lydia *carte-blanche?*' Gervase asked, shocked.

Gordon sat back in his chair as if his labours were finished. 'Well you may call it that, if you want. I have in mind a little town house with every luxury. In Mayfair.

Somewhere convenient. And well away from Harcourt, and Tolland, for that matter. Friends of mine, yes, but damn it, there is a limit. *Exclusivity* is what I want - but right now I need a brandy, or two.'

Gordon had obviously been touched on the raw.

'Well, good luck.' Leaving his friend alone Gervase limped off slowly, painfully and finally, to his own rooms, leaving Gordon waving the letter and calling for Nathaniel.

Once inside his bedchamber, Gervase went over to the window and flung it wide to let in some air but the atmosphere in the room was not improved. Had the unwholesome vapours followed him from the Farley household?

He discarded his jacket onto a nearby chair, removed his boots and threw himself down on his bed to contemplate his future. The duel had not resolved anything with the Duke of Albion. Caroline was now undecided and obviously worried about her fiancé, damn his eyes. Although Gervase himself was not entirely unworried. Albion had lost a lot of blood although Gervase had seen worse injuries in the Peninsula, much worse. His own for a start. He shuddered at the memory.

Gervase realised the events of the day had been extremely tiring. Tomorrow he must retrieve the letters he had written in case the duel had proved fatal for himself. But not now. Tomorrow he must see Roland.

As for Caroline… tomorrow he would … Gervase turned over and let sleep overtake him.

A knock on the door roused Gervase from his slumber but he did not feel refreshed as he heaved himself into a sitting position. Judging by the mantel clock only an hour had passed. 'Yes?'

In reply Nathaniel sidled in and stood close to the door with his hands clasped and without looking directly at Gervase.

'Yes?' Gervase realised he had woken up in a foul

mood.

'Being as you said you was going to be at White's last night, sir, I,' he paused.

Gervase felt guilty immediately, one must not take one's bad temper out on former comrades; Nathaniel was not responsible. 'There is nothing to discuss. The evening went on longer than I had expected.'

Disastrously so, under the influence of drink, leading to unwanted truth-telling sad to say.

'And then I had an early morning appointment. I did not want a bodyguard. I had others with me.'

Nathaniel gave him a keen look. 'Maybe you need one now, sir. I should say so. Word is out.'

It was only to be expected that the duel could not remain a secret; too many persons had been present from the gossip-mongering section of the *ton* if Gervase were not mistaken.

But he did not need a nursemaid. 'You must surely have more to do now that Gordon is back in society. I think I will have supper and then turn in.'

'As you wish, but don't say I didn't warn you. As for supper, there is a ham and some cold beef from the kitchen waiting for you, sir,' he said smoothly.

With a slight lightening of his mood, Gervase rose from his bed reached for his jacket, and, not bothering with his boots followed Nathaniel out into the living room.

He would feel better when he had eaten, wouldn't he?

CHAPTER 24

After a night of what must have been a sleep of exhaustion, the next morning dawned bright and clear for Gervase in the Albany. The sun was already up when he left his bed: another hot and soulless day in London town.

Another day without Caroline. How much longer could he wait? Then he reproved himself: years had passed during the Peninsular Campaign, years without a word from her, what would a few more hours signify. At least he knew what he was going to do.

On the other hand, if he were honest with himself he was no nearer his goal: to remove Caroline from the arms of the Duke. Would his plan work?

Consent was vital, he had no intention of compelling her, she must choose between them. It looked as though his opponent's injury had aroused her tender instincts, giving the bastard an unfair advantage. Would that he, Gervase, had been the one injured, he thought savagely.

Even to consider the Duke as a rival for her affections stabbed him in the heart. He felt sick at the thought.

But what do the sages say? Possession is nine-tenths of the law. At least her fiancé had not bedded her.

Round and round in his head the thoughts went, without a conclusion.

With an effort of will, he forced himself to concentrate

upon the present moment; before Gervase visited Caroline again a request to Roland was essential. Roland would not refuse him.

Gervase dragged himself into the sitting room and noted that there was no sign of Gordon: just Nathaniel busy clearing away evidence of a previous night's drinking session. No cheery whistling this morning. Of course, events had moved on as they have a habit of doing; Gordon was now lovelorn and pining.

Gervase hazarded a knock on his friend's door and heard an answering groan and a muttered 'Go away'. Emotional effort had been expended the previous evening which must have cost him dear, Gervase thought unkindly. The brandy too would have done its work.

Retreating back into their joint quarters, Gervase carefully removed the unnecessary last letters from behind the mirror on the mantel-piece. Long forgotten by the worthy Captain. Fortunately, they had not been needed. Easily disposed of by tearing up and throwing in the unlit fire. For later burning. It was doubtful whether the after effects of the duel could be tidied away so effectively.

On his way out Gervase had the thought to pick up Gordon's walking stick. It would ease the pressure on Gervase's right leg which had decided to play up again.

At least Gervase congratulated himself that he had managed to set off for Roland's town house in Mecklenburg Square before the noon day heat had reached its full strength.

The journey turned out to be a wasted one, for Roland was not at home: Gervase was forced to make his way to Tattersalls.

For he had been informed by Ingleby that His Lordship had left home hurriedly and unexpectedly, to look in at the auction house. The butler appeared to be on the verge of saying more but instead merely bowed and closed the door on Gervase.

A not unusual occurrence recently he thought grimly as

he made his way across town to find his friend. Soon all doors would be permanently closed against Gervase if his bad luck held and more especially if news of his duel with Albion circulated. Probably only a matter of time remembering just how many scions of the nobility, well, the *haut ton*, had witnessed the event.

Still he was surprised at the venue. Roland had not mentioned a particular interest in horseflesh of late. Not to Gervase's knowledge anyhow.

It was not difficult to find the Earl of Marlow at Tattersall's. He was surrounded by what looked to be a knot of his former fellow officers, all clad in regimental greens and reds. Just like at White's the other night. Always a popular companion at the best of times. This morning he had excelled himself. There must have been at least half a dozen of them.

'I did not know you had it in mind to enlarge your stables, Roland. I thought your thoroughbreds were second to none?' Gervase shouldered his way through the throng. Several of the officers moved aside to accommodate him and gradually there was a general dispersal. Not before he had noticed one or two searching looks being given him. It was difficult to be sure but he could not help thinking he had earned a degree of respect; and for once he was not thinking about the Peninsula. Were there others who disliked the Duke of Albion and his high-handed ways? Highly likely.

Roland swung around easily from where he had been leaning over the rail of the verandah watching the parade of horses. Negligently he rested back on his elbows. 'Gervase, how are you? Quite recovered, I hope? Well, as to that, I am thinking of retiring to the country and setting up a stud. Starting here is as good as anywhere, what do you say?'

'I say nothing of the sort! Retiring to the country? What are you thinking of? Have you had a touch of the sun?'

'Now, look over there, see that pair of matched grays?

They rival mine and I never thought to say those words! They are prime 'uns, aren't they?' Roland turned back to indicate the current high-stepping offering being walked around the arena. And causing their handlers some little difficulty at the same time. 'Lord Kendall of Colne has put them up for sale. Gaming debts is the *on-dit*. Yes, I have a stables second to none, I have often been told so. But one can always improve one's bloodstock.'

Roland paused, then continued. 'Let's walk over to my club, shall we? I have matters I would like to discuss with you and something tells me you have, likewise?' He shot a quick glance at Gervase as he drew on his gloves. 'That's if you are up to a walk? I see you are using a cane. I am aware that Tattersalls is not your usual haunt and we will be more comfortable there. Come.'

Gervase did not reply. Talk of physical pain could wait.

As the pair left the ring, Roland began again, 'By the by, no-one is talking about your little affair in Hyde Park. Mysterious moves are afoot and influence has been brought to bear, one hears.'

Gervase grunted, 'Does one?' Next Roland would be saying it had been deliberately hushed up by the Devil Duke.

Gervase's leg *did* hurt but he admitted to himself White's would be a better place for what might prove to be a difficult conversation. Or two, as it had turned out to be. They were both disturbed, with matters on their minds.

Turmoil was the human condition.

Later they were both conveniently ensconced in armchairs in a coffee-room at White's. In a quiet corner. But with a decanter at hand. Gervase was nursing a tumbler of brandy, while Roland still lingered over his coffee. A companiable silence had descended after the maelstrom of the past few days.

Gervase decided to confront Roland over the latest turn of events before Gervase himself asked Roland for help.

Again.

Another favour. But a small one. This time.

Not to be compared with Roland's clever arrangements for the transfer of Gervase to headquarters away from the lines, back in Spain. Not that he had thought so at the time, of course. Gervase had been unaware that *that* was due to the Earl of Marlow until much later. Gervase had not been grateful. *Angry* best described how he had felt. Help is not always welcome, especially when it sheds a light on one's inadequate state of mind. Had he been saved from himself? If so, even more was due to the Earl of Marlow and his connections than he had ever realised. Gervase quelled the thought.

Gervase eased his right leg into a more comfortable position. Ah, that was better, and began. 'Tell me why you are abandoning the Season here for an early retreat to your estates in Norfolk? I assume that is where you will go? Surely your passion for horses may wait? We have not been back in town for long yet it seems you are much in demand. Society hostesses will miss you and also your brother officers.'

Gervase knew Roland had effortlessly navigated the social scene. Naturally there had been an invitation for the Fifth Earl of Marlow to the Betrothal Ball. The event had held no qualms for him. Invitations aplenty were skilfully arranged on his mantel-shelf and cluttered the silver salver in the entrance hall awaiting a call to order. Yet Roland had been back but three weeks or so from the war. He was a catch and always would remain so.

Roland placed his cup down carefully on the side-table next to him and threw a cursory glance around the almost empty room. For a Monday late afternoon White's was even more deserted than one might have expected. Just the odd lord or two slumbering or otherwise comatose.

Roland went on. 'Well, I may not after all retreat to Norfolk as you put it. I have had second thoughts. It was

Whitby, believe it or not who put the idea into my head. Why not seek active service again? We all know there is a good chance Bonaparte will not be long on the Isle of Elba. My old army mucker, Lord, I should say Colonel, Falconbridge, has promised to see me at four o'clock today. He may be able to pull some strings. I know you sold out but I am on half-pay as you are aware, and the idea appeals.'

'Why now?'

'I have had a bit of a setback.'

Gervase looked at his friend carefully; he could see he was not his usual ebullient self. Gervase detected a sombre note in Roland's voice and waited.

'Truth to tell, I fear I am like to be a disappointed man.'

'Tell all.'

'It came from an unexpected quarter. Well, I applied to the Duke of Albion for permission to pay my addresses to Miss Susannah. Yes, yes, I know,' he said testily as if to bat away Gervase's remonstrations. 'I was well aware of how you would feel about *that* course of action. Even you must know that His Grace, in the absence of any relation at all of the Misses Langrish, must be held to be the rightful guardian of their best interests. Whatever you may say it is the proper course of action.'

'I have said nothing,' replied Gervase, affronted.

'My dear Gervase, you have just worsted Albion in a duel; you are hardly neutral.'

'Certainly. And I am pleased I did.'

Roland sighed. 'Leaving that aside, letters were exchanged…'

'Before he lost the ability to write…'

Roland looked at him askance.

Gervase felt a twinge of remorse. 'Temporarily, no doubt. An unfortunate turn of phrase, I apologise.'

'There was no guarantee that my suit would be acceptable to Miss Susannah.'

'What? I thought you and Susannah would be smelling

of April and May by now.'

Gervase admitted all his attention had been with Caroline. What did he know? Then another thought occurred to him. 'Are you sure that Albion does not have other plans for her?'

Roland spoke evenly. 'A better offer, is that what you mean? An earldom is not enough? Admittedly I have no further expectations as far as titles go. Debretts has my final entry.' And he laughed.

'No, that was not exactly what I meant...' He could not meet the Earl's eyes. 'No, forget what I said. What are your intentions now? Apart from rusticating in the country, or applying for a posting once more. India is recommended if you wish to leave the European theatre of war.' A suggestion that should give Roland second thoughts.

But his friend was not so easily deflected. 'What has Miss Langrish said? Do you know more than you have told me?'

It would be the honourable thing to do, to tell Roland of Gervase's suspicions; that Mrs Farley might wield undue influence. 'No, Caroline has said nothing. As you know we have spent far too little time together.' He hated to admit it. 'The delightful Mrs Farley. I do not trust her. She is in thrall still to the Duke; I was a witness.'

'Mrs Farley? Ah. But you know I do not think she is Albion's *maîtresse en titre*. She wields no power. I think she is merely a former *chère-amie* who looks after Albion's interests. Whitby told me there are others scattered around Mayfair in suitable accommodation: all housed at the whim of the Duke. Not the usual state of affairs for mistresses who have been given their congé. After all the Duke of Albion had a further appointment with a lady to be held after the duel. An appointment he would have missed. But I digress. There are doubts as to whether Miss Susannah will have me.'

Gervase was astonished at what he was hearing. The Earl of Marlow, charming, rich, landed and loved by all, was giving up at the first hurdle while he, Gervase, with little to offer as he was only too aware, was determined to pursue his love until… Well, until all was resolved one way or another. Although the outcome unfortunately at present was far from clear…

'You are meeting our old commander in the field here, I presume?'

Roland nodded.

'That's well and good. But really, Roland, you give up too easily. Ignore Mrs. Farley What are we doing here? You should address Miss Susannah Langrish directly. Have you done so?' Gervase kicked back a convenient footstool. The answering pain shot up his leg and made him wince. 'And by the by I shall never forgive him for that.'

'For the assignation that was not?'

'Certainly. To be betrothed to Caroline and to be still seeking a mistress! But you should speak to Miss Susannah. If you can find her amongst the bevy of admirers.'

'I will; you have inspired me. I will hear Falconbridge out though first though. And now to your travails. I think I should fortify myself.' And Roland poured himself a thimbleful of brandy.

Gervase took a quick look around but the coffee room was only slowly filling up with the odd lord or two, escaping the heat of another day in town, glad of the shadows and general air of torpor. 'Well, Roland. I have a favour to ask of you.'

CHAPTER 25

'Where are you going, Caroline?' Susannah entered the dressing-room with a flourish, closing the doors behind her quickly. She stood there, her eyes widening, her colour high, poised and, as so often, on the *qui vivre*. 'Well?'

Caroline sighed. Her sister's unerring ability to sense trouble or a situation of interest was uncanny.

'I am going on a visit.' Caroline replied. She finished tying the ribbons of her straw hat and caught the flimsy net veil so that her face, she hoped, would not be visible to curious spectators. Turning her head this way and that she was satisfied. It would be regarded as an attempt to keep the noonday sun from her complexion. As did all the ladies of the *ton*. And a disguise.

After another sleepless night, she had finally come to a decision. To wager all upon a reckless throw of the dice. In the manner of her Papa – surely she had not inherited *the fatal tendency* as her Mama had called it?

Susannah counted on her fingers. 'Let me guess. Gervase? Or The Earl of Marlow? Or?'

Caroline did not look at her sister but crossed to the other side of the room and, pulling back a curtain, regarded the street below. Distractedly Caroline said, 'You know it is you not I who have a tendre for the Earl. Am I right?'

'Perhaps.' But Susannah, as ever was close by her side, her arm around her. 'Let me see,' as she too peered down too. 'Oh, yes. So you will be accompanied by Finch. Now I know what you are at!'

Caroline thought she sincerely hoped not. She broke free from her sister's embrace and gathered up her stole and reticule. 'Susannah, once more I need you to divert Mrs Farley for me.'

Susannah pulled a face. 'Not again. Well, perhaps this once. Believe it or not, I am increasingly finding that time spent with Mrs. Farley is never wasted. One gleans so much from her knowledge of... But là, I do not mean to shock you! Caroline, you must tell me what you are about.'

'It is better that you should not know.'

Susannah turned her back as Caroline stood before her. 'You know I would never tell Mrs Farley.'

'I know.' Caroline prepared to make her departure. 'But you will know soon enough.'

Her sister did not reply, head down, still turned away. 'It is too bad that I am not in your confidence.'

'Goodbye, Susannah.' Caroline waited a moment and then left the dressing-room.

She waited on the landing and then quietly descended the main staircase and slipped out of the door, unobserved.

Finch would be waiting outside. The first part of her plan of action was complete.

If Gervase would not resolve the circumstances in which they found themselves, she would. After all, Susannah had had her season, she was out now. Her suitors were many, the Earl of Marlow not least. A match would be made there.

Once outside the doors, Finch came up to her and bowed. 'I am ready, ma'am. Wherever you want to go.'

Caroline smiled. 'Thank you, Finch. To the Duke of

Albion's. I am expected,' she lied easily.

Finch allowed himself a slight change of expression but she had no fears of his behaviour. After all these years he would not tell.

An encounter with the most gracious Duke of Albion, Hugo, would be to wager all. Ruin could ensue but Gervase was worth the risk. They could retire to Hampshire and live out the rest of their days in peace.

But her heart sank as she remembered the duke, her fiancé, and all his power and influence.

'Miss Langrish? I will apprise His Grace. Please to follow me.' The Duke of Albion's highly superior butler gave a slight bow in Caroline's direction.

'I have my man, Finch with me,' Caroline replied.

'Quite so,' was the reply and a click of the fingers followed. One of several footmen stepped forward and bore Finch off to the nether regions of Number One, Grosvenor Square. She was not concerned: Finch was more than capable of holding his own.

Caroline adjusted her veil to conceal her face more fully. A surprising number of members of the household were around the lobby, entrance hall and grand sweep of stairs as Caroline was led away by the butler. None were apparently taking any interest in the proceedings but one could never be sure. The numbers were to add prestige or were they? Surely they were not spying on her? She drew the veil even tighter around her face in spite of the heat. Enough gossip attended her and the duke's attachment; there was no point in adding to the rumour mill.

The butler would have had much practice in dealing with the duke's affairs. She had only to think of Mrs Farley, although maybe she never darkened these doors? Perhaps the duke visited *her*? And left these portals unsullied.

The more she thought the more complex the web of his entanglements proved.

Inevitably there was an air of secrecy. Caroline herself was neither a mistress nor a respectable fiancée. Why had he not proposed to a lady of equal rank? There must always be a degree of scandal associated with her name after her father's untimely demise. Why had the illustrious Duke of Albion chosen her to be his bride?

The question would never be answered.

After a detour or two, the butler alighted on what he must have thought to be a suitable chamber. He ushered her in, bowed and left with the words that His Grace had been informed.

The room was not inviting.

Two wing-backed chairs upholstered in a dull moss green, brocaded in an indeterminate pattern, with cushions to match, stood either side of an empty grate. Curtains in the same shade were looped back at the far window. There was very little other furniture of note, just a footstool or two, and a low table on the nondescript but deep-piled carpet. And on the mantelpiece, next to the clock, there was an unremarkable vase of dried flowers set amongst palm fronds unwavering in the afternoon's dusty heat.

What was the purpose of the antechamber? For whom?

A receiving room for a Duke's visitors: second-rate visitors perhaps. Small, undistinguished, worthy of an uninvited guest, even if a fiancée.

Or had the butler using his sense of decorum, ushered her somewhere quiet, away from the main reception areas, knowing his master's finely-tuned, even antiquated, notions of propriety? Whatever the reason she was unlikely to be given the honour due to a fully-fledged duchess until she and the duke were married. Maybe even the servants were aware of the tenuous links between the affianced pair. There was no way such secrets could be hidden from a ducal household.

The heat had been building since she left Brunswick Square. The stale air oppressed, making it difficult for Caroline to breathe. It was certainly not conducive to the marshalling of her thoughts, to her peace of mind.

Panic rose through her but it was vital she should control herself before the meeting with His Grace. She reached into her reticule and drew out her soft pink feather fan, her favourite in times of heat and stress. After unfurling her treasured possession, she wandered over to the window. The fan's long, swaying motions wafted air in her direction but to no avail. Deep breaths relieved her little; there was to be no respite.

There she looked down: a cobbled courtyard below, devoid of servants, but immaculate in its emptiness. But some muffled sounds reassured her that the abode was not deserted. The Duke of Albion's retinue were at work: to provide for his every comfort.

Well, she hoped so. She closed her fan and put it back in her reticule. Smitten with a sudden attack of guilt, worry possessed her. After Gervase's sorry tale, in what state could she expect to find her fiancé?

A murmuring sound beyond the doors leading from the corridor and then they swung open. She caught a glimpse of two footmen, one with a Paisley shawl over his arm, before the doors closed again behind the Duke of Albion himself, alone.

Caroline did not know what she had expected but when she saw him she took a sharp intake of breath. Yes, Gervase had told her he had injured the duke but she had not expected such an alteration in his appearance.

Leaning heavily on a walking stick, the duke halted in front of her. A pallid complexion, almost grey, his eyes dulled and his usual upright bearing no more but his dress was as correct as ever. His right arm was in a black sling of dull cloth, the sleeve of his tailcoat hung by his side, but his neckcloth had been carefully tied and his boots were polished to perfection.

'Caroline.' He gave her a formal bow. As he straightened up, he winced. 'I am at a loss as to why you have come to visit me,' he paused, 'unaccompanied.'

A deep curtsey followed on Caroline's part. 'I came with a manservant.' As his mouth tightened she added, 'Finch has been taken below stairs. To await my return, Your Grace.'

'*Hugo,* please. That is as maybe but I am not content. Under no circumstances should you be unescorted. Without your maid. What were you thinking of? It is as well we are affianced.'

The duke heaved himself across the room to one of the armchairs. 'Pray be seated Caroline. There are things I want to discuss. And regretfully I need to rest.' He indicated the other chair with his cane. 'Caroline.'

Caroline obeyed him.

His appearance was ghastly in the extreme. How could he have lost so much, well, presence, in so short a time? As she looked at him, a faint change of expression was visible in his face. Was he trying to smile? Aware of what she was going to do to him, she steeled herself.

'Hugo,' she began.

He stopped her. 'You are concerned for my well-being.' It was a statement of fact. 'No doubt you have heard rumours of the event that took place early yesterday, in the forenoon?' He leant forward, almost animated, 'Have you, Caroline?'

She nodded in agreement and prepared to go on. 'Yes, I have, but -

He would have none of it and waved his hand dismissively. 'You need not concern yourself. Naturally I would have preferred that no knowledge would have come to your ears. But people talk. There were too many persons present.' He sighed. 'However I have taken steps to ensure that there will be no further repercussions. For anyone.'

Incredible. Startled out of her train of thought, Caroline could only stare.' You have?'

As if unable to conceal his pleasure the Duke smiled and replied. 'Yes. Word has been sent to the highest quarters and I am pleased to report all will be well.'

As if he registered her air of surprise for the first time, he added. 'The gentleman in question will not be pursued for his part in the lamentable events of *that* morning.'

Caroline felt some of her tension dissipate. She sat back. Then her conscience smote her. 'I trust Your Grace will soon recover from your wound.'

Once again a faint softening of his expression, around his eyes. 'Thank you.' And he inclined his head. 'I am as well as can be expected.'

Firming himself in the chair, he spoke more strongly. 'I think it is time we made plans for our marriage. Yesterday's regrettable little episode has given me cause for thought. I expect you feel the same way.'

He leant forward and made as if to take her hand.

With a jolt to her heart she noticed the ring on his third finger was still being worn, a reminder of their contract.

And why not? He did not know yet what she had come to say.

Caroline rose up from where she was sitting, knocking one of the cushions onto the carpet. 'I have something I need to tell you, Hugo.' Her voice was high. All her careful planning was slipping away out of reach.

'No need to be shy, Caroline. Compose yourself. I know how you must feel...'

'No, indeed you do not.'

'I see.' He sat back in the winged chair – his gaze was fixed upon her intently. 'Shall I need some sustenance to help me hear you out? Ring for attention, I beg you.' He indicated the bell-pull adjacent to the doors.

'I think it advisable.' she replied.

If he was going to be reasonable her task would be made more difficult. Was it possible he had an inkling about herself and Gervase?

Her fear must have showed in her face because he raised his hand. 'No, I think I would prefer to hear what you have to say, without the benefit of strong liquor. Pray continue, Caroline.'

Now that the moment was come, speech threatened to desert her. The vase of flowers, she would look at that, concentrate on each leaf frond, that would help. 'I want you to release me from our engagement.'

The only sound in the room was the ticking of the mantel clock.

Mesmerized Caroline looked at the duke. What had she done?

Suddenly she saw him as she had not seen him before and as she continued looking at him it was as if for the first time they were communicating and she saw his position, power and influence with all its glory fall away and they were as close as they would ever be. Was this what it had all been about in the end? He wanted her, desired her and it was just possible, just possible, she was throwing away an opportunity she would regret and would never again experience …

Then the moment passed but she thought she might remember it for ever.

No, it was Gervase she loved.

The duke's face was once more devoid of expression but his left hand gripped the arm of the chair, knuckles whitened.

'Why are you telling me, Caroline? 'Are you afraid of being name-called a jilt?' His voice had deepened.

Caroline shook her head. No, it was not that. Running her tongue over her suddenly-dry lips, she replied. 'I wished to tell you face to face.'

He inclined his head a trifle, a very little. Calm had descended upon him once more, she thought. Could nothing shake his iron resolve?

'You know you are at liberty to leave me at any time.'

It was true. Was that what he would expect her to do, to run away?

She tried again. 'I am deeply sensible of your' she fought for the right words, 'generosity in providing for

Susannah's come-out…' His gaze did not leave her. 'And providing for our …'

'Keep.'

Caroline swallowed. It could not be denied. What would he demand now, and what was she prepared to offer?

He rose and drew himself up. 'Pray forgive me, Caroline. I must take a turn around the room.'

As she made as if to assist, he brushed her off. 'I rescind all debts. All.'

He walked up and down while she watched. Then, 'I have an arrangement to suggest to you.'

Here it came. She had known it would.

'I am not unaware of the previous entanglement between yourself and the Peninsular War's latest hero.' He shifted his right arm within his sling and with his left hand made a few adjustments. It must have served because he faced her once more. 'Marry him if you must. But it should be not beyond the bounds of possibility that we should, in the future, the not too distant future, I trust…'

'But –' Caroline tried to interrupt him.

'No, no, let me finish. We can come to an amicable arrangement. I repeat – marry him if you must.'

The same air of distaste. 'But afterwards …'

She was not entirely surprised after all. 'No, no, Hugo.'

'No matter. I shall ask you again.'

Silence fell between them once more.

'We may remain friends.' Caroline said without thinking.

'Friends? No. Not enough.'

Then he began again. 'Will you have funds?'

'Gervase, Mr Thorpe, has a small property in Hampshire.'

'And Miss Susannah Langrish?'

Caroline's gaze slid away from the Duke's. 'Mr Thorpe will support her until…'

'She is wed? There is one score upon which you may

rest easy. The Earl of St. Cross and the Earl of Marlow have both offered for your sister. The Duke of Lanchester has shown an interest.'

This was news indeed. Caroline started up. 'I did not know.'

'There is much that you do not know.'

He walked over to the bell-rope and rang it. 'I shall send you home in one of my carriages. No one shall accuse the Duke of Albion of a want of conduct. And you may remain at Brunswick Square as long as you wish.'

'Thank you, your Grace.' Caroline gave her deepest curtsey. There was nothing else left to say.

The same two footmen entered together, one with the shawl, and stood impassive. 'Miss Langrish is leaving. Send for Drayton. The Duke waved his hand but as she prepared to leave he came forward and took her hand and kissed it. 'I shall saw adieu not goodbye. And remember I have said that there is much you do not know. This is not over, Caroline.'

CHAPTER 26

'Miss Langrish! A word, if you please, with my mistress.'

Mrs Farley's abigail, Roberta, called down to Caroline from the top of the staircase.

Caroline stood in the darkened entrance hall, untying her veil, removing her straw hat and sighing with relief at the welcome respite given. It was cooler here. She had never thought to be pleased to be back at Brunswick Square but she was not to be left alone with her thoughts; more was to be demanded of her. She made her way to the stairs.

So Caroline would not escape the wrath of the Duke's principal chaperone, the chatelaine of Brunswick Square, the watcher, or maybe Susannah had been right all along, the wardress?

Although lately Susannah had shown a worrying eagerness for Mrs Farley's guidance on matters of dress, deportment and who knew how many other avenues of interest to a young girl.

'Please to accompany me to Mrs Farley.'

Acquiescing, Caroline followed Roberta.

It was an expected development. Although sooner than she would have thought. No doubt some servant had already passed the knowledge on, perhaps communicated by someone accompanying the duke's carriage in which

Caroline had lately returned in such comfort.

Maybe she deserved the scene which would play out she felt sure.

In silence the pair walked down several corridors before the abigail stopped and flung open a door. 'Miss Langrish,' she said in a tone without interest, and gave a brief curtsey before leaving.

Caroline entered the dimly-lit room to see Mrs Farley standing by the window with a letter in her hand. Wrenching back the curtain from one of the windows she turned to face Caroline. 'Let me look at you, Caroline Langrish.' She advanced across the room until Caroline could feel her opponent's breath on her cheek. 'How dare you refuse His Grace?'

'How do you know?'

'Because His Grace had the forethought, the kindness, to warn me.'

'I still do not understand.'

'He sent on ahead a rider. To explain! To explain the situation. It beggars belief. To reject His Grace, the Duke of Albion.'

'What has happened between myself and the Duke is private. I shall be leaving Brunswick Square as soon as …'

But when? Caroline was dependent upon Gervase's return, his offer of marriage, and he had not yet returned for her answer as promised and he had promised to return today, hadn't he?

Caroline began again. 'As soon as…'

'And when is that, pray? You do not seem very sure, indeed.' Mrs Farley scrunched up the letter. 'As far as I am concerned your leaving cannot come soon enough for me. Meantime I shall have to endure your presence. The Duke of Albion wills it.'

Caroline said nothing. It would not look good to give way to the strictures of someone so wholly on the duke's side.

'Wait.' Mrs Farley went on. It was a command but not quite on the previous level. The tone had changed. 'Your sister is not of the same mind.'

Caroline paused and then left the room without answering. She would find out soon enough.

Wearily she made her way up the stairs. Susannah would be waiting for her.

Caroline entered the sitting-room she shared with Susannah and caught her breath as, leaning back against the door-knobs, she regarded her sister. What a change since Caroline had left earlier in the morning!

Lying full-length on one of the two sofas, Susannah's feet, in pearl-encrusted slippers, resting on a cushion, the sweep of her flowing iridescent lilac gown reaching the carpet on one side and catching the light in a glimmering, shimmering torrent, Susannah was the very picture of indolent luxury. She was surrounded by flowers in vases on every surface – the mantel piece, the hearth, all four of the small tables arranged near the window, where the doors to the balcony were wide and flimsy nets moved in an almost imperceptible breeze.

Of all the bouquets it was the roses, damask roses, which principally caught her eye, a flaunting pink, shocking in the intensity of their colour. In spite of the season, they were hothouse-reared, come from some ancestral estate, and lovingly tended by a phalanx of gardeners whose attention was totally given to indoor beauties, not the relative rough and tumble of the outdoor beds…

Without thinking she found herself by the showy, gorgeous, resplendent bouquet. Leaning over, she immersed her face in the blooms and was rewarded; the fragrance was overwhelming. Surely it would be heaven to die here and now.

Caroline realised her sister was looking at her strangely.

'In case you are wondering, yes, the flowers came before noon this morning. By the by, the pink roses with which you are in love are for you, from the duke, Caroline.'

'Oh, no.'

'Oh yes.'

Hurriedly Caroline re-focused: next to *that* vase was a more tasteful arrangement of palest blush pink and cream rosebuds with a spray of delicate ferns and orange blossom. Surely evidence of the exquisite taste of the Earl of Marlow, Susannah's lovesick swain? Caroline forbore to ask. For now, at least.

Caroline noted the large open box of sweetmeats on a small table next to Susannah. The ribbons attached to the offering cascaded down towards the floor; unbelievably, their shade of lilac complimented the colour of her sister's dress.

Her sister, who had been engrossed in reading a small green book, placed it down carefully on the table. 'Caroline, where have you been? Have you visited Gervase at last? I hope so. While you were out I have been enthralled by Mrs Edgeworth's latest from the lending library. It is too, too delicious! But you must tell me all!'

Susannah rose from the sofa but Caroline evaded her sister's embrace and crossed to the window. Perhaps there she would feel cooler but it was doubtful. 'Who sent you the other flowers?'

Susannah, with a downturn of her mouth, turned away to resume her seat on the couch. 'The ones other than the overpowering roses with which you are so entranced, you mean. If you will not answer my question I think I will return to my book; but you will tell me in the end, you know. Let me see: the orchids are from the Earl of Saint Cross, Sir Clarence Hampden sent the lilies - I forget the rest...' So saying she selected another delight from the box and resumed reading but some concentration had obviously been lost for the book had to be turned the right way up after a minute or two.

'Who sent the rosebuds? Which of your many other suitors?' Caroline asked.

Susannah dropped her novel and sat up straight. 'I think you can guess. They are beyond tasteful, are they not? So elegant, just like His Lordship.'

Caroline leant back against the open balcony door, lifting her head in the vain hope of catching a breeze. 'The Earl of Marlow? I hear you have had more than one offer.'

Susannah chose another sweetmeat, turned it one way and another and popped it into her mouth. 'Well, you know, you have been so busy with your own affairs... Who told you?'

'The Duke of Albion.'

'Mrs Farley said that several gentlemen have requested an audience with me and have spoken to the Duke of Albion. He stands in the position of our guardian. Let us not argue the fact.'

'You are in Mrs Farley's confidence, I see.' Caroline said.

Susannah waited a minute before replying. 'So what if I am. Well, a little perhaps.'

'Mrs Farley is not to be trusted; I thought we were in agreement there at least. She reports back you know. Where did you get the slippers? They are uncommonly *à la mode*. By the by, you are wearing a new gown. Is the colour entirely suitable? For someone who has only recently come out?'

As soon as the words had left Caroline's mouth she regretted them.

Susannah did not look at Caroline. She picked up her book again and holding it up in the air, she turned a page. 'Well, I know Mrs Farley is watching over us but she has the entrée to several exceptional *modistes*. She escorted me there this morning. While you were out. She has *much knowledge* which she has decided to impart to me: of an intimate kind. I expect it to be useful to me: in the future.'

Here she put down the little book on the side-table nearest her and faced Caroline. 'When I am *married*, Caroline.'

Silence followed.

Susannah smoothed the drapery of her skirt with care. 'It is just a morning-dress. I shall not wear it out. It will be just the thing for quiet times when my lord visits me, in my private rooms.' And she giggled. 'I am returning next week to have fittings for several more such gowns. It will be so amusing.'

'And the slippers?'

'I borrowed them from Mrs Farley if you must know.'

Caroline repressed any further comment; she had said enough.

She came over to the couch and sat down on a footstool near her sister. 'Susannah, I have broken off the engagement with the Duke of Albion. I am going to marry Gervase. He returns today for my answer.'

'So you are a jilt! Poor man.'

Caroline felt a stab of pain. 'Who do you mean?'

'The duke, of course. He will be heartbroken. I am sure of it. You do not know your own power, Caroline.'

'And nor do you, Susannah! He will find someone else; someone who is more suitable for the role of Duchess of Albion. Besides, you were the one who reminded me of my attachment to Gervase,' Caroline could not resist saying so. 'And now you are feeling sympathy for the duke! You are fickle.'

'I cannot help it. Yes, your love for Gervase has been rekindled but you were going to marry the Duke of Albion! Surely I am entitled to feel some pity for your rejected fiancé?'

Caroline had no answer for her sister. What had she said? Heartbroken? No. Caroline rejected the idea.

Now, on the verge of a departure, it became important that Caroline knew what her sister would do. 'But I would like to know that you too are going to follow your heart?'

Susannah let go of her book and leant forward to clasp Caroline's hands. 'I shall almost certainly accept the Earl of Marlow. You'll see, we shall deal extremely well together. Now let me return to my book because I have not been in your confidence, dear sister. So, neither shall you be in mine.'

'Very well.' Caroline waited for a moment but her sister resumed her reading.

Caroline sat back on the footstool. She questioned Susannah's words, did Caroline really believe her sister would settle for the earl? And Gervase's best friend? And why was she, Caroline, worried that her sister might, just conceivably play him false?

As she herself had done so with the duke, with the best of intentions some would say, but others would not be so forgiving. Hardly credible though it was, would a life, of sorts, like the life of Mrs. Farley suit Susannah? After all, Mrs Farley was supported, not in want, with a reasonable amount of comfort... a measure of independence, within confines, of course...

No, surely the handsome and elegant Earl of Marlow would win through...

There was reason to doubt. Deep down, she knew she did not want Gervase to suffer another blow: the dismissal of his best friend's love, lost to the world of the *demi-monde*.

Her heart smote her; Susannah's happiness must come first; but surely it would be in the world of the *ton*, would it not? The safe world they had left behind; their world; the world of Beauminster Priory. The Earl of Marlow would ensure Susannah's return, if she married him.

As if Caroline could read her mind, Susannah lowered her book and looked Caroline directly in the eye. 'I must follow my own path, dearest sister. I will see you at dinner.'

Caroline nodded, rose to her feet and crossed to the doors. As she prepared to leave the room, she looked back over her shoulder to see Susannah blow a kiss in Caroline's direction before returning to her reading.

Enough words had been spoken; any more would be interference and Susannah was showing every sign of maturity. But what would she ultimately decide...

As if aware of Caroline's scrutiny, Susannah cast a look in Caroline's direction. 'I hope you manage to escape His

Grace's web; you will have to disappear. He has spies everywhere and it will not be easy.'

It was true. Now all Caroline had to do was wait for Gervase. But he had not come back as he had said he would, to receive the answer to his proposal.

CHAPTER 27

Gervase set off from White's Club with renewed vigour in his stride and hope in his heart. The boon had been granted. The boon that was essential and he was on his way to carry out the next stage of his proposed plan to make Caroline *his* again.

To take her away from *all that*, from the future with Albion that might almost constitute self-sacrifice. A life of servile domesticity, enlivened by the occasional required attendances at a stultified court. Was not the Duke a personal friend of the Prince Regent himself? Yes, with all the appurtenances of wealth, the town houses, the hunting boxes, the country estates, and always the limitless acres of land…

Where did that leave Gervase? Offering a small town life in Hampshire? She would not care, he thought stoutly. Or would she? Caroline had not accepted with alacrity last night, had she?

Surely she would have come to her senses by now.

Gervase reproved himself; he must devote his energies to the task in hand. The thoughts that went around and around in his head must cease. Well, that should not be difficult, for suppressing his wayward thoughts had become second nature to him lately.

Turning the corner into Mecklenburg Square, Gervase took a glance upwards. The sky was clouding over but if anything the heat had increased. Thunder clouds were rolling up, with a promise of a storm. He was amazed London had had to wait so long for relief from the oppressive weather. In Spain a tumultuous downpour would have occurred by now. And passed over, cleared the air, albeit temporarily, resulting in the dreaded heat resuming. Well, perhaps there were things to be grateful for, in England. The whole process taking so long that is, if nothing else. Realising quite how hot he was, he wrenched his already loosened cravat still further from his neck, moved his shoulders under his jacket and stopped, leaning on his cane. Idly he noticed that it incorporated a swordstick, cunningly concealed. Captain Howard, Gervase knew, was renowned for being ready for anything. Well, in the past Gordon had been certainly, not so much recently.

It was good that Gervase had such a devoted friend in Roland. As usual, the Earl of Marlow had come up trumps. Gervase had full permission to take what he wanted. And what he wanted was in the stables at Mecklenburg Square. In his pocket he had a note in Roland's scrawl, a note of authorization from the Earl himself.

Swinging his cane, feeling cheered, he resumed his journey.

Gervase crossed over into the middle of the Square by the railings fronting the gardens now deserted in the soporific heat.

Afterwards, he found it difficult to believe, *again*, how unobservant he must have been.

What had he been thinking of? But he knew. Caroline. Her creamy skin and her abundant dark hair, only waiting for the pins to be removed so that it could cascade down to her waist and capture him in such a way that he could never escape. And would never want to.

He had been followed from White's that much was certain.

The stables were over on the other side of the Square out of reach even with a sprint of which he was sadly not capable anyway. The view was obscured by a bank of trees in the centre and as luck would have it there was no one about.

Apart from the two men who had stepped out from behind him and now barred his way.

A stolid, brutish pair of similar height and girth, he judged. Not much to choose between them when it came to a fight, he thought as he sized them up. It was unlikely to be to his advantage to tackle either before the other.

What did they want, bold-faced in the daylight hours, not even having the decency to wait for darkness?

Money he had in his purse but he suspected that was not the purpose. Pretending to reach into his waistcoat he slipped his hand to the swordstick as it had turned out to be.

Gervase unsheathed the blade and confronted the two men. 'Well, sirs?'

Neither stepped back and as he looked at them more closely the garb they both wore was remarkably similar; made of dark, not inexpensive suiting. Even though well-worn. But neat, with discreet, covered buttons to match. One might almost say, *livery*.

Perhaps of the kind to be worn by former villains now gainfully employed by His Grace the Duke of Albion. To do tasks the like of which other members of his staff would not wish to soil their hands.

Realization dawned as, in shock, he lowered his sword.

More of His Grace's henchmen.

Gervase felt a stab of recognition. Perhaps they were same two who had manhandled him away from Caroline at the Betrothal Ball.

The somewhat burlier of the two spoke. 'Nah, this ain't about money. Pity, though. Expect plenty of *that* on you, milord.'

The other spoke next. 'Yes, sir, you can be sensible. Put up your sword now, sir. No point in a fight being as you are coming with us in the end. After all you want to know what His Grace has to say, don't you? Especially about a *lady*.' The word was emphasized with a leer. He grinned, showing uneven teeth. 'Nice and reasonable does it. Carriage around the corner.'

'Or?'

The sight of cold steel should have given them pause, but the man Gervase was mentally calling *assailant minor* thereupon drew out a knife which glittered in the bright sunlight, thereby in the process turning him into *assailant major*.

A few moments passed before the start of the inevitable fracas.

Two against one was at least better than having three opponents, thought Gervase as he tried to give himself heart. What a pity Roland was otherwise engaged crossed Gervase's mind also, especially as he knew he himself was not in the best of shape. Damn his leg.

Anyhow timing was all and the will to succeed, as he lunged forward, aiming for the stomach of the one while wielding his sword towards the other with a sweeping motion.

The coarse sand of the ground beneath his feet gave him purchase. It must have helped, or else the gods were on his side for once, for the armed ruffian doubled up almost immediately - but not before causing damage of some kind to Gervase's face. At any rate he tasted blood. Meanwhile, yelping, and clutching his leg, the other man hopped around. The sword had made contact.

Undeterred, the pair of them as if of one mind, barrelled in together. Gervase was soon on the ground, face in the dust, but not before landing a punch on the one and kicking out with all the strength he had, towards the other. In the direction of the wound already inflicted it was to be hoped. Unfortunately, in the process Gervase had stupidly mislaid his sword.

The fight was over.

Between them, the ruffians forced him to stand up and locked him into a hold; Gervase had a cut lip, was swallowing blood, and his leg ached like the devil, but he also felt better than he had in ages.

The sword belonging to Captain Howard was no longer to be seen: probably thrown over the railings into the Square gardens.

'You're more trouble than you're worth,' grumbled the man who was now emulating their prisoner's limp while the other squinted at Gervase through the beginnings of a black eye, as they dragged him away. Again.

The whole business was reminiscent of the Betrothal Ball episode but at least this time Gervase's opponents had not emerged unscathed.

He was bundled into the carriage as predicted.

No more words were exchanged for which Gervase was thankful.

One or two servants had appeared from across the Square during the mêlée, probably attracted by the noise, but to act as bystanders only. He could not make out whether they were from the Earl of Marlow's residence or not. Gervase had other things on his mind at the time. If they were, he hoped they would inform their master. They may even have recognised Gervase, who knew? Frankly, he did not care.

Roland had had a prior engagement after White's or he would probably have accompanied Gervase. Roland had seemed reluctant to let Gervase out of his sight since they had been back in England.

Well, and with good reason, the voice of sanity spoke in his ear, as he sat back uncomfortably in what was surely one of the least used of the Duke of Albion's carriage stock.

To add insult to injury, as Gervase stared blankly out of

the window nearest to him, he saw Nathaniel in the distance. The self-appointed guardian had failed miserably in his volunteered task.

The carriage ride continued.

Every rut they passed over caused a tremor in his leg that he could do without. The two henchmen were with him too, making the carriage interior uncomfortable full, and odorous, and reminding him of the unavoidable closeness of an army encampment. Obviously they had decided not to travel up top. Not that he was any danger now. He hoped they did not know how little he would relish any further trouble. It would take some time for his leg to settle down again.

But the voice carried on remorselessly, questioning his actions since he had returned from Spain, not least towards Caroline. Had Roland resumed his watchful mode because of Gervase's erratic adventures?

His behaviour during what he liked to call the Episode at the Betrothal Ball was entirely justified, of course.

A jolt and the carriage stopped. He heard the carriage steps descend.

In consolation, now he would come face to face with the Duke of Albion again. Another chance to wreak further havoc, Gervase hoped. So be it.

He wondered in what state his nemesis' arm would be now. Had the duke made an unexpected recovery or had some obscure nameless disease set in. Gervase knew which he would prefer.

There was a further worry; Caroline's dismay at her wretched betrothed's injury might have led her to make further enquiries.

But a servant could have been sent.

Loyal Finch, for example.

Gervase shook his head, as with one mind the pair of lackeys rudely forced him out and down the carriage steps to the ground where he stumbled on the gravel. He was back at the duke's residence he presumed; his thoughts interrupted. No, Caroline would never have visited the Duke of Albion herself.

CHAPTER 28

'I have a proposition to make to you,' were the first words of the Duke of Albion to Gervase.

The destination had turned out to be Grosvenor Square, as expected. Gervase had been strong-armed through the portico and up two flights of stairs. Feeling tired, for once he had shown little or no resistance. Let fate take a hand.

Gervase lifted his head, and breathed deeply, as he took in his surroundings. He had been marched into a very large reception room: a room hung with gold and red brocaded curtains from ceiling to floor on each of the several windows lining the wall ahead. The sun streamed in from every quarter and threw patterns on the gold and purple carpet. Dust motes danced through the shafts of sunlight.

At the far end of the room, in front of the light, His Grace, the Duke of Albion sat behind a wide table, draped in what looked to be gold cloth. Obviously it had been pressed into service for more mundane reasons as a desk: a desk fit for His Grace. To his side a tall thin young man stood, holding a sheaf of documents and appearing to be deeply preoccupied in reading one of their number. He gave the usual impression of a secretary remote from the event which was unfolding before him. Gervase recognised him. It was Charles, who had ushered Gervase in previously, before the glove-slashing exercise leading to the subsequent duel.

Gervase feared history was about to repeat itself.

Could one fight another duel with the same person? What was the etiquette on *that*?

No, another duel was out of the question.

In any case, the Duke was still *hors de combat* regretfully from that point of view; Gervase did not count his own leg injury; it had not incommoded him before.

More to the point - *What would he have to do this time to raise the ire of the bastard at the other end of the room?*

Well, at least the setting made a change from the small chambers in which he had been berated recently: first the retiring room with its pungent aroma off the ducal Ballroom, then Mrs Farley's broom cupboard or whatever it was. Had he been in a better mood he might have been overawed. The damned Duke certainly lived in some splendour. Perhaps it suited him to receive Gervase in such a sumptuous chamber, or maybe he just didn't care. The usual inscrutable face gave nothing away.

Gervase felt a distinct nudge from the henchman on his right. Realising the fight must have taken more out of him than he was aware of at the time Gervase moved forward a few paces. He felt done in.

But he must rally.

Shrugging his shoulders, he spoke. 'I am here under duress. On that matter I shall have more to say, but otherwise I have nothing to say to you. On any subject at all.'

'That's as maybe, but I have something to say to you.'

The Duke made a small gesture of dismissal to the two lackeys either side of Gervase. They left the ducal chamber. Just himself, the Duke and Charles now, who looked somewhat uncomfortable and was nervously shuffling the papers he was holding.

Reluctantly Gervase answered; the sooner the conversation was concluded the better for all. 'Well?'

'It was imperative that you and I spoke. The situation is fast moving so I used the means at my disposal to bring you here. Any damage to your person will be subject to recompense. After we have spoken you may repair to my quarters so that your injuries, such as they are, may be attended to. Is that clear? You may not wish to talk but I have something to say to you.'

Surely Albion's longest speech since Gervase had had the unpleasant honour of being within the devil's orbit!

What had happened? Had there been a change of circumstances? Did this smack of desperation, perhaps? If so, Gervase's spirits rose. He needed to find out. Had Caroline rebuffed the Duke?

It certainly seemed likely.

The moment he had longed for was upon Gervase, the moment of long-awaited triumph. It must be. He crossed the floor, crossed the deep-piled Aubusson carpet, across the mingled purples and reds, useless colours of the aristocracy, useless now for the grand Duke of Albion.

Until Gervase was standing over the table, hands flat on it, on the rich gold velvet, staring down into the glacial personage of the illustrious Duke of Albion. The Duke's face was white. A small nerve jerked in his cheek.

Gervase said slowly as a statement of fact. 'She has jilted you.'

His voice had been unnaturally loud.

There was a long silence broken only by the sound of the ticking of the mantel clock and a very slight suggestion of thunder in the distance.

Charles had moved away abruptly. Gervase watched the Duke rise to his feet, step back and adjust his arm in its sling, to face his adversary. 'As to that, you must speak to Miss Langrish herself. Your presence was required to discuss another matter.'

'What other matter?'

'I am aware that your circumstances are not, shall we say, easy?'

Money, that was what it always came down to, in the end, wasn't it? Money.

Was the Duke of Albion actually going to say what Gervase thought he was going to utter? If so, it was beyond belief...

'We can come to an arrangement.'

He was.

'An arrangement?'

Instinctively Gervase's hand went to where in better times his damn sword would have been. To no avail.

Now it was Gervase's turn to step back, first steadying himself, then pushing away from the table. He drew himself up.

Why was the Duke's behaviour still shocking Gervase? It was the way of the world; women were merely pawns, playthings of the gods to the aristocracy.

But the infamous Duke continued in the same vein, in a voice devoid of emphasis. As if, as if he were arranging a lease on a property, or... Here, even Gervase's imagination failed him...

'I envisage a long-lasting liaison between myself and Miss Langrish, so the amount will be not inconsiderable. Accommodation will be provided for yourself and Miss Langrish - in town. Yes, a town house in an admirable quarter, nothing not of the first stare.'

The man had lost his senses.

Bereft of words, Gervase could only wonder. If the Duke of Albion was no longer in the world of reason, perhaps the thing to do was to humour him. It would certainly provide some entertainment. 'Mayfair, I trust?'

'Of course. And shall we say, a stipend? I wish her to have every comfort.'

'How much?'

'Ten thousand a year, would that be enough?'

'Twenty.'

'My secretary will provide a document for you to sign.'

The Duke beckoned Charles forward.

Charles had now shown a renewed interest in the proceedings, and was actually looking Gervase in the face. Perhaps he was no longer afraid of blood being spilt, thought Gervase mockingly. The man should be wary; it was not a foregone conclusion.

Charles selected carefully a piece of paper from the sheaf he was holding. The rest were placed on the gold cloth for later perusal, Gervase assumed. The sheet of vellum crackled as the secretary thrust it towards Gervase.

Gervase took it, registering the bold black lines of writing.

The Duke of Albion meanwhile had removed his signet ring, as Charles moved a pen, ink and it looked like a small tin of red sealing wax nearer towards his master. A candle would be pressed into service soon by the secretary. Then the deed, almost like a marriage settlement, would be signed, sealed and placed in a safe somewhere.

The ring removed. Ah, it was significant the sign of betrothal, if indeed it was so, was no longer being worn on the left hand. Proof positive.

Time to end the farce.

Gervase could no longer carry on the charade.

He tossed the vile document back onto the table. 'I have no intention of signing. Nor entering into any kind of *arrangement*. I will make my own way out.'

He did not intend to stay to hear the response but one particular aspect of the events of the past few days still bothered him. The rest he consigned to history. Caroline was his. If she still wanted him. He must confess he was not entirely sure on that point.

Since neither the Duke nor Charles had spoken, Gervase turned around to see the Duke whispering to Charles, who bowed and hurried over to Gervase.

'I am to escort you to the door,' the secretary said quietly without looking at Gervase.

Gervase nodded. He bore Charles no malice and

wished extremely to leave the Duke's presence before some other preposterous proposal loomed.

Once they were out of the doors, swiftly opened by smartly suited footmen, they were back on the landing, richly carpeted in red velvet, muffling and deadening any sounds that might have the effrontery to obtrude upon His Grace's noble ears and above one of the two flights of stairs to freedom.

'Do you wish your injuries to be dressed first, sir?' There was a look of concern on the secretary's face, as he spoke quietly to Gervase.

Gervase shook his head. He was not aware of any injuries apart from the bruising to his face and his cut lip but maybe his limp was more pronounced.

However, now was the time to seek the answer to one question at least; after all Charles had appeared not entirely unsympathetic.

'The appointment that the Duke of Albion had, the one that necessitated that the duel was held in Hyde Park... I have heard it was with a lady?'

Charles hesitated.

'It can do you no harm to tell me. I am leaving London, probably forever,' said Gervase recklessly.

'Very well. It was with a diamond of the first water, I am told, Miss Fairburn.'

'Why? When he was about to marry Miss Langrish?'

Charles looked him in the eye. 'You do not understand the rules. It is expected of His Grace. A gentleman in his position.'

'What?'

'Since His Grace's betrothal to Miss Langrish, a lady had been dismissed, so the role was vacant. The lack was noticed, in the best of circles. At Court. It was necessary. To have a *maîtresse en titre.*'

Well, Gervase had his answer. He must have revealed the disturbed nature of his feelings in some way and Charles must have taken pity on him because the secretary added, 'I can assure you His Grace has the utmost respect for Miss Langrish, but form is all, to His Grace. Do you see?'

Gervase did not reply, he was too busy trying to beat down the painful thought of Caroline and the Duke again...

Another worry. Had Caroline herself made a contract with Albion? He certainly was fond of the damn things. He had made two attempts to suborn his rival to date. How could Gervase be sure? He would not put it past the Duke to try again.

Charles indicated the stairs to him and they commenced their descent at speed.

Finally, at the heavy black oaken entrance doors, Gervase held out his hand. He bore the man no ill will and he had attempted to help. The fact that more concerns had arisen, was not his fault. Charles shook it but said, 'I must hurry back. His Grace will have other plans now.'

Yes, a foregone conclusion, devil take it. One of the most powerful men in the land with nothing to occupy himself with but to concentrate on his machinations...

There was nothing further to be said. What would the Duke of Albion do? He was not going to give up easily.

Gervase's next course of action ought to be put into practice immediately; he should retrace his steps to the stables at the Earl of Marlow's town house with all speed, as already agreed with Roland. The favour requested when they were together at White's been granted with alacrity but Gervase knew beyond a shadow of a doubt that he needed a rest. Perhaps Nathaniel could patch Gervase up before the journey onwards.

He would set off early the next morning. Before that however, he still had one or two important errands to discharge before the journey to collect Caroline and embrace their future together. At the same time, for amusement, he could torture himself with dreadful visions of Albion's next move!

That paled into insignificance though when Gervase considered that he had told Caroline that he would return today for her answer to his proposal. Never mind, he would see her tomorrow, the arrangements must be put in place. Besides she would wait for him and with the jubilation which he had not allowed himself to feel before, his heart sang.

For she had rejected the all-powerful duke for himself!

CHAPTER 29

A full moon had already risen and the night sky was clear as Gervase entered the Albany for what he hoped would be the last time; his important errands completed. The document he wanted was in his pocket, again through Roland's influence. Gervase laughed inwardly at the idea of himself, lowly Gervase Vyvyan Thorpe Esquire, being friendly with a bishop! But Roland had contacts aplenty amongst the *ton* and the upper reaches of good society as it was called, including clerics. Fortunately, Gervase only had to deal with the bishop's secretary who had looked askance at Gervase's facial injuries but had said nothing.

And as for Caroline, he was confident she would understand why he had not returned for her answer today when he explained how he had been abducted en route to her …

Which brought Gervase to the consideration of Nathaniel. Well, Gervase would have to have a word with his protector, last seen disappearing into the distance from the rear carriage window when Gervase was hauled off to Grosvenor Square to have an unwelcome audience of the Duke of Albion.

Now all Gervase needed was hot water, some attention

to his wounds, a light supper and a retiring to bed early in preparation for the following day. For tomorrow promised to be long and tiring.

It was quiet in the quarters but as Gervase made his way through the sitting room towards his private apartments he realised he was not alone. Moonlight shone through the open window revealing Gordon was there too, in the semi-darkness. Captain Gordon Howard was seated motionless in his now familiar position at a desk staring out at the evening skies. If Gervase had given any thought to the matter at all, he would have expected the Captain to be *en flagrante* with the Lady Lydia Vellacott somewhere.

At the noise of the door to the kitchen area swinging open with a crash Gervase turned around with a jump. Nathaniel came bustling into the room with a taper and began furiously lighting candles in their sconces, muttering to himself all the while as he concentrated on his task and ignored his two masters. Not that Gervase had ever called himself so.

But from Gordon there was no movement. Gervase walked over to his friend, bypassing Nathaniel for the time being; it looked as though Gordon needed some support.

Gervase stopped by the window and looked down at his friend with the furrowed brow. 'And how was Gunther's Tearooms, may I ask?'

Gordon looked down at the table on which another letter was being written. 'Oh, as to that, Lady Lydia tried the violet ice and pronounced it prime. Tolland was also there,' he added as an afterthought.

'And?'

'I persuaded him to make a hasty exit. Then she refused me!'

'Why, pray? Did she give her reasons?'

'Too many, there's the pity. Not interested in *carte-blanche*. Says she has other plans and lots of business to attend to, although I don't know what. Doesn't fancy becoming respectable yet, if you please. And she left me alone in the middle of Gunther's!'

Gervase was not entirely surprised at the turn of events. He doubted whether the Lady Lydia Vellacott would take kindly to a life of splendid confinement in a town house, even one as luxuriously appointed as Gordon had promised.

Caroline had rejected a similar offer, thank God. But not immediately, a voice inside him cried; true, his love had certainly considered a life of luxury with the dreaded Duke of Albion. More than considered; she had become betrothed. Ignoring a brief stab of pain, he thought to himself that after tomorrow Caroline would be his, Gervase's, again. Wouldn't she? Barring 'perfidious Albion'! 'What do you intend now?'

'Think I'll apply for a transfer to the Isle of Elba. May as well join old Boney in his exile; we will be miserable together. Must be posts in the garrison there.'

'I would not give up so easily, my friend.' Gervase replied. 'Napoleon probably is not. Even now *he* is probably scheming to return to the mainland. In my opinion Elba is not far enough away but never mind we are not discussing the former French Emperor. Why don't you take the Lady Lydia Vellacott for a drive in the Park? Wendover has carriages aplenty and to spare. You may ask him courtesy of myself; only mention my name and all will be well,' he added recklessly. If Roland felt so beholden it was time to take advantage on behalf of a friend, call in the favour. Gervase owned the idea gave him a measure of satisfaction.

'An assignation! And I'll show my face again, in society. Avery recommended it. Besides still plenty of people about, season not over.' Gordon sat up straighter and called out. 'Nathan, bring me a candle over here, will you? I must get on.'

Nathaniel had been standing by the sideboard on the other side of the room all the while, Gervase remarked; no wonder the manservant missed so little. He picked up a candlestick, set it down next to Gordon's right hand and then retired to his former watchful position.

Gervase sat down on the sofa realizing how tired he felt. Gordon's back was now turned, he had his extra light and there were sounds of a nib scratching on paper. Judging by the concentration, the letter was not easy to write.

When Gordon finally sat back in a rest from his labours Gervase spoke. 'By the by, I am likely to be out of town for some considerable while, from tomorrow.'

Gordon shot Gervase a surprisingly keen glance. 'Your arrangements have come about?'

'They have – providing I can leave town tomorrow.' It was best to be honest. 'I may not return.'

Gordon whistled. 'How fortunate.' Then in the space of a beat. 'Your rooms will be vacant then.'

Gervase nodded; he could not resist it. 'Maybe Tolland might be interested?'

'Tolland be damned; I shall make good use of them, never fear.' Gordon picked up his pen and dipped it into the inkwell. 'When I have finished this I think I'll go down into Piccadilly.' And he continued writing.

Gervase moved away to give Gordon the space he needed.

At this point Nathaniel chose to stand in front of Gervase and assume an obsequious air which would have fooled no one, least of all Gervase. 'Sir, I regret I was not with you when the two gentlemen from the Duke of Albion's household, er,'

'Yes, yes, when I was unceremoniously conducted to the household of the duke,' interrupted Gervase. 'It is all in the past. I grant you, at the time, I would dearly have liked to have had you there, fighting my corner, but do not blame yourself.'

Nathaniel looked away. 'Am having trouble with the Captain.' He lowered his voice and whispered. 'He is all over the place. First it's dress uniform for Gunther's –

tried to reason with him – wanted to cut a dash, he said then he wants to be in two places at once.'

'It will all come right in the end, you'll see. I have encouraged the Captain not to give up. The die is cast, for me, by the by – I'm leaving tomorrow. For Hampshire. No need to keep watch anymore.'

'You'll need to get far away to escape attention, if you don't mind me saying. And that's a nasty cut there on your lip, an' no mistake,' Nathaniel said, screwing up his face in concentration. 'Could do with a dressing. I'll fetch hot water now, sir.

He went off towards the kitchen quarters but just as Gervase was about to enter his own rooms, Gordon spoke again, gazing out through the open window. 'I love her, you see, Thorpe. Legshackled is what I want to be but it turns out Lady Lydia is of age and may please herself.'

A moment of truth; Gervase was shamed by his previous flippancy. Was Gordon now writing a letter with a proposal of marriage?

Without a word Gervase readied himself for some painful ministrations from Nathaniel and left Gordon alone with his reflections.

Later, as he waited impatiently in his dressing-room, he found himself admiring his reflection in the mantel glass; the extensive colourful bruising on his face and the drying blood around his mouth, all acquired in a good cause; the proxy fight with Albion. Dearly would Gervase love to cross swords with his rival again!

A further cause for reflection was his new role in life. After his last conversation with Roland Francis Sebastian Wendover, Earl of Marlow, a belted earl no less, of all people, at Tattersalls on the subject of Miss Suzanne Langrish, and a recommendation not to retire defeated, he was found giving sage advice to Captain Gordon Howard. Though that in its way was more understandable. Poor Gordon often seemed to lack direction. The effects of the War were long lasting, some said.

But Gervase was worried that he, of all people, was fast becoming a mentor of sorts, heaven help him!

CHAPTER 30

'You have a visitor, miss, in your sitting-room.' Eliza, one of Mrs Farley's housemaids, had whispered the words after quietly entering Caroline's bedchamber.

Eliza closed the door and gave a quick curtsey, her eyes wide. It was rare indeed for any of Mrs Farley's household to attend upon the sisters. Unless, of course, they were to be summoned for a reprimand.

Startled, Caroline rose from where she had been sitting listlessly on her bed. The hour was late, she realised. How long had it been since she had left Susannah? Caroline's thoughts untrammelled had been rushing hither and thither to no apparent purpose but none of them, coherent or otherwise could possibly allay her fears; Gervase had not returned for her answer to his proposal.

Was the visitor, Gervase, at last? No, impossible at such an hour. Although it was just the kind of action she would have expected from him. But in that case how had he managed to evade the ever-watchful eye of Sawyer on the doors?

'I will come down,' Caroline replied.

'A lady visitor, miss, being the Lady Lydia Vellacott.' There was breathlessness in the maid's voice. 'The lady gave me a guinea, to fetch you. She came to the area steps. Out back. I don't rightly know how she knew about them. I mean, exactly where they was.'

'But she did?'

'No-one but me saw her, I dare swear.'

Eliza opened the door and the pair of them hurried along the corridor to the stairs which led to the sitting-room.

Caroline did not know what to expect, why could she possibly be of interest to a titled lady, hitherto completely unknown to her?

Most worrying of all, was the lady some kind of emissary from Gervase? If so, did she represent another emotional entanglement? Caroline and Gervase had been apart for so long and their circumstances so different...

Gentlemen have their needs, as her mother used to say.

Refusing to encompass such thoughts, Caroline opened the door and entered the sitting-room, her head held high. Eliza followed her closely but the girl left quickly after bobbing a curtsey. Perhaps she was afraid of losing the largesse so liberally bestowed.

The Lady Lydia Vellacott dominated the room for there was no sign of Susannah. The lady, who had her back to Caroline, was resplendent in a rich salmon-coloured soft velvet pelisse bordered with a ribbon of a deeper hue and a fetching orange hat in the military style of a shako. Caught looking at herself in the over-mantel looking-glass, the lady swung around gracefully and smiled at Caroline.

'Yes, I think it really is *de trop* but the mood took me, and one knows how it is!'

So saying she took off the hat and cast it aside, to be followed by the pelisse, onto one of two armchairs ranged either side of the empty grate.

She came forward to Caroline with an outstretched hand. 'I am Lady Lydia Vellacott, my dear, and I have heard so much about you that I felt I must see you at once!

I have something to tell you too!'

There was no mistaking the warmth of the greeting but it was almost as though the lady was extending her welcome to Caroline in her own home, such as it was!

Some of her mixed emotions must have been displayed on Caroline's face because Lady Lydia, dropping her hand, looked away and said. 'There I go again; I have been told so often to moderate my over-affability! The Captain, Gordon, you know, reproves me constantly! Can we not be seated in your comfortable armchairs as I have not much time before I am found out. I have been here before but Mrs Farley and I nearly came to blows years ago – why I cannot immediately recall but la, I think it was over some premises we both wished to acquire in South Audley Street, for I am in business, Miss Langrish!'

So saying she moved to the armchair she had already purloined and sat down with a flourish, pushing the pelisse and hat to the carpet.

Obviously Lady Lydia did not stand on ceremony so Caroline sank down in the armchair opposite her, still bemused, but managed a few words. 'Captain Gordon Howard lodges in the Albany, I believe?'

She felt immensely relieved that so far the connection with Gervase appeared to be via his rooming companion only. The Earl of Marlow had mentioned the Captain when Caroline had beseeched Gervase's address. Already *that* episode had receded into the past.

Gervase was always so single-minded and bent on his own path. *It is you, Caroline, always you*, he had sworn more than once, she remembered. How could she have doubted him?

Lady Lydia gave Caroline a direct look. 'Speaking as one woman to another I have come here to tell you the real reason for your lover's injuries. There is this ridiculous code of honour whereby ladies are protected from the details of what goes on in a battlefield. We are not supposed to have the stomach for it! If I do not, you will never know the truth. Men can be so protective of one another; don't you find?' Another sharp look was directed at Caroline.

Caroline was not conscious of having had the experience to agree with the sentiment but she nodded. Her desire to keep her visitor talking was paramount. 'Oh yes, please tell me, my lady!'

'Lydia, please.'

'Lydia then, but I do not understand how you can know of such things.'

'Well, let me tell you the story; Gordon, when asleep, talks; and I am half-ashamed to say that I listen. In case you are concerned I have his permission to tell you.'

'I thought you said there was a code!'

Lady Lydia smiled at Caroline. 'I have made a conquest, you see. It took all my arts to extract the full story though. But time is short, let us press on, I have no wish to meet with the delightful Mrs Farley again. Your beloved intervened to save the life of the Earl of Marlow and in the process took a bullet for his friend. There that is the sum of things.' And she sat back as if the words had caused her some effort. 'Well, I find that I have no desire to tell you more after all! But without me I very much suspect you would have heard even less or most likely nothing!'

Caroline sat back too, feeling sick. '*Is* there more? What else is there?'

Lady Lydia sighed. 'Only that Gordon feels guilty because Mr Thorpe was not attended to immediately. No, it is more than that, he is excessively distressed because he feels it was his responsibility. I tell him that in the heat of battle who knows what happens.' She rose, collecting her outer garments as she did so. 'I feel I have caused you pain, but it is all for the best, is it not?'

'What did happen, pray, Lydia?' Caroline heard the anguish in her own voice.

'Gordon swears he and the Earl of Marlow were separated from your man.'

Caroline found her mouth dry but she managed to speak. 'And then, for how long? How long was Gervase left?'

'I gather he was stretchered away the following morning. Gordon was instrumental in his rescue, you know. If it is any consolation, my love has had many sleepless nights. And taken to drink, but he is on the mend now. It is always the way – gentlemen find the scars of battle do not easily fade.' She trailed her hand over the cover on the back of the armchair. 'I must take my leave of you as my carriage is waiting in the mews.'

Caroline swallowed and fought to retain her composure. She rose too and held out her hand. 'Thank you, Lady Lydia. It was good of you to tell me.'

Lady Lydia came forward and enveloped Caroline in a warm embrace. 'Take care, Miss Langrish. You must be very sure that what you are about to do is your own choice.'

Caroline responded in kind and was released.

The Lady Lydia Vellacott swept to the door. 'I can find my way out of this establishment,' and she gave another wide smile. 'I wonder whether we will meet again – I am not entirely respectable, you know! Are you, Miss Langrish?'

A question which Caroline found unanswerable. She had long suspected she was no longer so she merely curtsied in response.

And her visitor was gone with a click of the door before Caroline could answer.

She felt she had found a true friend in Lady Lydia whether or not their paths crossed again.

Caroline, appalled at what she had just heard, made her way slowly back to her bedroom. If her thoughts had been in turmoil before, they were spinning fully out of control now.

Well, she had wanted an explanation of Gervase's leg injury.

She spared a little thought for Captain Howard's remorse but poor Gervase!

The immediate need now was for Gervase to see a physician.

A growing realisation dawned on her that the Earl of Marlow was heavily indebted to Gervase.

Already friends, they had fought in the same war, in the same regiment; the bonds were close and now closer still, for Roland owed his life to Gervase.

CHAPTER 31

'These are the horses in question?'

Gervase looked at the two grays in adjoining stalls, both apparently peacefully at rest. Until he looked more closely. It was certainly true of the horse furthest away but the other had a hint of devilry in its alarmed eye as it lifted its head to look at the stranger in the stables. Perhaps the horse sensed he was about to be taken out by someone other than his master.

When Gervase had arrived at the Earl of Marlow's town house, still tired in spite of the overnight sleep, or rather lack of it, but primed and ready for the next step, he had found Roland more than willing to assist. They had wasted no time in going to the mews. A couple of interested grooms stood nearby in attendance, with the head groom a few paces in front.

'Do not concern yourself. You will find the pair sweet-goers and they will cause you no trouble. At Richmond you may pick up my post-chaise. Take Wilson, my Head Groom, with you if need be. Or he could ride separately. If you need privacy, that is.' Roland gave Gervase a swift glance as he leant against the wooden stall.

Privacy Gervase did need. He had much to discuss with

Caroline. And he hoped for more, but it was likely that his late arrival would come first. A day late! To have left her waiting to give her answer to his proposal – it really was unforgiveable! He saw that now.

'By the by, I was expecting you yesterday,' continued Roland.

'I was delayed.'

'How so?'

'Another intervention from the deplorable duke.'

'I guessed as much.'

It is becoming tiresome but will no doubt get worse.' Although Gervase profoundly hoped not. He needed to conserve his depleted strength for Caroline.

'Ah, the duke. Did he use physical violence or was it his men? I quite thought you had gone five rounds at Jackson's.'

Gervase snorted. His appearance was immaterial; Caroline would not care. Although truth to tell his superficial injury was still a little sore. But what was a bruised mouth after all? He determined to change the subject. 'It is no matter. All in the past. And what about your words with old Falconbridge?'

'Well, you know, he is always high in the instep but he condescended to wish me every success in my venture. A return to the service would be welcomed in all quarters, or so he thought. So many are on furlough now but a call to arms would not be totally unexpected. Bonaparte has been on the Isle of Elba only a matter of months but one never knows. *He* probably thinks it is long enough.'

Gervase snorted again. 'I only asked you for form's sake. It is not far to Brunswick Square. Why are you not there plying your suit with the beauteous Miss Susannah Langrish?'

Roland reddened. 'It is my next port of call. But I think we should not arrive together. I shall be on a formal errand and you are proposing an elopement.'

Gervase laughed. 'Certainly not an abduction. My

suggestion will be a drive to begin with. Even the dubious Mrs Farley must sometimes allow Caroline out for air. If not, I will have to resort to subterfuge.'

Roland raised an eyebrow. It was Gervase's turn to look guilty; he knew he was often accused of a predilection for confrontation. It was difficult to know how he could force his way through the impenetrable defences of the Farley household but somehow he would. Ignoring Roland Gervase continued. 'Once we are away, well, it is time I clarified the situation between Caroline and myself. By the by, my guess is that my beloved has thrown the duke over. It has cleared my path.'

He hoped.

Roland looked at him. 'You do not know,' he said tellingly.

'No, not for sure. But something has passed between them. I know it. I was in Grosvenor Square yesterday, not by my choice.'

'I was expecting you to take the curricle yesterday, which was why I wrote you the *laissez-passer* when we were at White's.'

The chiming of a church clock in the square reminded Gervase; he needed to set out on his way. 'My thanks, Roland. For the loan of your curricle, and the carriage later too.' He held out his hand.

Roland took it and clapped Gervase on the back. 'My men will harness the horses and make the curricle ready. I'll send a message to Richmond. Maybe I will try my luck with Miss Susannah and if the answer is nay, I swear I will take up colours again.'

Gervase was not done; Roland had excelled himself in friendship. 'Thanks do not do justice.'

They faced each other.

Roland spoke quietly. 'I have not forgotten how you rescued me at Salamanca. You did me a great service once: taking a ball for me, I mean. At great cost to yourself.'

Gervase turned away. 'It was nothing. I will wait in the

Square while the horses are put to.'

Roland nodded and they parted company.

Once out in the open air, sultry and oppressive as it was, Gervase felt a measure of calm.

At least he had some small consolation. He *had* assisted his friend it was true on one grievous occasion but it was nothing compared to Roland's unrelenting support throughout their time together in the Peninsula. The unpleasant business at Salamanca was best forgotten.

He had, but it seemed Roland had not. Not that Gervase's leg was likely to stop reminding him for the foreseeable future.

In spite of himself he fell to thinking about the past.

Yes, Salamanca, that dreadful summer and outweighing all other memories of the battle ... the incident that had maimed him, perhaps. He prayed his leg would regain its strength.

How had it started? July, 1812, the march, both armies marching across the plains towards Salamanca ... Wellington and Marshal Marmont, some would say equally matched in cunning, both skilled at manoeuvring to gain advantage.

Some would say now and there was truth in it too, that of the two commanders, Marmont was the superior. Gervase, ever loyal, disputed the received opinion. No, Wellington always had the edge. Gervase would defend his leader to the end. And yet, and yet ...

Certainly the French were faster on a march.

Gervase could not deny it.

How he had longed for the shade of the rumoured green cypress trees of the hill-top town of Salamanca, rising out of the dusty plains, the cool fountains, the plashing of water...

Then the rumour, then the fact, that another army was approaching led by another of Old Boney's commanders, he of pseudo-royalty, King Joseph, to augment the French contingent...

A partial retreat was ordered but the dust of the baggage trains confused the French enough to cross in front of the line and then the fight was really on ...

How had it happened? One moment all was well, the fighting rough but only as expected and during a lull, they both having dismounted, Gervase saw someone lining up a shot and called to his friend, Roland who was speaking to Gervase at the time, and might have taken the full force, had not Gervase thrown himself forward ...

It was the work of an instant.

What he had done and why he had done it he had many times asked himself...

What he did remember most of all was crying, 'Leave me here. Leave me here to die.'

Of course he had not been left.

Only overnight. By which time, delirious as he was, rescue was just a hazy recollection, a time of hallucinatory pain and later fear of losing his leg.

Rescue by Roland, it transpired later.

Ably assisted by that stalwart heavyweight Captain Gordon Howard, or so Gervase was reliably informed later by a brother officer, possibly Tolland. Tolland, now reincarnated as Gordon's love-rival, it would seem.

Nothing was to be gained by dwelling on the incident.

Only now, ridiculously, Roland considered himself to be beholden to Gervase.

The past, was well, the past. Best forgotten. Except perhaps where Caroline, his faithless inamorata was concerned.

Nevertheless, he hoped when he was safely down in Hampshire work on the small estate would ease his leg; or he *really* would have to see a physician, preferably someone other than the *ton*'s favourite Dr Jamieson.

No, a setter of bones, a country doctor with true knowledge and experience of men working hard on the land to earn a living; not a charlatan charging exorbitant fees to his spoilt and wealthy clients.

Perhaps the exercise would calm Gervase down; he reckoned he needed the fresh air and punishing toil, in the fields, preferably. Otherwise Caroline might find him hard to bear. He hardened at the thought. Time had passed since they had been alone together. Too long. He was not sure how much longer he could wait. Please God she would not turn him down as she had the viper Duke of Albion. If so, everything would be lost.

Everything.

Thunder rumbled in the distance. Still too far away to be concerning.

But he hoped they would make Richmond and one of the Earl of Marlow's closed carriages before the storm broke. And storm there would undoubtedly be. Although what were the odds? He did not care. One can make love in a thunderstorm as much as any other kind of weather.

There was only one possible impediment.

Would the Duke of Albion intervene again?

Some would say it was inevitable on past form. But it remained to be seen how much the duke knew of Gervase's plans. How much had Caroline told him? Very little he hoped, but there again the duke appeared to have limitless power and connections everywhere.

Gervase thought he would like to see Albion try.

CHAPTER 32

'Miss Langrish is at home without a doubt. I must see her. Let me pass!'

And as an afterthought, for form's sake, and regretting the words as soon as they had been spoken, for the foolishness they were, 'No need to announce me!'

Gervase pushed past the usual immovable block of granite, Sawyer, otherwise known as the Gatekeeper of the Farley household.

This time it proved surprisingly easy. Was the Janus-like figure losing his touch? But the whiff of brandy on his breath explained at least some of the reason although perhaps not all. Surely the massive bulwark, employed by Mrs Farley, or rather the Duke of Albion, could not have some glimmerings of sympathy towards the recalcitrant suitor? No, more likely Sawyer had detected some subtle shift in the balance of power within the household. Maybe Mrs. Farley's star was no longer in the ascendant, on the downward path even? Staff were always the first to know.

Anyway Gervase was in and at the foot of the stairs, looking upwards again at the glass atrium roof, marked now with dust trails, no longer in harmony with the gold and black tiles of the marbled entrance hall.

Taking the stairs two at a time, he reached the first landing and using a prescient gift strode out along a corridor, hearing some laboured panting behind him and the tones of a man not to be outwitted easily. 'Wait on it. There's the ladies' apartments! You have no right going there. Mrs Farley will hear about it.'

What Sawyer did next, Gervase cared nothing for it. Let him fetch her.

Was Caroline at home? It was no longer early in the day; Gervase had hoped to surprise the household in Brunswick Square but as usual fate was against him. But he had the curricle waiting outside; the horses, those admirable grays, at this very moment being walked up and down by Wilson, his own mount tethered conveniently nearby. Thanks largely to Roland's help, everything was prepared.

On an impulse, Gervase took the first set of doors and opened them wide.

The room was in darkness, the curtains pulled to and the heat was oppressive. When his eyes became more used to the somnolent gloom, he saw Caroline was seated alone, utterly still, her hands in her lap, by the empty grate.

At the sight of Gervase, she leapt up and came towards him with her arms outstretched, 'You are here!'

'Yes, I am here, beloved, tell me yes, Caroline!' said Gervase and he swept her up in his arms, kissing her with passion. 'At last. But we must make haste. I have come to take you away from this,' he gestured wildly, 'from all this madness. This cage. Come. I have squared everything with the duke.'

'*He* can no longer hold us back.' He added confidently. 'Let us leave immediately. Bring what you can in as short a time as possible and we will be on our way. We are eloping as agreed and failing that I am abducting you, but I know you are willing!'

'Gervase, I have broken my betrothal to the duke.'

'I knew it!'

Hardly had he spoken when the doors swung open with a crash and the slight figure of Mrs Farley entered, Sawyer towering over her just a step or two behind, his gaze blank.

Gervase heard Caroline's sharp intake of breath beside him.

Mrs Farley.

In spite of an unsteady gait, negligent mode of dress, and a hint of something being not quite as it should be, she still drew the eye. 'Mr Thorpe, Sawyer has been most remiss in not turning you away. These are private apartments, the domain of His Grace, The Duke of Albion. I must ask you to leave immediately!'

The voice as always was beautifully modulated but the venom behind her words was barely concealed.

Yes, Mrs Farley was far from than her usual composed, elegant self. A thin-lipped smile belied her words and her hands were shaking as she grasped the folds of her flowing gown, an afternoon ensemble of delicate shades of orchid pink silk, with an occasional hint of red beneath. Rich chestnut hair partially escaped from a snood of silk. The silvery mesh, studded with tiny seed pearls, had given way beneath the weighty and importunate demands of mass. Her slippers were scuffed as if, as if, she was clinging to the last remnants of her previous life…

The heady scent she wore, distilled from heavy, overblown hot-house roses, had undertones of laudanum or some other opiate.

Undeniably her territory was enclosed spaces, bounded by conservatory glass, spaces set within humid, vaporizing air. Or curtained bedchambers remote and airless awaiting hot and impatient lovers desperate for release at any price.

True, the air of a chatelaine could never quite leave her, Gervase supposed, and likely never would but he was willing to bet that she had in the past lured many a man to lose his very reason…

Shaking himself and wondering whether the

atmosphere of the Brunswick Square house was tainted by a kind of poisonous miasma, he replied, hardly knowing what he was saying, 'Miss Langrish and I are leaving. We have an arrangement and I have a curricle and pair waiting outside.'

At his words, Caroline had drawn even closer; he was aware that she had taken his arm, closing her fingers on the sleeve of his jacket, her nails digging into the rough cloth. She felt hot to the touch. 'Gervase,' she breathed, 'Take care.'

'Arrangement? What kind of an arrangement, pray? The Misses Langrish are here as guests of the Duke of Albion and I am their companion. Sawyer will escort you to the door.' Mrs Farley's colour was high.

Had there been a momentary hesitation before the use of the word 'guests'? Gervase thought that there had; it gave him hope. He ploughed on regardless. 'Miss Langrish is no longer betrothed to the duke. Send to His Grace himself, if you do not believe me. Come, Caroline.' And he turned towards the doors, placing his hand over hers on his arm to bind her to him.

Another pause in the proceedings while Mrs Farley waited, but for what? She had no answer. Did she know the truth?

Then she hissed, 'Remove Mr Thorpe from my house. Sawyer!' When there was no immediate response she repeated with a screech, 'Sawyer!'

Gervase laughed, there was a comical element to the entire episode, in the nature of a farce almost, and then he was amazed by Sawyer moving with surprising haste across the room.

Before Gervase could credit it, he was in an arm lock from behind and being dragged out of the door. He felt, rather than saw, the pressure of Caroline's fingers falling away from him and heard her calling his name.

Once in the dark corridor another two men stepped forward from the shadows, but their assistance was refused with a curt nod of the head. Unfortunately, Sawyer needed no help and Gervase was ashamed of it. Already his head reeled and his leg ached as he was dragged along to the top of the main staircase.

'Let me go!' The grip tightened.

Came late and was ineffectual anyway, Gervase cursed himself. Caroline was well-entitled to think so.

A surprise was in store however when they reached the bottom of the stairs, a process that required considerable effort on Sawyer's part, Gervase was pleased to think.

For he was released.

Everything was quiet here, in the entrance hall, amongst the gold and black tiles, the air heavy with dust and hazy sunlight from above, but the sky was darkening. Far away came muffled sounds of servants about their business. There was no-one about.

Sawyer coughed as he brushed down his jacket sleeves, and without looking at Gervase, said, 'Off you go. And get on with it. His Grace will soon know right soon enough. I've sent word.'

'That's nothing to me,' Gervase lied.

But he was aware that he had stored the comment away for future reference.

Gervase turned to make for the stairs and Caroline.

'Oh no, you don't.' Once again his adversary grabbed him, this time by the lapels of his jacket. 'I shall bring her out too. All in good time.' He opened his mouth to smile, revealing his yellow teeth. 'There's things going on here in this house as Mrs Farley don't know and my orders have changed.'

Gervase began to protest but Sawyer shook his head and opened the front doors, propelling Gervase out into the street.

Disconsolate, Gervase needed a moment or two to compose himself. Then he turned, eager to re-enter the house, in search of Caroline. To his amazement, the heavy oaken doors had not been properly closed and he managed easily. The entrance hall was deserted; Sawyer had wasted no time in removing himself to his quarters. What had he said, something about the house being in upheaval?

Gervase's boots clattered on the worn tiles as he made his way back towards the stairs.

'Mr. Thorpe!'

He had not heard anyone else, he had not thought anyone else was around but there looking down at him from above, her hands tightly gripped on the bannisters was the beauteous Miss Susannah Langrish.

'Pray a moment of your time, I beg you. I wish to speak to you about your friend, the Earl of Marlow.'

Her hair hung loose about her face in such a way that one would almost have thought her a practised courtesan. Her robe was open from the throat, and the cascading folds promised allurements – for Roland.

As Gervase gazed at her, still convinced that Susannah though *an incomparable* as the old saying went, was no match for his Caroline – although was Caroline really *his*? No, he was in thrall to her, not the other way around but…

Yes, he saw Susannah's beauty. A portrait of an odalisque came to mind… a fear came over him. What did she really know of Roland? He, Gervase, would not leave the house of sin without doing the right thing. The house where Caroline and her sister had been watched over, and for what purposes? Well, it was known that the illustrious Duke of Albion had marriage plans for Miss Susannah Langrish.

Or could it be that the mistress of the household, Mrs Farley envisaged a different future for her charge?

Gervase took a deep breath and came to a decision. He owed it to Roland. Yes, hell's teeth Gervase *would* interfere. Half an hour o' the clock and then he and Caroline would leave for Richmond. It was after all the least he could do, knowing what he did.

'Miss Susannah,' and he bowed to acknowledge her, 'In

what way may I be of assistance? We, Miss Langrish and I, are leaving immediately.'

Susannah swept down the flight of stairs to stand before him. 'I have a note from your good friend, the Earl of Marlow. I fear I may disappoint his lordship.'

Unexpectedly a wave of anger came over Gervase. Was she a worthy mate for Roland? Or was she like her sister, prepared to be bought for a worthier suitor? He must find out how she viewed the duke's proposals for her future.

Her beauty would undoubtedly sway many a scion of the *haut-ton,* if not *royal* personages themselves but naturally marriage *there* would be unlikely with the background of the Langrishes…

Casting aside any remaining vestiges of remorse at betraying a confidence, he plunged in. 'I understand His Grace the Duke of Albion has other suitors in mind for you, Miss Susannah.'

Susannah gave a graceful little laugh. 'Dear Mr Thorpe, I am not beholden to the Duke. He may say what he wishes but I have other avenues in mind.'

Dear God, what was she about? Had she no idea of the ruinous opinions of the ton? One misstep and a woman's reputation was damaged beyond repair. It was known, everyone was aware.

He continued speaking in an even tone. 'You wish to join the demi-monde, I take it. Mrs Farley has painted a false picture, I fear.'

There was a toss of the beautiful hair but she did not meet his gaze. 'I shall insist on a bijou residence in a select part of town. I shall have my own independence. It will suit me very well.'

There it was: independence of a sort, as against a landed lord, but what of love? If Gervase possibly could, he would try to influence her.

Now for another betrayal. Hell, if he did not tell her it was certain Roland never would.

'Well, the Earl will be disappointed.'

'How so?'

'After all he has suffered in the Peninsula.'

'Is he unwell?'

'It was after Badajoz. We stormed Badajoz in the April, but enough of *that*, Gervase added hastily. *That* was a subject he did not want to discuss.

'But before Salamanca, when we were crossing the plains,' he continued, realising he was going back now, again. Away from the marbled halls and the ways of the *ton*... Back to dusty plains and heat immeasurable; memories he was unable to escape.

'The Earl of Marlow, Roland, well, he was on the staff, as close to Wellington as he could be, you see...'

'Pray continue.' Susannah had moved nearer to Gervase. The scent of roses was all-pervading.

'He was sent on ahead, in charge of several men, to reconnoitre. Volunteered as usual, always too ready to do so, if you want my honest opinion. A tradition of the Wendover family, I would have you know.'

'No. I didn't know.' To do her justice, Susannah had not looked away since Gervase had started the story. He was not sure he had seen her attention so unwavering since he had first clapped eyes on her at the fateful Ball. Well, concentrate she should.

He resumed the narrative. 'We lost two men in that little excursion, I regret to say. I am not sure it was worth it.'

'To cut a long story short, there was an explosion. Not entirely unexpected after all. They came upon some ordnance. Hazards of war exist on all sides. It was some time before the forward column caught up. By that time...' He paused, remembering coming upon the scene of devastation, remembering the event well, too well. It was seared in his memory.

'And he was injured.'

'Yes, it was a mere flesh wound,' here Gervase hesitated but Susannah made a small gesture, so he continued, 'but Roland must have lost a lot of blood that day. Naturally he carried on.'

'But he seems quite well now.'

'According to the army physician it would take a year before the Earl of Marlow fully recovered.'

Susannah moved away, as if she had heard enough. 'Yes, as you say the hazards of war.' She looked at him again. 'I have heard your exploits were mentioned in despatches also.'

'We both were,' he replied shortly.

Gervase had no intention of going into any further details about Badajoz or Salamanca for that matter. It was unnecessary.

Susannah came up very close to Gervase and laid her hand upon his jacket. 'You must tell me more; it is important to me.' Susannah's interest, once roused, appeared not easy to halt.

Gervase looked down at her and carefully removed her hand. 'If you insist. But I have not much time. We are leaving…'

'Yes, yes, I know. You are driving to Richmond. My sister has already told me. I wish you well. I shall do nothing to interfere. I am only pleased that Caroline has had the good sense, at last, to come to the right decision. It will suit her very well. But I…'

'You are different, I understand,' he said, realising he had raised his voice.

'I insist.' It seemed she was not to be deflected.

'Very well.' To give her further details had not been his wish. Perhaps he would indulge her, it was all for Roland, after all.

'It was not the usual weather one associates with Spain. No, not by any means, a chilly spring, that March. Mud everywhere.

'The 52nd Regiment, our regiment, you understand, was heavily involved in the siege of Badajoz.

'There were storming parties, wave after wave of them. About fifty men, led by an officer. All volunteers, I may add. Up the cursed scaling ladders. Into the two main breaches in the walls, well, no, we were beaten back constantly. Back down into the ditches. Foolhardy in the extreme.'

'Or admirable?' She whispered. 'But you were successful.'

Gervase did not answer. He continued. 'Attempt after attempt was made, forty in all, in the space of two hours, to gain entry, each one 'a forlorn hope', ours included. Everything failed. The town was so well-defended.'

'But eventually?'

Gervase shook his head. 'No. A little-regarded diversionary attack to the north succeeded, led by General Walker. Roland later told me Wellington was quite shocked. He had been on the verge of acknowledging failure.'

'Yet both of you were mentioned in despatches.'

'Yes.' His glance slid away. He saw her need for answers, he just wished he could give them.

Susannah gave him a slight smile. 'I think you are not telling me the whole story.'

'Maybe.'

Gervase would not tell Susannah about the sack of the town afterwards. It did not bear discussion. *That,* at least, had left no blood on their hands. He watched her carefully but it looked as though there were to be no further questions.

It was a bald account, a partial explanation, which he had no intention of elaborating upon. She must read 'The Gazette' to learn more. The little he *had* said, left him feeling drained. Now she knew a little, just a little, of the fortunes of war. Had he done right?

It was done however.

Susannah moved away from him, her head bowed, as if deep in thought.

Now Gervase must leave.

Meanwhile, earlier ...

Caroline had cried out when Gervase was wrenched from her and dragged away by Sawyer, out of the doors, into the corridor, leaving her alone with Mrs. Farley.

Nor was it the first time Gervase had been forcibly removed from her presence... she was reminded of the Betrothal Ball ...

It had all been done in a trice. One moment Gervase was there and the next he was gone.

Caroline made a convulsive movement to follow him out of the slammed doors but Mrs Farley stood in front of them in all the glory of her dishevelled state. 'Oh no, Caroline. It is completely impossible that you should leave His Grace's protection for this man!'

Caroline swallowed. 'The Duke of Albion has released me from our betrothal. I have his permission to leave his house.' Caroline said firmly. 'You cannot keep me here, as you are well aware.'

Perhaps, at last, the truth was beginning to sink in. Certainly Mrs Farley's face tightened and the colour had left her fine complexion. Her lips were now set in a firm line. With a sick feeling, as Caroline watched, she had a premonition that Mrs Farley would shortly tell her something she would not wish to hear.

Gathering her skirts together, and avoiding Mr Farley's eyes Caroline made a determined effort to force her way past. Mrs Farley put out restraining arms and held her in place. 'Your lover owes much to his friend and mentor, the Earl of Marlow, enlisting as they did at the same time. Without him I doubt your Mr Thorpe would have advanced his career as he has done. Thorpe, such a plain name is it not? Of course, no-one would have expected the outcome that your poor cavalier has endured. No wonder he has sold out. Or was he discharged? Or invalided out?'

'What do you mean?' In spite of herself, Caroline's attention was caught, distracted. 'Naturally he has sold out – the war is over.'

'But I will say no more on that score. Men will have their secrets. You should try asking him someday.'

'Certainly, Gervase owes him more than he can ever repay,' said Caroline haughtily; she hated the idea of discussing Gervase with Mrs Farley.

Mrs Farley had not finished. 'On the contrary. It is more the case that *the earl* is indebted. Ha, you did not know that, did you?'

Caroline looked away, desperate not to show prior knowledge. It was fortunate indeed that the warm and effusive Lady Lydia Vellacott had visited Caroline the previous evening, otherwise Caroline would truly have been at a loss over the slant of Mrs Farley's remarks.

Yes, Gervase had taken a bullet for his friend, Roland.

Mrs Farley moved on; she obviously had other weapons in her armoury. 'Very well. I will say no more on *that* score. Now, to return to your present role, there has been an agreement reached, ask Gervase Thorpe. A very particular arrangement. You are to be allowed to marry, but it will be a sham. His Grace will still avail himself at every opportunity... You are being deceived at every turn.'

'It's lie!'

Mrs Farley smiled. 'Ask your sainted lover. Ask him. And never forget - when you leave here you will never be free.' So saying she stepped back from the doors and made an ironic gesture of dismissal.

With her heart racing Caroline's hand closed on the door knob and with her face turned away she was about to leave Mrs Farley forever, she hoped.

But Mrs Farley said, very low. 'You would have done better to remain with the Duke of Albion. You are not worthy of him.'

By this time Caroline was struggling to make a frantic exit.

In the corridor before the doors closed behind her, she heard the final words, '*I* would never have left him, and in such a way!'

Caroline ran along the corridor but she hesitated on the landing overlooking the downstairs entrance hall. She needed to gather her wits about her, to summon her strength or perhaps even to calm herself.

There was dawning realisation that Mrs Farley had been made more dangerous by her feelings for the Duke.

And how had she so much knowledge of his affairs? Had she his ear? Or had she a network of spies in his household?

More to the point was the question regarding herself and Gervase. Was it true that Gervase had been suborned into an 'arrangement' with the Duke?

This is the way the world is ordered, my darling, she remembered her mother saying, speaking from bitter experience, *we are only chattels, worthless goods in the hands of our masters.*

But not with Gervase, never.

The situation at Grosvenor Square had worsened. It was too late to gather any of her possessions together, they needed to leave immediately. But what of Susannah?

Gervase heard sounds from above and saw Caroline at the top of the staircase, looking down at himself and Susannah.

'Caroline, I think you should be on your way.' The sister said, with just a quick look upwards. Then she held out her hand to Gervase and he took it. It seemed appropriate to bestow a kiss. After all, he had done his best for Roland. Not that *he* would be grateful.

Somehow he thought Roland would never know about the revelations.

I have behaved like a green girl, he thought ruefully. But it was all done for the best.

Not that that was ever a justification. But still…

'Come, Caroline,' he called out but she was already descending the stairs.

The two sisters exchanged an embrace and then

Caroline was in his arms again.

    The doors opened with a creak and a groan and they were outside.

CHAPTER 33

Releasing Caroline, Gervase took several gulping breaths, and then sat down on the steps of the town house rather more suddenly than he had intended. Once more shooting pains in his leg reached up to the top of his thigh. His injured leg. Soon, very soon, he would have to see a sawbones. Hadn't those been Roland's very words?

As he sat there, *wallowing* in his pain, as he thought to himself, he recalled the episode at Salamanca, *again*...

Not that Gervase regretted his action in the slightest. Roland would have done the same, had the situation been reversed, but sometimes, just sometimes, Gervase almost wished he had not... he had not ...

Taken a bullet for his friend.
All shall be well, and all manner of things shall be well...

Gervase wondered whose words those had been... the pain seemed to be easing. He closed his eyes.

'Gervase, are you ill? What is the matter?'

With a start he realised Caroline had crouched down beside him and was shaking his shoulder. An elusive scent of garden flowers reached him, only half-remembered yet never completely forgotten. Always he associated her with the rose garden at Beauminster Priory, years ago when all things military were ahead of himself and Roland.

With an effort he roused himself and stood up. What had happened? He must be more tired than he had thought. 'Yes, yes, we must set off for Richmond. Where is the curricle? Your sister, Roland said he would... but I betray a confidence...' He was hardly making sense, even to himself. Goodness knows how he must sound to Caroline!

Raising Caroline closely against him, melded one to another, they clung together for a moment. Her lips tasted like heaven. If only, if only ... Then she carefully detached herself from him. Gervase ran a hand down his face - really he was becoming even more maudlin now!

'The curricle is there.' Caroline pointed. 'Is that your groomsman, Gervase?'

The road was quiet save for the solitary curricle being walked gently up and down by Wilson. Gervase's curricle. His curricle. Well, courtesy of Roland.

Together they watched as Wilson, as if aware of their emergence from the house, began to make his way back towards them. The horses, also, as if anticipating an approaching journey, showed every sign of wanting to force the pace. It was all he could do to hold them.

Then several events happened almost at the same time. From behind the equipage, a rider came cantering into view, leaving a dust storm in his wake, and overtaking the curricle with ease. Disturbed, the excellent pair tried to shy away but Wilson showed his mettle and all was under control once more.

As the rider approached, Gervase recognised Roland, on Aristides.

He admired the way in which Roland brought the magnificent thoroughbred to a halt before them. Had his friend finally taken to heart the advice Gervase had given him, and come for Susannah? It must be so.

Swinging down easily, Roland handed the reins to a groom, who had appeared smartly from the direction of the mews behind the Brunswick Square house, closely followed by a stable-hand eager to assist in the privilege of serving the earl.

Roland advanced, hat, gloves and riding crop in hand. 'Your servant, Miss Langrish. I am seeking your sister, Miss Susannah.' He bowed gracefully to Caroline.

The massive doors to the Brunswick Square house swung open and Susannah appeared in a carefully arranged state of *déshabillée*.

What was she about?

Susannah stepped forward. 'Then I think you should come with me, my Lord. Mrs Farley, I regret, is indisposed and the house is presently at sixes and sevens.' Her curtsey was of the deepest and her look under lowered lashes was artful, Gervase would give her that. He watched as Roland bowed, his colour heightened, as the pair made their way into the house through the double doors. For a proposal and who knows, what else? Caroline's sister was making her presence felt. He had no doubt that *there* at least the path would be easy.

So unlike his own situation. Was Caroline truly with him and would the Duke of Albion really relinquish his hold?

Restored to a sense of urgency, he glanced up at the darkening skies above. They must be on the road; he was not sure the weather would hold.

'I want to make Richmond as soon as possible. The weather is far from certain. Wilson will accompany us as an out-rider.'

With these words, and an almost bruising grasp, Caroline felt herself hustled down the steps from the house into Brunswick Square. Did Gervase think he was leading her away from that house of correction, Mrs Farley and the Duke of Albion for ever? Caroline wondered at it. It was hard for her to believe even now: that she would ever truly escape…

She looked more closely at the curricle. It displayed a discreet crest on the side of its shiny black carriage and the horses were a fine pair of grays. All stood waiting, with a groomsman in attendance.

Gervase however was back in his nervous, agitated state of mind, Caroline felt sure; he was pale and limping again quite badly: always a sign of inward distress. She was still no nearer an explanation of his facial injuries: the cut lip, the bruising to his cheek. Never mind, she would find out during the course of their ride together.

She watched as he signalled to Wilson, the long-suffering groom, or was he perhaps more senior? Certainly he had a decided air about him even though he had probably been walking the horses back and forth since Gervase's arrival. Wilson now favoured Caroline with a polite nod of his head and a murmured greeting.

And how had Gervase acquired a curricle with such a fine pair of thoroughbreds? No need to ask, the Earl of Marlow, Gervase's friend. The crest on the carriage was his. The equipage had obviously come accompanied by the head groom; perhaps the Earl was unwilling to allow what must be such treasured possessions as the grays out of his sight, even to his best friend, without assistance from the mews.

And was the indebtedness that Mrs Farley spoke of so spitefully responsible for such largesse?

Caroline became aware of her surroundings; Gervase was right, a dark and ominous bank of clouds threatened from the West. 'Richmond?' She repeated. A sudden and unexpected gust of wind tugged the ribbons of Caroline's straw hat and occupied her for quite some minutes, distracting her.

'We must make haste.' Gervase was close now. His face, the same as always, but now with fine lines at the corners of his deep set eyes and a worrying frown on his brow. 'Come with me, we can talk as I drive.' There was a pleading note there which caused her heart to leap.

She remembered how she had thought once she would follow him to the ends of the earth if need be and her heart smote her. What had happened to her? To doubt the strength of her feelings for him?

A cold, hard voice spoke to her in her heart of hearts.

Life had intervened. Gervase had gone to war and she had remained to pick up the pieces after her Papa had left herself and Susannah to fend for themselves. Abandoned, orphaned, destitute.

She had chosen wrongly, was her thought, *she should have struck out, she should have taken a position as a governess, Susannah would have managed. Instead, she, Caroline, had sold first her soul, and ultimately she would have sold her body, to her first male suitor, the Duke of Albion.*

Why? Had there perhaps been some temptation, some lure of position, wealth, or heaven help her, some glimmer of attraction?

She shivered and refused to pursue the idea.

'Where are you, Caroline? You are not with me.'

There was no more to be said. The die was cast. She had chosen.

Caroline was handed up into the curricle by Gervase, who took his place lightly beside her. He signalled to Wilson at the grays' heads to let go and they were off. Looking back over her shoulder she saw Wilson swiftly mounting his horse to follow on. As an out-rider, Gervase had said. Was Gervase, or even the Earl of Marlow, expecting further trouble?

Surely not.

Caroline faced ahead once more. The journey had begun.

Well, a curricle and pair, with an out-rider. And a crest on the side of the carriage. She was travelling in some style. Already eyes had been turned towards them as they bowled down the street.

She suppressed the thought that once again Gervase was availing himself of his friend's generosity and that Susannah too would be most happy to spend the undoubted wealth about to come to her, if she so chose.

The roads were dusty, the heat had not abated and it was as if all London town were on the move.

Gervase's lips were tightly together, his face was set, his mood had not changed. It was to be hoped the air and the concentration necessary would remedy the situation. She sat back prepared for the long conversation to come.

'Gervase! Take care!' Ahead an overloaded post-chaise slowed to a halt.

The grays swerved, causing her to hold on to the side of the curricle with one hand, and the seat with the other. She felt her straw hat slipping from her hair, the ribbons loosening.

Gervase swore under his breath. For quite some minutes he was fully occupied with handling the reins. The high-stepping horses were now showing signs of veering out of control but Gervase was not to be outdone. Although Wilson took it upon himself to ride forwards and steady them before dropping behind again.

They were on the road to Richmond.

Conscious that Gervase's grip had eased and that he had sat back, she was about to speak when he forestalled her. 'It may interest you to know that I have had the honour, the *extreme* honour, of a meeting with the duke.' His voice was hoarse. He gave her a quick glance before returning his attention to the dusty road ahead.

'When?'

'Not two hours ago.'

Just when she thought she had escaped from the duke's toils.

Ahead of them the road opened up giving a clear ride for a little way; the horses settled into a steady pace.

'What had he to say to you?'

'You must understand I had no choice in the matter; I was taken forcibly to His Grace's presence.' Gervase gave a short laugh.

'Oh, no.' As she had suspected, he had sustained injury at the hand of the duke, even if indirectly. 'I see the result in your face, Gervase. What happened?'

'That was nothing, it was what he had to say!'

'What did he say?' she asked with alarm.

She waited. It must have been after she had broken off the engagement. 'Tell me, Gervase.'

'Well, he had the audacity …' Here he stopped speaking and must have tightened the reins because the horses once more showed signs of a will of their own and he was temporarily pre-occupied before he resumed. On this occasion Wilson forbore to come to his protégé's aid. 'To say that after you were married to *me*, and after an appropriate amount of time, probably incredibly short no doubt, he would come to an arrangement…' Here Gervase choked, raised his whip, thought better of it, and they continued as before.

'An arrangement, what kind of an arrangement?'

'Oh, he envisaged a permanent liaison with you, my wife, and I would be merely an escort for form's sake, a kind of chevalier, one knows not what the appropriate term might be, certainly not a husband. Well may he fantasize!' Here he pulled the curricle to one side of the road and turned to face her. 'What do you say to that?'

There was the very faintest hint of a question in his tone. She must disabuse him of the notion that she would even consider it. So much for Mrs Farley and her insinuations! Now Caroline knew what had happened. How could she ever have doubted Gervase?

'Gervase, he has proposed the same arrangement to me.' Even now, time having passed, it seemed the most fantastical idea she had ever heard.

'He did?'

'Naturally I refused.'

'Naturally.' Was there relief in his tone? 'Thank God. I could not have borne it. You do know that, don't you?'

'Yes.'

Gervase was not looking at her now, his mouth set in a grim line. 'He proposed financial compensation or something of that ilk, but fortunately a little sense must have returned to him, because when I refused, he let me go. I considered calling him out for a second time. God forbid! Well, I did not want another duel. Impossible. Although I would like to have taken out his other arm. Yes, that would have been very satisfying.'

He shook his head. 'It was insufferable!'

'I can hardly believe it. Let us forget my former fiancé.'

'Most willingly. Then there is no more to be said on that score. His Grace is no longer a threat.'

Caroline wished she could be so certain.

There was silence for a while after they resumed their journey.

CHAPTER 34

The dark and threatening clouds had still not produced any expected rain, nor had the promise of a cooling breeze made itself felt but the swaying of the curricle gave a little movement of air, and Caroline was grateful.

The horses settled themselves into a steady rhythm and later into a smart trot so that Gervase should have been less preoccupied with keeping them under control but still his concentration held firm. Wilson kept up with casual ease but stayed as close to the curricle as possible. The road ahead widened out and promised a clear ride to Richmond.

A worry that would not go away was still present in her mind; she remembered the Duke of Albion's parting words to her, that *it was not over.*

Yet he had let her go, hadn't he? She had been told she could stay in the Brunswick Square house for as long as she wished but was that enough? Had he expected her to depart quite so soon?

Would the flight to Richmond truly be unimpeded?

Gervase's hands gripped the reins as he leant forward urging the grays on. Did he feel the same?

As if he could read her mind, Gervase spoke, still with

his attention fixed ahead. 'The old bruiser Sawyer let slip that he had sent some minion or other to tell your ex-fiancé that I was taking you away.'

Caroline's suspicions were confirmed; the truth was best. 'The Duke of Albion told me that all was not over between us.'

'Just so, I did not expect him to deal fairly; he has released you but there again he has not! The devil! Excuse my language, Caroline but might is right in his eyes.'

After a pause, he added, 'I have the satisfaction of knowing that he does not have any inkling whither we are bound! Does he, Caroline?' And he turned briefly to look at her.

'I told him, Gervase. I told him that you had a small property in Hampshire.'

'But not the exact whereabouts,' she added hastily. After all she did not know; that was true at least.

She waited for Gervase's reply to her honesty with some apprehension, especially when he did not answer immediately. Only the sound of horses' hooves broke the silence and then, 'Well, then we must be prepared for any eventuality, I suppose,' was Gervase's mild reply. 'I for my part welcome the chance for another set-to!'

A feeling of relief swept over her and she leant back in the curricle.

'In any case, the dreaded duke cannot possibly know the route I have chosen to take. Many roads lead to Hampshire,' Gervase added confidently.

Caroline was not certain; surely there was hardly a choice. She owned she was not entirely convinced. But with the resources her former fiancé had at his disposal he could no doubt afford to keep a watch on all the main roads out of London town!

Desperate for some relief from the prevailing sense of unease that followed Caroline everywhere, she turned her attention to the future. Even though they were well on the way out of London and the time was ripe for the answers to more questions about the events of the past few hours, it was the future that was her immediate concern.

'What do you intend when we reach Richmond, Gervase?'

'Well, as you know, we are going down to Hampshire, to my property; it is in Whitchurch. I intend that we shall arrive there by tonight. I need to get you away from all the influences of His Sainted Grace the Duke of Albion, your beloved sister, and that witch, the Mrs Farley. But above all, I fear *his* power. You could say that I am abducting you, after a fashion, but as you have given *him* his dues, it cannot be so.'

Gervase went on. 'I am unable to consult with your guardian, whomsoever he might be and as you are not of age, we are eloping. But I do have your permission!'

'Yes, Gervase, you do.' Eloping sounded a very grand and romantic term to describe their departure together from Brunswick Square but Caroline supposed that it suited him. But such a distance and in such a few hours… 'Surely not all the way in a curricle and pair?'

'By no means. We will pick up Roland's post-chaise at Richmond and continue in that fashion. Wilson may return with the grays, when they have been rested.'

He added, 'I myself do not intend to do so, ever; I have had my fill of London.'

'Never? But there is Susannah to consider; I know I have left her now but I hope to see her again.' But Caroline knew in her heart she had abandoned her sister.

He looked at her. 'Unless of course you wish it. Indeed, if I could offer you a house in London I would, but, as you well know, my means do not stretch so far!'

When she did not reply, he halted the curricle and pulled it into the side of the road. Wilson followed but at a discreet distance, eyes averted. 'The main thing is, we are never going back to that house of sin! Your delightful sister will deal very well with Roland, one way or another. I am sure of it. She will make him a very happy man, once he is leg-shackled.'

Caroline nodded but made no answer; she hoped that it would be true.

'It is you, Caroline. You are all that matters to me. I have to ask you again, are you with me? Tell me yes, Caroline!'

Caroline smiled at him. 'Yes, Gervase. Yes, I am.'

Transferring the reins into one hand, he flung one arm around her and holding her against his side, he kissed her.

After a space of time, the curricle wended its way on again; there was no signs of the grays tiring.

At last Gervase spoke again. 'By the by, I have a special licence with me.'

'How did you obtain it? The Earl of Marlow?' *As with the grays and the promised post-chaise, surely thanks to Roland?*

'Yes, indeed, his help has been invaluable.'

'Mrs Farley hinted to me, more than hinted, that your friend Roland is heavily indebted to you.'

Eyes fixed on the road, Gervase did not reply.

'Gervase, I had an unexpected visitor last night, the Lady Lydia Vellacott.' Then it all came out in a rush. 'She has acquainted me with the story of what happened at Salamanca. And why the Earl of Marlow is so indebted to you. That you took a bullet for him, and, and that is why your leg is so injured.'

Gervase, still leaning forward, his shoulders hunched said nothing but Caroline heard a sigh. 'The Lady Vellacott is a singularly resourceful woman, so I am not surprised that she found you. And it is to be expected that she should acquaint you with a tale I would wish you not to know. I am sure Roland would agree.'

He sat back and gave her one of his rare smiles. 'You know my story and now I am at your mercy, dearest Caroline. I do not wish you to say any more. Not now, not ever. Not to anyone. Will you promise me?'

'Only if you swear you will visit a physician when we are in Whitchurch.'

'Oh, if that is all, most certainly I will!'
It would be enough for now.
They rode on for some miles in what Caroline felt to be a state of bliss, saying nothing to one another.

The way passed underneath some dense overhanging branches; part of a small wood that stretched on either side of the dusty road. 'The next turnpike will be soon,' Gervase said.

The curricle swung around a corner where the vegetation was even denser and the road became dark.

Out of the gloom, coming towards them, travelling at a leisurely pace was a great, lumbering, creaking carriage helmed by a single coachman, two footmen up behind - and with a set of four outriders.

Up until now the road had been, if not deserted, at least quiet. In the past hour, if her memory served her, she had only witnessed a post-chaise or two, and an overcrowded coach.

Caroline knew immediately.

It was after all a shock. But later, when she had thought about it, and more than once, only to be expected. Had she really believed her erstwhile fiancé would give up so easily?

With a loud crack, a pistol-shot rang out.

Caroline jumped, Gervase swore and the frightened horses whinnied and danced around as he fought to control them.

Once again it was their companion Wilson who rode by to assist at their heads and with calming words and much dexterity brought them back onto the straight and narrow.

All the outriders were masked, wearing black, and as Caroline now saw, armed. The leader, with the smoking gun, smiled as he wheeled his horse about. The men re-grouped and melted away into the trees. As if they had never been there in the first place.

But they would not be far away if required she felt sure.
All that was left was a whiff of small shot in the air.

'What the devil!' Gervase, still holding the reins, forgot himself enough to attempt to stand, thereby threatening the balance of the curricle. Caroline held onto the side nearest her but Gervase sat down again almost as abruptly and stability was restored.

'It must be the duke,' Caroline said. 'It must be. We will face him together.'

'I cannot credit it,' was the reply. 'But it is *his* coat-of-arms on the side of the carriage, I know it!'

As Gervase had obviously regained control of the horses enough to satisfy Wilson, the groom relinquished his hold and rode back towards them. 'I could do little against armed men, more's the pity, sir. The Master warned me to expect trouble on the road. I think we should wait – unless you wish me to ride on to Richmond? It is not far.'

'No, indeed. Certainly not. I may need you, Here, be good enough to take the reins will you?' Gervase did not sound in command of himself; his colour was up and Caroline wondered what he might do next.

After dismounting and tethering his own horse to a convenient nearby tree, Wilson came forward ready to replace Gervase in the curricle. Gervase leapt down and seeing Caroline had already gathered up her skirts and was preparing to follow, he assisted her to alight.

It was obvious the duke must be confronted yet again. Only on this occasion it would be the pair of them, Caroline vowed. When Gervase snatched a quick look at her, she made an effort to control her expression. She was with him; he must know it.

As they watched and waited, one of the two footmen from the coach dismounted and let down the steps. Ponderously, the Duke of Albion, his arm in a sling, was assisted to the road by the servant. Another gentleman, carrying a large box of some description, followed him from the confines of the coach and stood back discreetly.

Shaking off his support, the duke walked towards

them.

How unwell he looks, Caroline thought. But the air of consequence would never leave him however many rebuffs he encountered.

'Miss Langrish and Mr Thorpe.' The duke bowed. 'I crave a few words with you both. I apologise for the rather direct way in which I caused you to halt.'

Caroline gave a brief curtsey but moved closer to Gervase.

Gervase answered. 'I will speak to you, Albion, but at least let Miss Langrish travel on with Wilson here.'

'I am afraid that will not be possible. I wish to speak to you both. Together.'

Caroline spoke quickly. 'Certainly, Your Grace.'

'I have a proposition to make. There is a small house I have in Winchester which has been much neglected - I will have a document drawn up leasing the property to housekeeper and general handyman. It would be yours for life.'

Caroline was amazed; to what lengths was the duke prepared to go. It seemed there was no end to his plots, subterfuges or whatever one chose to call them... she hardly dared look at Gervase but she could feel his anger like a powerful force beside her.

No wonder he had not wanted to release Wilson from duty. Whatever befell them both now, he would bear witness if the worst should happen and Gervase murdered the duke in front of her.

'Gervase,' she hoped she sounded a warning note to her lover, who was obviously beside himself. She expected any minute to see Gervase attack the aristocrat who had just made such an astounding offer. Again.

'And what are your expectations should I accept the offer?' Gervase's voice was surprisingly cool.

The Duke of Albion had the grace to look away. 'The expectation is that I should visit by prior arrangement at an agreed time.'

'Impossible!' Gervase snarled. 'You have had the impertinence to make the self-same offer to me before.'

'I wish you both to consider my arrangement. Together.'

Caroline stepped forward. 'Your Grace, you released me from our betrothal; the arrangement of which you speak is not agreeable to me.'

'Then there is no more to be said, for now.' The Duke of Albion bowed to Caroline. 'Forgive me, my dear Miss Langrish but I must speak to Thorpe. A final word.'

CHAPTER 35

A final word.

Gervase felt a quickening of interest. Maybe the old devil had still more to say? Words that could not be spoken in front of Caroline; it was highly likely!

But Caroline was no longer looking at Gervase. Maybe she was tired of the histrionics. Gervase caught her hand and pulled her closer. 'I will give him the courtesy of that.'

'If you must.'

'Draw a little farther off.'

'This is madness.' Caroline turned her back and retreated towards the curricle, which was still in the care of Wilson. At least he would be able to recount the day's events later to his master, Roland. Though what he would have to say, Gervase dreaded to think.

The Duke of Albion's supporters had withdrawn. *His* carriage now moved slowly away to the shelter of some trees but was ready for whatever might ensue. Gervase's heart rate increased.; the decks were being cleared for action.

The air was quiet, somnolent, yet heavy with anticipation.

Gervase snapped his attention back to Albion, who had

taken a step closer. In a measured tone the duke said, 'My arm for your leg.'

Gervase stared. *What did he mean?*

'We are equally constrained, are we not?'

Gervase conceded grudgingly that Albion had a point. 'As you say.'

'Well, then, I suggest we settle this man for man. With swords. First blood to decide the matter. Denbigh here has come provided.' And he gestured towards his companion, a slight, spare man, who gave the semblance of a bow. With a self-effacing manner highly suitable for the duke. 'Unless you prefer fisticuffs?'

Gervase shook his head. 'Hardly. In your condition.'

The duke gave the smallest of acknowledgements: a slight incline of his head. 'As you wish.'

Gervase continued firmly. 'Swords.' There was a definitely different tone to His Grace's voice. He had sounded almost, well, alive, for want of a better word. In the present, awake, involved, whatever one wanted to call it.

Yes, *alive*.

Gervase, too, felt as he had not done since Spain; the hairs on the back of his neck had risen, his stomach was gripped, in other words, his body was gearing up for action. For a fight.

No more dancing around the subject.

The rivalry of suitors and the only way, the primitive way to sort out the business.

Albion must be shown the error of his ways.

But there was the small matter of the duke's arm. But before Gervase could speak Albion forestalled him. 'I am left-handed, you see.'

That was all there was to it, after all. The last obstacle removed, the last cause for concern.

'Very well.'

The duke beckoned Denbigh forward and the box was opened, the swords presented. Gervase could not have cared less by this stage. Already unfastening his cravat, he chose one at random and the sword was held ready for him by the duke's companion.

'By all means then, let us begin!' Gervase threw off his jacket on to the parched grass nearby. He unbuttoned his cuffs and rolled up his sleeves.

On his part, Albion carefully removed his arm from its support and flexed his fingers gently. Denbigh received the duke's jacket after it had been eased off slowly and painfully. Albion winced at any rate. Gervase looked away. The man must really be in need of a fight of some description. What was the matter with him?

Denbigh handed the garment to the footman. The carriage was used as the depository for the garments, and the underling disappeared from sight. Denbigh, ready for the next request, stood to attention.

The duke indicated with a slight nod of his head. 'There is a suitable clearing, where we shall not be disturbed; I have made sure of it.'

The power of the lofty Duke of Albion extended to the domain of Richmond? Well, it was to be expected.

The wooded copse had a small path leading through it. There the land opened up into a grassy sward with fitful dappled sunlight catching the leaves of the trees: their sway alternately dazzling and disorientating or darkening and obscuring.

For now, the promised storm had held its breath for a clash of wills.

Gervase felt dizzy. Just for a moment the scene swam before his eyes. What was he doing? Jeopardizing everything, at the risk of losing Caroline, his love, for the sake of what? The old, old, masculine need for the shedding of blood. And a token at that, for what did the gentleman before him know of the actuality, the reality, the truth of war, as he, Roland and Gordon had experienced …

To the present. It was indeed a space suitable for a duel

with swords.

Once more Denbigh was kept busy, measuring out the paces.

When all was done and the swords were handed out, the two men faced each other.

'On guard!'

There was a grating clash of steel as the swords met. Jarring and unsettling. The antagonists circled around for quite some minutes before engaging once more. The pattern was repeated. Over and over again.

Long enough for Gervase to realise they were evenly matched. The tortured leg, the damaged arm, or rather shoulder, balanced out. No doubt of it.

He might have the advantage of agility, but Albion, being more heavily-built, had the force.

Gervase gasped, sweat dripping from his brow, realising the bitter truth. Was he perhaps failing? Had the events of the past few days finally caught up with him?

What next?

With a supreme effort of will Gervase rallied and lunged forward. With his sword he caught the edge of His Grace's fine white linen shirt, near his exposed throat, and ripped the garment open down to his waist.

Regretfully Gervase realised he had not drawn blood. Yet.

He parried the next thrust of the duke's blade, and the next.

Pausing only to note that his opponent might be slowing down, or was that a ruse perhaps, Gervase attacked again, unsuccessfully. And was beaten back.

Then it happened.

Gervase slipped on the turf and found himself on the ground, with his opponent leant over him, sword point poised at the midpoint of his chest, and Albion's foot slammed down on Gervase's wrist.

Gervase's own sword gently slid from his nerveless hand.

He swallowed but it was enough for him to feel the very slightest movement of the blade; he was truly cornered.

An inconsequential thought occurred to him — that under no possible circumstances would he ever again wish to view his rival at such close quarters. Goddamn it but the duke had an unprepossessing visage!

He laughed and felt the sharp edge again.

Nonetheless, the fight must continue. 'Release me, Albion. Let us follow on.'

'I wonder, shall we?' There was a mocking edge to the duke's voice. 'I think you are done in.'

'This is not a fair fight. Not a capitulation. You have not drawn blood.'

'No, true, you have the right of it. You must concede that I may do so at any moment however.' The point moved again almost imperceptibly. 'I am the victor. You will allow me then to remain in contact with Miss Langrish. Whenever I wish it.'

'No!' Gervase heaved himself forward and felt blood trickle down his chest. He noticed his shirt too was now torn.

Albion must have been caught by surprise because he lost his balance and his sword, and in the end they were indulging in the fisticuffs avoided at the start of the whole thing.

This was a definite improvement. Much better. A *mill*.

How long it would have proceeded was anyone's guess but they must each have been more tired than they knew …

Inevitable then that there would be a pause.

Feeling himself unable to carry on, Gervase collapsed. Drawing breath, he faced Albion, likewise grounded, and wondered what the pair of them must look like. Running a hand through his hair, he knew he was in a sorry state; the Duke of Albion just looked dazed.

Aware that his own leg was hurting damnably and that

the duke appeared not to be at all incommoded by his injured arm, Gervase pulled himself upright, determined to fight on, to the death if needs be. If only they could resume with swords, he would ...

'Now, sirs, I have it in mind that the fight should cease.'

There was a pleading note in the voice that broke into Gervase's thoughts. Looking up, he saw the duke's companion, Denbigh, close by and realised for the first time that he might be a personal acquaintance of Gervase's adversary, his almost *permanent* adversary, he thought ruefully. Difficult as it was to believe that Albion had friends as such.

The Duke of Albion was staring down at the ground. Then quite quietly he leant over and a slight amount of what looked to be blood issued from his mouth in what would be called in a lesser mortal a spitting action. Presently Albion moved his left arm forward and supported his right, which was resting on his knee, as he sat awkwardly, almost cross-legged, on the grass. The grass was now scuffed and in parts worn away and stained in places. He mumbled a few words but Gervase could make no sense out of them.

Denbigh was bending over his superior in an attitude that could only be described as concerned. What was he about? Anyone would think the duke had not started the fight in the first place!

Although to be honest it had given him, Gervase, great satisfaction, he thought to himself. Pity it now seemed to be at an end. Anyhow the scion of upper-class incivility was worsted. Or was he? Best make sure. Wiping away some blood still dampening his shirt, Gervase struggled to his feet, for Albion, heavily assisted by Denbigh was now standing in an upright position. 'I am the victor here. Admit it, Your Grace!'

The duke waved away his assistor and drew himself up to his full height. 'I must remind you, Thorpe, that the first blood went to me.' He paused. 'However, in the circumstances, and as I prefer not to continue, perhaps a draw would be fair.'

Gervase looked at him.

Tall, thickset, a giant of a man, with all the advantages that wealth and privileges of birth, *rumoured royal connections even*, could bestow on him. All his for the taking. To use as he wished or dispense at will, thereby ensuring a reputation for good works.

But still, a man who had not achieved what he really wanted? Although, God knows, the bastard had used all the means at his disposal, barring brute force. For which one should be thankful.

Caroline.

'Very well,' Gervase said. 'And you will leave Miss Langrish and myself alone in future.'

There was a change in the expression on the duke's face. Always expressionless, he looked, if anything, even blanker. The façade was truly in place again.

There was the very faintest inclination of the head.

That was all. He turned slightly and the ever-present Denbigh shouldered his aristocratic burden away, whispering to him not to mind, and other inane comments, in the direction of the Albion coach.

Well, it would have to do. Gervase had had enough. He was beginning to worry about Caroline. Was she still there? Or had she left in disgust for Richmond? With or without Wilson, on foot maybe. How far away were they? If so, she could hardly be blamed, and he smote himself.

But before he could restore a semblance of order to the torn remnants of his shirt, and his dress in general, Denbigh had re-appeared, alone. 'Well, what now?' Gervase snarled.

'Your behaviour was most ill-considered,' Denbigh sniffed. 'Rest assured your conduct will not be forgotten.'

Gervase did not think that riposte was worthy of a reply, so he ignored it and continued wiping the blood from his chest, flinching as he did so.

Denbigh waited a moment, then scuttled off through the undergrowth down the path from whence he had materialized.

By the time Gervase had followed him through the clearing towards the road, he was feeling more himself. He was just in time to see the Duke's coach moving off in its usual slow and stately fashion back towards London. A few minutes later the posse of black-garbed riders followed. The last man had the gall to turn and wave a salute to Gervase, smiling as he did so. Perhaps they had been only for show.

But where was Caroline?

Gervase felt the back of his neck; it was damp with moisture. A distant rumble of thunder provided an answer – the weather was about to break. And not a moment too soon. He wiped the sweat from his forehead with what was left of a fine linen shirtsleeve. Where the hell was Caroline?

Feeling a few spots of rain, he pushed on through the undergrowth. He saw her then. She was standing in a glade, another clearing in the copse, in the same small wood where he had fought the Duke of Albion.

But *he* is not here now, Gervase thought.

How could he have doubted her? Of course she would wait for him! His heart raced in his breast.

Ah but, then the terrible voice in his head began again. Reflect, she had barely waited for him to return from war. It always came back to the burning question; had she betrayed him?

Had she? Not in a physical sense maybe but in thought, word and deed, she had taken the Duke of Albion as a fiancé, in indecent haste.

He sought answers. Now.

Could he really forgive her?

Caroline turned, as if she had heard him. Perhaps he had spoken aloud. Her hair was unpinned; her beautiful hair; its rich, dark locks cascaded down over her shoulders, over the flimsy muslin dress she was wearing. Never had she looked so beautiful, so enticing, so tempting…

He was not sure how much longer he could endure it…

The truth was – he wanted her.

And there was no holding back now, the Duke of Albion was defeated, he had relinquished his hold.

CHAPTER 36

The green foliage of the thicket parted and Caroline saw Gervase, bloodied, his breathing shallow, stumbling through the undergrowth. Returned from the folly of another fight with the Duke of Albion.

She took in the sight before her: a shirt ripped to shreds, an upper body barely clothed, exposing his honed and muscular physique.

Was he still bleeding? Her question was answered when he passed his hand across his forehead, took it away and gazed down in disgust.

She went to his side. 'Gervase! Let me look at you! What were you thinking of? To fight again!'

At that, he looked up sharply. 'Blame the duke for instigating the fight, but I was willing! Oh yes, only too willing!'

'I do not doubt it!'

'Tell me the truth, again, Caroline, I beg you, or I swear I will not touch you although, I am almost beside myself – it has been so long, since we were together. I beg you.' His tone was fierce, as if the words had been wrenched from him, as if he were choking.

'What do you want to know, Gervase? How many

times must I tell you, yes, I was the Duke of Albion's affianced bride. I was weak, yes, I accepted him, I thought it was all for the best, for Susannah, and, yes, for myself, if you must know. But we were never lovers! It is the past, Gervase, the past. Now we have the present, to do with as we wish.'

Surely her words would be enough? Must he still doubt her?

'Always, always, I thought you had betrayed me, Caroline. I had some very dark days, when I was in the Peninsula. Now I believe you.' His voice had dropped; he sounded quiet again, controlled. 'We will speak of it no more but I have waited a long time. I cannot conceive of waiting any longer.'

'Neither can I. I am yours.' She replied.

A look came into his eye then, a quick flame of some emotion, and as quickly was gone. He passed his hand across his face as if he were shielding himself from her and she could not help but think that she had seen something he would rather she had not. Was he on the brink of breaking down? When she looked again, he laughed. 'Forgive me, I need to see to myself.' He half turned from her and began wiping the blood away, ineffectually, with the ruined linen of his shirt and as quickly gave up in apparent distaste. He sighed. 'You will have to accept me as I am. Come, we will find somewhere more secluded.'

She came to him then and he swept her up in his arms so that she was firm against his chest. She felt the beating of his heart as they moved together, the hardness of his wanting against her.

The tracery of overhanging branches ahead parted. Gervase pushed through, lowering his head, his feet crushing underfoot any foliage not already burnt by the interminable summer.

Ahead, another clearing was revealed.

And a small miracle.

The grass there, shielded from the heat of the sun, looked fresh, green and inviting: a soft cushion, made to be a resting place, a lying place, a fitting setting for their coming-together.

Away from the rest of the world, even the sounds of twittering birds had ceased, as if they had entered a paradise all their own.

Gervase laid Caroline down on the grassy bank and threw himself down beside her. He gazed, holding his banked fire, savouring the moment, the moment he had waited for, for so long.

In his fantasies, and who knew how often he had dreamed of her in the hot hell of Salamanca, of their lying together, it should have been in a bed, his bed, the first time. Not here, and yet, and yet...

Her eyes were bright as she returned his gaze. No holding back, for her. 'Gervase.'

He crushed her to him then and, frightened at the intensity of his feelings and wishing to prolong the moment, he held her away from him. 'You are mine, Caroline.'

Gervase heard her sharp intake of breath; it was enough to provide a distraction. What had he done?

He realised. 'My blood has stained your dress.' He said, and paused, long enough to rip what remained of his shirt from him and throw it aside. 'Never let there be anyone's blood on you, but mine,' he muttered, hiding his face in her lustrous hair, now loose about her shoulders.

He felt her body move with a quiver of emotion.

Gervase kissed her. Gently, at first. Then demanding, seeking her response. And it was everything he had hoped for. He deepened the kiss but she matched him.

Reaching instinctively for his falls, his mind, his vision, everything clouded over, at last, Caroline would be his. Then he held himself back, he must never forget it was the first time – for her.

'Caroline, Caroline,' he murmured, hardly knowing

what he was saying. 'Are you sure, really sure?'

'Yes, yes,' she replied, her gaze still locked on his.

'I would have waited, but...'

In answer she reached up and pulled him down on top of her. He felt his arousal against the soft silk of her dress. He gently caught the soft material of her bodice so that her soft, creamy breasts were freed against him. His mouth came down and took first one and then the other.

His hands explored beneath the silk as he reached for her core, the soft lips of her folds, and she was wet, wet for him. Now was the time, now, now, he choked, his eyes closing with the delirious joy of it all.

Later, later, there would be the luxury of tantalising disrobing, acres of time in which to savour the moment but not now, not now. Words were not needed between them and had she not agreed...

'I may hurt you, Caroline. Please God I do not, but I may.' Even to his own ears his voice sounded hoarse, guttural, as if driven to desperation. He heard the pleading note and was ashamed. Did she know? Did she hear it too? He hoped not.

There was no time to waste, no time to have second thoughts, as this time he freed himself minimally, all that was necessary to be done, from his constraining garments and ready to enter her. And held back.

'Caroline,' it was a warning he needed to give her, a warning as he exerted self-control beyond all imagining.

Now it was her turn. 'Please, Gervase, please.' It was as if she knew. Yet, how could she?

He moved to enter her, a thrust that he knew took her maidenhead, heard her gasp, but then they were together, in the age-old rhythm.

Entwined, their bodies close and warm together, bonded, for life as it were. Oblivion came to him then; merciful oblivion. All the memories, savage and discordant, fell away. At least for now.

His last waking thought was to ask himself; when had

he last felt the blessed sleep of satiated passion?

Gervase felt the first drops of rain: a cooling caress on his face. He looked down, hardly daring to hope, yes, Caroline was still asleep in his arms. It had after all not been a dream; the future lay ahead of them. A future in Hampshire, away from the machinations of the *haut ton* in London. Meanwhile, he must act. The journey proper was to begin at Richmond where Roland's carriage awaited them.

He kissed Caroline awake, her hair silky under his lips, her body pliant and yielding against him. But there was no time, no time. He gasped in anguish.

'Caroline, we must make haste, the day draws on.' He kissed her again passionately, as he drew her to her feet.

She clung to him, 'Gervase?'

Gervase cursed himself then, and letting go of her, he flung himself down on one knee. 'Caroline, my dearest, will you marry me and make me happy for the rest of my life?'

'You know I am yours,' she said simply.

He kissed the hand which she held out to him. 'I cannot offer you the splendour of a wedding ceremony in London but I have a special licence with me. We will be married quietly as soon as arrive in Hampshire.' He broke off and looked around in despair, 'My jacket!'

Caroline laughed and together Gervase and Caroline walked back towards the road, the curricle, and their future together away from the constraints of London society, Gervase hoped.

But would they ever be free from the malign influence of the Duke of Albion?

He was not sure.

Epilogue…. Hampshire, late October, 1814 *Three months later…*

A Love Betrayed

'La, are those all your acres, Caroline? To the woodlands yonder?' There was a note of awe in Susannah's voice as she threw open the dormer window and gazed out.

It was the first visit of Susannah and her aristocratic cavalier, the Earl of Marlow, to the new home of Caroline and Gervase, her husband now, a visit to the long-promised smallholding. With a little trepidation, Caroline had taken her sister up the rackety wooden stairs at the back of the house to the small bedchamber Caroline shared with Gervase.

'No indeed, Gervase's demesne extends only as far as the brook,' Caroline replied dismissively. Yet more land would have added to their worries.

Susannah leant out and lifted her face to the sun for a moment or two before she retreated back into the room. 'The scent of your flowers is too delightful. And so *comme il faut* – pink roses around the door, Caroline! I do so adore a cottage! But now the light hurts my eyes.'

Yes, the sun still shone brightly on the hawthorn hedge that wandered down to the brook at the end of the kitchen garden. The kitchen garden that Caroline had tended so lovingly over the course of the remains of the summer spent in rural seclusion. For Caroline was aware she must think of the future.

A flock of birds rising from the rushes and heading upriver heralded the end of yet another balmy day. But before too long the lengthening season would turn misty, and settle into the crispness of autumn. But for now all was still warm and sunny. Time enough to worry about her and Gervase's winter on the smallholding…

Caroline smoothed down the sable wrap which Susannah had thrown down carelessly onto the bed, Caroline and Gervase's marital bed, still a hallowed place....

Her sister swung around, turning her back on the window and fixing Caroline with a straight look. 'Can you truly be happy here, in such reduced circumstances? And what does Gervase do all day?'

Caroline looked away. 'Yes, I can. Do you make your way to Hurstbourne Priors tonight?'

Susannah moved restlessly around the room. 'Yes, my lord wishes it. Wendover, I should say the Earl of Marlow, has such a comfortable residence there, I'm told, with a veranda and French windows, it will be such a change from the humble hunting lodges. *There* one may as well stay in lodgings. I must confess I am rather tired of them! And we were so secluded from society.' Here she stole a quick glance at Caroline, and with a touch of the old Susannah, her smile shone through. 'Not that there were not compensations. But it does not signify because after we are married I shall have the town house in Mecklenburg Square, as well as Marlow Grange, you know.'

Caroline could only marvel at the number and variety of the Earl of Marlow's residences. She comforted herself with the thought that at least she would always be settled *here*.

The looking-glass now claimed Susannah's attention and she leant forward as if to admire her reflection. Since becoming a mistress, for how else could one describe her position at Roland's side, Susannah's taste had developed remarkably. Caroline's glance lingered on the ruby and diamond ear-drops, the curling plumage of the high-crowned hat, and the sables on the bed. 'Are you not a touch over-dressed for an afternoon call upon your sister? I know that you have been travelling,' she added hastily.

Susannah pulled a face. 'There will be time enough to be matronly when I am a married lady. I am become odiously spoilt, I do declare. Besides Roland likes me to dress in this way. *À la mode,* I swear I am all the crack!'

And she giggled but she removed her hat and tossed it onto the bed to join the furs.

Caroline wondered whether it was likely that a mistress would be so but Susannah was undoubtedly blissfully happy in her role. 'In answer to your question, by the way, Gervase works on the land.'

For once Susannah had nothing to say.

'It helps him, he says, to recover from the horrors of war,' Caroline continued.

'And is he recovering, do you think?'

Caroline answered. 'Yes, I think so, little by little. But he does like to punish himself it seems to me. Why I am not sure.' And she wondered why she revealed herself so. Susannah always had that effect upon her.

'Perhaps he blames himself for only being able to offer you a cottage as your marital home,' was Susannah's quick reply. 'Instead of an estate such as Beauminster Priory.'

Before Caroline could utter the sharp retort that was on her lips, Susannah made her way to her sister and pulled her into her arms, 'But let us forget that now. Dearest, you will, you simply must, return to London to see me wed. Gervase must support Roland, you know. Even though my darling and I did not attend your hasty nuptials!'

'There was not time. It was all arranged in a hurry.' Caroline could not meet her sister's gaze. She would not tell Susannah how Gervase had worried so about their unwed state, in spite of the special licence. Until they were safely married. For herself she found she had cared not.

How I have been affected by Mrs Farley and her machinations, she thought.

'Because of the Duke of Albion, no doubt. Why are you all afraid of him? I am not, I swear.' Susannah held Caroline away from herself for a moment and pouted.

Overwhelmed by her sister's perfume, powder and persistence, Caroline allowed herself a few moments respite. If only it were so for herself and dare she say it, her husband? 'Yes, no, I must consult with Gervase.'

'Why?'

'You know why.'

'Oh yes, the august Duke of Albion!'

'Have you any news of him? How does he?'

'I fear he has buried himself in the country. But I heard...' Susannah clapped a hand over her mouth. 'Oh no, I promised Roland.'

Caroline dug her nails into her palm behind her, careful to hide the tell-tale signs of her discomfiture. 'Tell me.'

'Roland says, the duke has been sighted in Hampshire - near here. He has been buying up land. For some fell purpose I expect.' She released Caroline and moved away.

'Why?' Caroline's heart began to thud in her breast. Not again.

'No one knows. But I have an idea.'

'And so have I,' replied Caroline. 'Let us go down to take a dish of tea. I have baked a cake, especially for you. I am sure the men will have returned by now. It would not have taken long for Gervase to have shown Roland his land.'

And now Susannah's rattling on had given Caroline quite the headache. One thing she knew for sure; she could not live in alt all the time as her sister chose to do.

Susannah laughed. 'Yes, refreshment will be most welcome. I declare I am in dire need. A cake made by my own beloved sister will have a taste beyond compare.'

They reached the door together.

Susannah placed a hand on Caroline's arm. 'Tell me, are you increasing, Caro?'

Caroline caressed her stomach. 'I am.'

Caroline knew that all the minor privations that she would bear, and bear willingly, in order that she might be with Gervase could not compare with Susannah's future responsibilities. Susannah was condemned to be a countess with all its attendant duties and occasional boredom but there would be entirely suitable compensations aplenty for her.

Besides, Susannah need have no fear. Her errant reputation would be ignored, the illicit and ill-concealed months with the Earl of Marlow would be forgotten, once she had been admitted again to the safe, secure world of the titled, and entitled, ton. All forgiven. Adoration amongst her circle of friends, and admirers so many as to be tiresome.

Charm was in Susannah's nature and to be spoilt her condition; the Earl, finding nothing too good for her, her loving subject for the rest of his days.

And Caroline was happy for her sister. All the memories of their father's ignominy, their tainted past, washed away. Susannah's comeout, her tutoring by Mrs Farley and her natural aptitude made her a fitting consort for that most estimable of gentlemen, the Earl of Marlow. No longer tempted by the louche attractions of the demimonde Susannah would play her part in the milieu most favourable for her.

Perhaps the sisters' paths would cross less but Caroline felt that the earl was too good a friend to ever lose touch with his former comrade-in-arms, her husband, Gervase.

Everything would be well.

'A fair piece of land,' Roland clapped Gervase on the back. 'Good man!'

They stood together looking out over the fields in front of them, acres currently awaiting the plough. The soil was rich and should prove profitable, Gervase had little doubt. It had better be, he thought grimly for soon the need would become more pressing, with another mouth to feed.

'To tell you the truth, it is as much as I can handle,' Gervase replied, 'The damn leg is getting stronger but could do better still.' He flexed the limb in question and then winced. 'However, I have help from the village.' Which he could ill afford, he thought but had proven necessary if they were to survive the winter.

Roland gave him a quick look, narrowing his eyes and with a crease between his forehead. 'Well, my estates in Norfolk require a manager very shortly and you have a modicum of experience now… '

Gervase shook his head.

Roland continued. 'Anyhow, there may be other opportunities soon… I do not think Elba will be able to hold Napoleon; it is not far enough away. We can always return to the fray.'

Gervase tensed. 'It would be worth considering indeed.' He preferred not to think about that now – there was too much to occupy himself with, here in Whitchurch. 'I think we should return to the house. Do you rest at Hurstbourne Priors tonight?'

Roland nodded. 'And I am glad of it, for another change of horses would be too much I fear, especially for Susannah. It has been a long journey.' The two men walked back down the path towards the cottage as the light began to fade.

'Have you any news of Captain Gordon Howard by the way?'

Roland laughed. 'I gather the fellow is still pursuing the Lady Lydia Vellacott but without success as yet. It keeps him out of mischief but to my mind she will shortly yield and accept his suit out of sheer weariness. And of course he is certainly well-heeled.'

For his former Albany companion's sake Gervase hoped she would. Everyone deserved a chance of happiness as well as himself.

'And what of Mrs Farley?' Gervase was not sure why he asked but feared to delve too deeply into his motives; his excuse was that she had been intimately bound up in his reclaiming of Caroline.

'Oh, I hear she has been taken back into the Duke's household and the house in Brunswick Square is quite shut up, for now at least.'

A circumstance that would please Mrs Farley extremely, Gervase thought.

Roland halted and said 'There is another matter of which I must acquaint you, I fear. Albion has had dealings with this parish, I'm told.'

Gervase had expected it. 'It is no concern of mine.' He took a deep breath. 'But I will fight him every inch of the way. If His Grace as much as sets foot here, I swear I shall...' He stopped, appalled at the strength of his reaction.

'Well, I would not make too much of it, my friend. Albion has interests all over the country. The fair Miss Georgiana Lane has recently been rumoured to be His Grace's latest *chère-amie*. And don't forget to keep a weather eye on the news from abroad. I do confess I would like to cross swords with the French again. It is a natural thing. I can get you a commission. Now that you fulfilled your uncle's wish and have taken possession of his smallholding. What do you say to that?'

'Let us go in,' replied Gervase carefully, 'I respect your willingness to help but I would not want to leave my wife here alone.' It was still a pleasure to use the words. 'Especially not in her condition.' He added.

'Oh, that way, is it, I congratulate you. By the by, you must come to our wedding ceremony, in November. My Mama, the Dowager Countess, you know, will soon be made acquainted, I'm sure, with how I have been carrying on. It can only be a matter of time.' Roland sighed. 'I have not taken Susannah to Marlow Grange for that reason. My Mama lives in the Dower House nearby. And, and it would not be seemly. Regretfully, for the past few months have been paradise. We have visited others of my properties, not all of them entirely suitable, I'm afraid. Including Stretton Manor, where we both grew up and had such escapades, you remember.'

'Yes, I remember,' said Gervase slowly. How could he forget?

'Poor Susannah! Truly I have been most ill-behaved. Now I have made an offer and I have been accepted. Our wedding journey, our *voyage de noces,* I may call it so, however, will be to Brussels, so a decided improvement. I am told there is quite the social scene there so it will delight Susannah.'

It had been ramshackle, disreputable, not at all what Gervase would have expected from Roland. 'Yes, it came to my ears, even here in Hampshire. We are not completely out of touch with events in London and elsewhere, you know. I am glad that you are putting everything to rights. Caroline will be pleased too. But the rumours concerning Boney are news to me. It bears thinking about. Come, Caroline is waving to us.'

A pretty picture indeed, Gervase thought; the two sisters in the cottage doorway, framed by the wandering climbing roses of a dusky pink, already losing petals to the autumnal days, Caroline's burgeoning figure masked by her long country apron and Susannah's town manners forgotten as she too waved.

Gervase felt his good fortune and perhaps Roland felt it too because they both picked up pace and went forward together, each destined to certain happiness.

Gervase knew that all the burdens and worries he now endured, and endured willingly, for Caroline, his wife, and would endure soon for his child as well, could not be compared with those of his friend, Roland. For Roland was a belted earl, with cares and duties, with estates to be managed for good or ill, with attendance in the House expected.

But Roland had a natural grace, not at all determined by his rank and breeding and education. Already fêted wherever he went, he would now be doubly sought after. For his future wife, the fair Susannah, was capable of stunning a room into silence merely by entering into it; and thus his sum of happiness would be increased.

Yet Roland was already secure in his position in life and did not need Susannah as much as Gervase needed Caroline, Gervase thought, and then berated himself for his selfishness in thinking of Caroline as his mainstay. But so help him, he did, he did.

There would now be a gulf between the friends. Separated not only by sheer distance but also by the strata of society in which their

respective futures lay.
However, Gervase felt that the earl was too good a friend to ever lose touch with his former comrade-in-arms, Gervase.
Everything would be well.

Both the Duke of Albion and the former Emperor Napoleon Bonaparte alike could wait.

Any future war was, as it was said, in the future…

ABOUT THE AUTHOR

Sylvia Robins grew up in Plymouth, England, after the Second World War and moved to London in the Sixties., where she still lives. She has always loved telling stories and as a child she made up tales to tell her dolls. At school she had prose and poetry published in the school magazines. After a career spent as a computer analyst/programmer she has recently returned to writing.

Her first Historical Regency Romance, 'The Desire of a Lord' was self-published in May 2020.

Printed in Great Britain
by Amazon